Angela Thirkell

Angela Thirkell, granddaughter of Edward Burne-Jones, was born in London in 1890. At the age of twenty-eight she moved to Melbourne, Australia where she became involved in broadcasting and was a frequent contributor to the British periodicals. Mrs. Thirkell did not begin writing novels until her return to Britain in 1930; then, for the rest of her life, she produced a new book almost every year. Her stylish prose and deft portrayal of the human comedy in the imaginary county of Barsetshire have amused readers for decades. She died in 1961, just before her seventy-first birthday.

Of the contemporary English novelists . . . none offers a more solid texture of plot and situation than Mrs. Thirkell, or can manage a more sustained lightness of touch.

— *Saturday Review of Literature*

[Angela Thirkell's] humor consists of a subtle understanding of the characters and conversations of ordinary intelligent people.

— *The Times Literary Supplement*

O, THESE MEN, THESE MEN!

Other books by Angela Thirkell

Ankle Deep
August Folly
Before Lunch
The Brandons
Cheerfulness Breaks In
Close Quarters
Coronation Summer
County Chronicle
The Demon in the House
A Double Affair
Duke's Daughter
Enter Sir Robert
The Grateful Sparrow
Growing Up
Happy Returns
The Headmistress
High Rising
Jutland Cottage
Love Among the Ruins
Love at All Ages
Marling Hall
Miss Bunting
Never Too Late
Northbridge Rectory
The Old Bank House
Peace Breaks Out
Pomfret Towers
Private Enterprise
Summer Half
Three Houses
Three Score and Ten
What Did It Mean?
Wild Strawberries

O, THESE MEN, THESE MEN!

A Novel by

Angela Thirkell

MOYER BELL
Wakefield, Rhode Island & London

Published by Moyer Bell
This Edition 1996

LIBRARY OF CONGRESS
CATALOGING-IN-PUBLICATION DATA

Thirkell, Angela Mackail   O, These Men,
These Men

1.
2.

PR6039.H43A82   1996   96-46714
823'.912—dc20   CIP

ISBN 1-55921-173-3

Cover illustration: *Henry Davidson, English Poet* by Louise Breslau
Chapter illustrations from *Samplers* by Susan Mayor & Diana Fowle

Printed in the United States of America
Distributed in North America by Publishers Group West, P.O. Box 8843,
Emeryville CA 94662, 800-788-3123 (in California 510-658-3453).

To
J.H.
with my love, and always

CONTENTS

O, THESE MEN, THESE MEN!

CHAPTER I

UNHAPPY PROLOGUE

Caroline Danvers's parents had long been dead. Her best friends and companions while she was growing up were her distant cousins Hugh Mannering and Francis Lester who lived together in an old house in Bloomsbury belonging to the Lester family. Francis had inherited a solicitor's business from his father and Hugh worked on a newspaper. Both were devoted to their young cousin Caroline, and when she married James Danvers Hugh managed to get James onto the staff of his paper.

James's family consisted of a father and mother, a younger sister Anna, and two yet younger brothers, Wilfred and George, who all lived in the country. Wilfred and George came up to town every day to their father's office, while Mr. Danvers only came up two or three times a week. Thus it happened that Caroline, though very fond of her husband's family, especially of Anna who was about her own age, rarely saw them. Once or twice in the year the Danverses used to come up to their house in Cadogan Square for a few weeks, and occasionally Anna stayed in London with her brother and his wife.

Caroline after three years of marriage was thankful that her husband's people saw so little of her home life. When his father and mother came to town James was as charming to them as ever, finding considerable relief in misusing his wife more than usual when they had gone. To his young brothers he was something of a hero, and the only one of his family who guessed what he was becoming was his sister Anna, whose further visits he did not therefore encourage.

Among Caroline's many griefs not the least was the forcible estrangement of her cousins Hugh and Francis. In his drink-clouded mind James had conceived an unreasonable and intolerable jealousy of them both, finally forbidding Caroline to ask them to the house or see them at all. The cousins were anxious and unhappy at losing sight of Caroline, but as any attempt at a meeting only meant that she would be exposed to James's senseless rage, they stayed away.

For several months they saw and heard nothing of Caroline. Hugh indeed saw James at the newspaper office, but avoided him as much as possible, alternately praying and fearing that his unpunctual ways and brawling habits would lead to his dismissal. Neither Hugh nor Francis knew whether James's father and mother suspected his downward ways, and they came to the conclusion that interference would be useless and all they could do for Caroline was to wait, hoping for matters to mend. Once or twice Francis was able as a lawyer to extricate James from some piece of folly in which his own weakness had involved him, hating at the same time to send the wreck that James was becoming back to the uncomplaining Caroline.

One morning while Francis Lester was still at breakfast, the elderly parlormaid Rose brought him a telephone message saying that Mrs. James Danvers would be glad if he or Mr. Hugh could come around at once, urgently. Mrs. Danvers, Rose said, had rung off. Filled with certain foreboding of trouble Francis left word for Hugh, who was away for a weekend, where he had gone, and drove to Caroline's house.

Within three hours he was at Beechwood where the Danvers family lived. Before he could get out of his car, Anna Danvers, James's younger sister, came running out to meet him, pleased at the surprise of seeing Caroline's delightful cousin Francis at such an unexpected hour.

"I have brought Caroline with me," said Francis. "Anna, be an angel and ask no questions, but take her up to your room. Where are Mr. and Mrs. Danvers?"

"In the library, I expect. Oh, Francis, what is the matter? Is it James?"

"It is."

A very quiet, polite Caroline got out of the car.

"Can you have me for a day or two, Anna?" she asked, sitting down on a low window seat in the hall. "I seem to be rather unwanted, and if it isn't a bother I would very much like to lie down. If you could explain, Francis, it would be very kind. I might cry and that would be so mortifying."

She looked anxiously from one to the other as she spoke, more concerned to keep up her part of a well-bred visitor apologizing for an intrusion than for anything else. In clinging to this symbol of convention she felt she could avoid the way that madness lies.

"Yes, I will explain," said Francis. "Go upstairs with Anna. Shall I help you?" he added, looking with concern at her pallor, the effort she made to get up.

"No thank you, I can manage so well. None of my arms and legs are broken, thank you. Will you come and see me before you go?"

"Of course I will."

Anna and her sister-in-law went upstairs. Francis went down the passage towards the library, hearing Caroline's voice as she labored carefully through the politeness expected of a guest, Anna's perplexed responses. Outside the library door he stood in thought. No one could have devised a more repugnant or difficult task than to tell a father and a mother that their eldest son was a complete failure, without decency, courage, or kindness. He could not even guess how they would take it. He must be prepared for disbelief, tears, the resentment which is felt against the bearer of bad news, possibly a refusal to shelter Caroline. In Anna he knew he had an ally, but her father and mother were unknown quantities in this horrible game of family affairs. So were the younger brothers Wilfred and George, now he hoped safely out of the way, at work in London in their father's office. Knowing that nothing could be much worse than his own anticipations, he went in.

Mr. and Mrs. Danvers were surprised to see Francis at twelve o'clock on a Monday morning, but as he was a solicitor they concluded that some kind of business had brought him to Beechwood, and asked him to stay to lunch. Francis fidgeted wretchedly and answered their questions at random, trying to remind himself that he had handled dozens of similar cases professionally and at the same time failing entirely to find any precedent for what he had to do. His distress was so apparent that Mrs. Danvers asked him point blank if he was in some kind of difficulty.

"I am," said Francis, "and the worst of it is that it affects you too. It's about James."

"Is he dead?" asked Mrs. Danvers, suddenly looking old.

Francis would have liked to say, "No, worse," but he realized that to a parent nothing can be worse than a child's death. Death is the only final and irrevocable disgrace. All others may be repaired or forgotten.

"No, Mrs. Danvers, he is quite all right in that way. I don't know how much you know," he said, temporising.

"We don't know anything. James hasn't told us anything in particular. Is anything wrong, badly wrong?"

"I'm afraid it is, Mrs. Danvers. It's about Caroline too. In fact I had to bring her here."

"But why? Is she ill? Is James ill? Where is Caroline? I must see her."

"Evelyn," said Mr. Danvers, "wait, my dear. Francis, please tell us exactly what has happened. We have been anxious about

James for a long time. He has been extravagant, that we know. What more?"

"Drink, sir, and pretty well everything that goes with it," said Francis, desperately anxious to get the worst out. "Caroline rang up this morning and asked us to go to her. Hugh was away so I went. Did you know that James had lost his newspaper job some time ago because he was always drunk? He was badly in debt too. They have been living on her money, which isn't much. Sometimes she hasn't known where he was for days at a time. I have found him once or twice and brought him back to her." He hesitated.

"Please go on," said Mr. Danvers.

"There have been women too. Caroline didn't tell me about them—James did. On Saturday night he brought one home with him. Caroline heard them both go out on Sunday morning. He didn't come back last night. She had been sitting up all Sunday night afraid to go to bed. Then this morning she rang us up. James had practically turned me and Hugh out of the house, or I might have helped her before. She could hardly talk at all. When she had told me what had been happening I thought she would collapse, but she wouldn't let herself. I couldn't obviously take her to my house, so I brought her here. Was I right?"

Mr. Danvers's face had been buried in his hands while Francis spoke. He raised it drawn and ravaged.

"Quite right," he said. "Our son's wife is a child of the house. Thank you, Francis. Evelyn, you had better go and see Caroline. God knows what is to come of all this, but that child has need of comfort."

"This letter came from James just as we were leaving," said Francis, taking it out of his pocket. "I opened it. It wasn't the moment to consider whether one was being honorable. He says he doesn't propose to come back and she can do what she likes."

"Cecil, what are we to do?" said Mrs. Danvers, looking imploringly at her husband.

"My dear, I can't tell you yet. Francis can advise us perhaps, but we can do nothing at present except to try to help Caroline. I blame myself. I have been deliberately blind to things I could have seen. I hadn't the courage to talk to James and now we are all punished for my cowardice. My poor Evelyn."

Rapid steps were heard in the passage and Anna came running in.

"Francis, please come at once," she said breathlessly. "I made Caroline go to bed. What has happened to her? She is ill, she can hardly speak. She said you promised to see her before you went. Mother, Father, what is it? What has Francis said?"

"It isn't Francis," said Mr. Danvers, "it is James. He has been unkind to Caroline and left her. Don't ask anymore just now."

"I hate James," cried Anna with sudden passion. "I saw him when I stayed with them last year. Drinking and bullying. I had a row with him and he said if I would promise not to tell father and mother he would turn over a new leaf. I was a fool and a coward and I promised. Did you know that Caroline was going to have a baby then, Francis? That is all over now, thanks to James, the hateful brute. She made me promise not to tell anyone, because she thought you would all be angry with James. It was then that I had the row with him. I wish I had told everyone in the world. Oh, Mother, Father."

She flung herself into her mother's arms in a storm of tears.

Mr. Danvers rose like an old man.

"You had better see Caroline if she wants you, Francis," he said. "Come up."

Francis followed him in silence to Anna's room. Mr. Danvers knocked at the door. There was no answer. Francis felt his heart beating as Mr. Danvers knocked again. Still there was silence and they went softly in. Caroline was lying in Anna's bed, quite still, her eyes closed.

"My poor child, my poor child," said Mr. Danvers compassionately. "I don't know what to say. You shall be safe with us. This is your home."

Caroline's lips moved, but neither man could hear what she said. Francis sat down by her bed.

"What is it, Caroline?"

"Tell Mr. Danvers not to be angry with James," said Caroline in such a thread of a voice that it sounded to Francis as though it came to him from far away and on her latest breath.

"We aren't thinking of James, only of you, Caroline."

"Please don't," said the other-world voice politely. "I am quite all right."

"Can I do anything for you?"

"No, thank you. Thank you for bringing me here. Give my love to Hugh."

The thin small voice ceased. Francis took her hand. It lay unresponsive in his own.

"I think you ought to have Dr. Herbert, sir," he said to Mr. Danvers, who was only too glad to find something definite to do. Mrs. Danvers then came in and took possession. Francis said good-bye to her, refusing renewed offers of lunch and promising to ring up in the evening for news. In the hall he found Anna, her eyes swollen with crying, but otherwise herself again.

"How is Caroline?" she said.

"I don't know. Your father is sending for Dr. Herbert. Anna—James is your brother and was once a friend of Hugh's and mine, but I could kill him with the greatest pleasure."

"So could I," said Anna. "Oh, Francis, what is going to happen?"

"I don't know. When Caroline is well enough to talk she will have to decide. She could divorce James if she likes, of course. Good-bye, Anna, and take care of her."

He got into his car and drove back to town. There were arrears of work in the office to be dealt with. It was not till nearly eight that he got back to his house in Bloomsbury where he and Hugh had lived together since his parents' death.

"You will have to wait till after dinner," he said to Hugh, who was anxious to know the meaning of his message. "Thank goodness it's Monday."

"Why?"

"Because it's the evening your paper lets you loose. I need you to talk to."

After a dinner which their fear of Rose the parlormaid and Maud who helped with the waiting prevented them from hurrying, the cousins went up to Francis's study, a comfortable room behind the drawing room. Here Francis took so long to fill and light a pipe that Hugh became indignant.

"Caroline sent for you apparently at cockcrow from what Rose told me," he complained, "and you go off all mysteriously for the day and come back late, and then pretend we can't talk in front of Rose, when well you know that she knows all about everything long before we do. Has James cut his throat in a fit of D.T.'s? I haven't seen him for about three months, not since the editor finally sacked him, so I am quite in the dark. Of course there's been a lot of talk in the office, but I haven't encouraged it."

"James is every kind of a blackguard," said Francis.

"Well, I know that. Do you mean more than getting tight and getting into debt and carrying on with women? I'm more sorry than I can say for Caroline."

"Did you know about the women?" asked Francis.

"Of course I did. James used to come in and boast about them in his cups, which were practically continuous in the last few months. I couldn't knock my cousin's husband down in the sub-editor's room, or I'd have done it. That sort of thing doesn't look well for the paper. What has he done now? Cat burgling?"

"I think he has killed Caroline. I left her at Beechwood. She was in bed and almost unconscious. All she could say was, Don't be angry with James. It would give me a great deal of pleasure to wring James's neck, very slowly. Angry! There isn't a word for the kind of rage it makes me feel."

"Steady," said his cousin. "I still haven't the faintest idea what really happened. Do you mean that James has done anything to her, hurt her? I'm in with you on the neck wringing if he has."

"Sorry, Hugh. I ought to be legal-minded. Of course you don't understand."

He repeated to Hugh, though at greater length, what he had told the Danverses that morning, adding some details which he had not thought it necessary to inflict on James's father and mother. Hugh listened with a darkening face and at the end relieved his feelings by remarking, Hell.

"Exactly," said Francis. "Hell for Caroline. And we have got to do what we can to help her out. James's people are splendid. They must have been hard hit. Poor Anna broke down, but she was all right when I left. She had seen James at it and knew more than her parents will ever know. They will take care of Caroline. Of course we couldn't talk of the future at all, and what to do about James. Have you any idea where he may have gone?"

"Not the faintest, but I might find something out at the office. Junior reporters have a disconcerting way of knowing what their betters are up to."

Just then Rose came in with the evening post.

"Thanks, Rose," said Francis, taking his letters. "And please get me Mrs. Cecil Danvers's number on the telephone—the country number."

"I say," said Hugh, "here's a letter from James."

"Confound his impudence," said Francis.

"You'll probably confound it even more when you've read this," said Hugh, passing the letter to his cousin.

"Dear Hugh," it said, "Please tell anyone I owe money to at the office that I shall probably continue to owe it. I have found someone who really appreciates me at last and don't intend to come back. Caroline can get any information she wants from my lawyers. I suppose one of you will be ready to marry your charming cousin when she is free. Francis is very welcome to her, though I doubt whether she will look at him while you are about. J.D."

Before either of the cousins could voice the anger which both felt, the telephone rang. Francis answered it and heard Anna's voice.

"Caroline is no worse," he said as he put the receiver back. "Dr. Herbert says it is shock and exhaustion, and they have doped her so that she'll sleep. Anna says she only spoke once, to apologize for being a trouble and to ask if you would be coming down. Oh, I didn't tell you she sent you her love when I left her this morning."

"Poor child," said Hugh.

"Look here, I'm going for a walk," said Francis. "I'll go mad if I stay indoors. I'll see you tomorrow."

For an hour or more Francis walked quickly through the empty streets, reliving every moment of the eventful day. In vain did he try to consider Caroline's case as a lawyer should. He could only see Caroline as she sat, intensely self-controlled, telling him with painful reluctance the ignominy of her story, defying him silently to say a word against the husband who had almost destroyed her sanity, making it very clear that she asked for no sympathy and only wanted to be allowed to hide her grief in some safe place. When she had finished she obediently and politely did as he told her, put on a hat and a coat, found her gloves and bag, and came with him to Beechwood. He had never had to make a decision more quickly and he prayed that it had been the right one. He believed that it was. Then he saw her again, white and drained of strength, lying in Anna's bed, unable to respond to word or touch, and his angry exclamation started another solitary walker whom he was passing at the moment. He saw Caroline as she was when she married James. He remembered how Caroline had grown quieter and often looked afraid, how she had tried to conceal her husband's downfall from him and Hugh till the day when James had turned them both out of the house and gone back to his wife to inflict no one knew what humiliations upon her. He and Hugh had been such friends of their cousin Caroline from childhood that they had accepted James with the affectionate jealousy that brothers may feel for a sister's choice. And there was no doubt that James had been infinitely charming. No wonder that Caroline had adored him with his good looks and his gifts. No wonder that everyone believed in a brilliant future for him, that his friends, and they were many, looked upon his newspaper work as only a step to an important career. Well, all that was gone now. There was no career for a man who couldn't keep sober to do his job. If only he had waited a few years, Francis reflected bitterly. A man who had arrived could afford to get drunk and even have a very successful career if his constitution were good; one could think of many men who had done it. But to be known as a hopeless drinker and slacker before one was thirty meant the end of everything. Poor, poor Caroline.

Then with a fresh surge of indignation he thought of James's letter to Hugh. It was obviously written when he was pretty tight, but nonetheless it stung by some of the crude truth in it. Francis knew now that he cared for Caroline more than for any living creature, but James's gibe was only a devilish shot in the dark. No one, not Hugh, not Caroline, knew what Francis hardly knew himself, so determinedly had he worked at not knowing. To think of Caroline took his breath away, so he would not let himself think of her. Now it seemed a profanation to think of her at all except as the object of any sheltering care that could be given. He saw her again lying almost speechless, using her last strength in words of polite deprecation, sending her love to Hugh.

As he remembered this, Francis again uttered an angry exclamation. If James had made another devilish and certain shot in the dark matters would be more difficult than before. Twice had Caroline sent a message to Hugh from the cold darkness where her spirit was holding its last defenses. If James conceivably was right, what hope for him, what hope for Caroline? So utterly had the revelation of James's brutality wiped him out of Francis's consideration that he found himself hoping and fearing for Caroline, for Hugh, for himself, as if she were a free creature, ready and able to choose, not the ghost of Caroline whom he had lately touched and seen, the wife of James Danvers. Realizing at last that he was very tired, and that the spectacle of a gentleman in evening dress striding along the Hampstead Road uttering ferocious words to the universe was becoming of excessive interest to policemen on point duty, he hailed a belated taxi and went home. Hugh had long since gone to bed, furious at James's letter, but in no way disconcerted by an implication which he treated as the ravings of the madman that James had become.

Meanwhile at Beechwood Mr. and Mrs. Danvers were dealing with life as best they could. After a constrained dinner at which Wilfred and George were simply told that Caroline was ill and asked to be quiet, a request which they both resented deeply as savoring of unnecessary parental interference, Anna went up to sit with Caroline. Wilfred and George, who at twenty-two and twenty found home life cheap and useful but cramping to the style, went off to spend the evening with Dr. Herbert and his wife, so Mr. and Mrs. Danvers were left alone. There had been neither time nor opportunity for them to face the wreckage of happiness that James had made. Caroline's almost desperate state, Dr. Herbert's visit, a nurse to be got, carefully constructed half-truths to be told to callers—"Poor Caroline had a kind of breakdown and as James is away we thought she had better come here"—evasions of the truth to be prepared for the benefit of the servants—"Mrs. James has been quite unwell and the doctor said she had better come here for a little rest," an evasion which everyone knew the servants would not for a moment believe, and indeed at that very moment they were happily discussing it all in their sitting room, tremendously enjoying the fuss and gloating on the increased attraction which first hand contact with a scandal would give them in their social circles, what to say to George and Wilfred, all these things had so occupied the afternoon that this was the first time that they had been able to meet in peace. Both would have been only too thankful to shirk all discussion of the subject, but time and circumstances pressed.

"I think, Evelyn," said Mr. Danvers, "that when that poor child is a little stronger we must see a lawyer. It is partly my fault perhaps that James has behaved so unspeakably. I shall never forgive myself for shirking my duty and not speaking to him earlier. I might have done some good."

"Not your fault, Cecil dear. Really no one's fault I think. Not James's fault. It is like being possessed. He can't know what he is doing. And must we have a lawyer? Can't Francis do anything that needs doing?"

"Francis is Caroline's cousin. It might be painful and embarrassing for them both if he had to arrange a divorce. It would be better to have an outsider."

"Divorce, Cecil? Oh, no. James could never bear it. Oh, Cecil, you couldn't think of such a thing."

"My dear, James is my son too. If I could spare him anything by my own suffering I would, just as you would. God knows I would. But you heard what Caroline told Francis, you heard what James had written to Caroline, you heard what Anna, his own sister, said about James. It may be possession, but nonetheless Caroline must be protected against it forever. We might have had a grandchild, Evelyn, but for this."

"But, Cecil, it can't be all true. Perhaps Caroline was a little hysterical, perhaps Anna exaggerated, perhaps—"

"No, my dear. It is all very dark and very hopeless. We can only do our best. I can't cast James off any more than you would, but our present duty is to Caroline. She must be protected and she must stay with us, then no one can say a word against her. Don't cry, Evelyn. James may have broken life for you and me, but Caroline is young and has a right to live and to mend her broken life. Hasn't she?"

"I suppose so, Cecil. Oh, why must people be wicked?"

"A question which a great many people have asked in vain, my dear. Will you see if Caroline is all right for the night now?" Mrs. Danvers put her hands on her husband's shoulders and kissed the top of his head. As she left the room Anna came in.

"Stay with father," said Mrs. Danvers. "I'm going up to Caroline. Is she still asleep?"

"Yes, Mother. Nurse is with her. And I rang up Francis to tell him. He sounded so tired, Father. He has had a frightful day. What a mercy that Caroline had him to bring her to Beechwood. I think Francis is a very safe kind of person to have for a cousin. I should think he would always be a help in difficulties. Father, what are you going to do?"

"I wish I knew, my dear. But I am very tired tonight and can't see clearly. Caroline will have to decide."

"Father," said Anna after a pause, "I am sorry I was so beastly about James this morning. I apologize. But it is every word of it true. I suppose if I had been more brave and told you and Mother you might have stopped him. I'll never forgive myself for being a coward. But Father, James did so promise to be reformed, and I thought you would be so unhappy if you knew. Please say I wasn't too cowardly."

"No, my dear," said her father, "you weren't. And in any case don't blame yourself. We are all trying to blame ourselves, so that we may think better of James, but it isn't much good. I have blamed myself too, I knew James was wild and extravagant. I thought no worse of it than that—and because I loved him so much I was afraid to speak to him. God help us all."

Anna, finding no comfort anywhere for herself or her father, sat silently stroking his hand, determining to make up for her own cowardice, her too easy belief in James's promises of amendment, by devotion to Caroline. She and Caroline, nearly the same age, had been more like fond sisters than sisters-in-law. The

glimpse—more terrifying to her from her happy life at
Beechwood—of a brutal and debased James had increased her
protecting love for Caroline. She felt, rightly or wrongly, that if she
had a husband like James she would have battered him morally, if
not actually physically, into decent behavior, and had no doubt of
her ability to do so. She saw that her sister-in-law was too gentle
and afraid to stand up to James and would have liked to take her
under her wing and fight her battles. What she did not understand
was the passive strength that Caroline had, a strength to suffer and
endure though not a strength to fight or conquer. She had come to
know Francis and Hugh since Caroline's marriage and felt for
Francis some of the protective affection she felt for Caroline. In her
romantic head Caroline pale and fainting, Francis as the desperate
rescuer, were all jumbled up together, and she was already more
than half in love with Francis because he had saved Caroline, as she
put it to herself. She sat thinking of him till Wilfred and George
came in.

"Hullo, you are home early," she said.

"Dr. Herbert was called off to a case and we all felt a bit
depressed, so we came back," said George. "How's Caroline?"

"Asleep or as near as. Go up quietly if you can. Was anyone
else there?"

"Colonel Beaton that has come to live at Whitelands, and his
daughter. She is called Julia and she is nineteen and very jolly.
Colonel Beaton is a widower, though he doesn't look old enough,"
said Wilfred, whose ideas of the right age for a widower appeared
to have strict limitations.

"He must be the Beaton who wrote that extremely able book
about Alexander the Great's campaigns," said Mr. Danvers, who
had a way, disconcerting to outsiders, of knowing a great deal
about subjects entirely unconnected with his merchanting business. His family accepted his wide knowledge as a matter of
course and treated him as a combined Encyclopædia Britannica,
Dictionary of National and Foreign Biography, and authority
on Modern English Usage. It was a family saying "Look it up in

father" instead of "Look it up in the dictionary." One evening at a dinner party in London he had, to his wife and daughter's intense admiration and delight, held his own brilliantly against a politician, a painter, an authority on astronomy in the classical world, and a very affected French literary lady. After this Anna had fondly christened him Universal Intellect, a name which had subsequently been shortened to Intellect, or by his irreverent younger sons, Old Intellect.

Mr. Danvers asked Wilfred, the elder of the two, who was in charge of a department at the office, a few questions about business. Having satisfied himself on one or two points he went off to bed, leaving Anna and her young brothers together.

"I say, Anna, what really is wrong?" asked George, as soon as he had shut the door behind their father. "Dr. Herbert gave us a hint that something was up, but wouldn't say what. Old Intellect looks as if the world had come to an end. Or is he just enjoying himself being pessimistic?"

Mr. Danvers's attacks of world pessimism were rather dreaded by his family, but they gave him such intense pleasure that no one grudged him his occasional fits of depression.

"No, it's not the world this time," said Anna. "It's even more depressing. Did either of you know how much James was drinking?"

Wilfred and George exchanged glances expressive of despair at the narrow-mindedness of women.

"Oh, come," said Wilfred, "I wouldn't call it drinking. I've seen James pretty tight once or twice in town, but nothing to worry about. You do take everything so seriously, Anna."

Anna, who was quite aware how much her affectionate young brothers despised her, and was privately amused by them, began to feel her temper rise. Both the boys adored James, partly because of the glamour of his being on the staff of a newspaper, and partly because he treated them as contemporaries and gave them such an amusing time in town when he remembered their existence. An elder brother who leads an idyllic existence of lunching at restaurants, frequenting cocktail parties, always meeting really important people like film stars and actresses, and then suddenly has to dash off to his newspaper in an aura of importance, is naturally a hero to young men who go to their father's office every day and work for regular hours.

"I wouldn't worry if it was only for ourselves," said Anna, "but Caroline had to live with him."

"Well, that's her job, and if she doesn't complain I don't see why you should," said Wilfred, not very kindly.

At this Anna completely lost her temper and let loose on her brothers the accumulated nerve strain of the day. She described Caroline's arrival, what Francis had told them, what she herself had seen of James in London, what James had written to Caroline, how Dr. Herbert took a serious view of Caroline's condition. When she had finished speaking, flushed and almost in tears of rage, there was an unnatural silence. Both young men were a little shocked and, what they deeply resented, made distinctly uncomfortable by their sister's outburst. These were things, they felt, which should be discussed without fuss by their parents, who would then vaguely do something which would make everything all right again. They were sorry if James had been a bit of a nuisance to Caroline, but women do exaggerate so dreadfully. Anna had probably seen James when he was a bit jolly and had invented the rest.

George, whose affections, nice though he was, were not deep or extensive, then more or less told Anna what he thought, taking a lofty man of the world attitude which she did her best not to resent, or at least only to resent inside herself. Wilfred, whose kinder heart was touched, though his feelings as a man bade him discount much of Anna's outburst, sat in embarrassed silence.

"All right," said Anna getting up, "I won't say any more. Divorce is bad enough without having family rows."

"Oh, that's too thick," said Wilfred, startled. "Divorce? But why? I'll see James myself."

"You can't," said Anna, with some satisfaction. "He has gone off with a woman leaving a lot of debts behind at the office, and no one knows where he is. Anyway a divorce will be much worse for Father and Mother than for us. They still mind that sort of thing. I must say I mind it myself too," she added, "though all in favor of it."

Wilfred found it quite impossible to explain that while he thought absolutely nothing of divorce, and indeed thought but poorly of any establishment in which at least one partner had not been divorced, yet he did not at all wish his elder brother to be associated with that necessary and sordid business. So he let his annoyance boil over onto the absent.

"I must say Father and Mother are the most maddening people," he said resentfully. "If it isn't one idea it's another. I should have thought they'd have been on James's side. Well, anyway, I shan't be here much longer. I loathe business and I know a man who wants me to go to Kenya. That's more the life. Well, I'm off."

He went rather blusteringly out of the room, but Anna noticed that though he made a parade of flinging the door open and closing it violently behind him, he took considerable pains to shut it noiselessly, and she felt comforted and able to laugh.

"Is it really as bad as that, Anna?" asked George, who had been silent for a long time.

"Worse if anything."

"Well, I'm terribly sorry for Caroline. I expect she nagged a bit. That often makes married chaps take to drink, you know," he said wisely. "As for James he's a bit of a rotter, but I dare say he hasn't any idea what he's doing. Lots of fellows haven't when they're a bit tight. Of course Mother and Old Intellect are angels, but they don't begin to understand the first thing, and Wilfred gets all hot and bothered when there's no need. You're a bit hot and bothered yourself, Anna. I must say there's one person that no one seems to think of, and that's me. It won't be much fun for me at the office if Wilfred is going off to Kenya and James is getting divorced. But I expect Caroline will come round. I'll have a talk to her myself. Anyway, thank God the Russian ballet will be here next year."

Knowing well that her mother and the efficient Scotch nurse would deal with George's well-meant suggestion, Anna said nothing, but kissed him good night. She remained alone for a little longer by the dying fire, thinking of Caroline and Francis, and then, more satisfactorily, of Francis and herself. But when she went upstairs it was only like her parents and Francis to find sleep fugitive and remote. Hugh, Wilfred and George had gone to sleep in various stages of indignation. Caroline, drugged to unconsciousness, lay still, her body quiescent, though no one could know through what abyss of cold horror her mind passed that night.

To such a pass had James brought the people who had loved him most.

CHAPTER 2

PICKING UP THE THREADS

Caroline Danvers had slept badly as she often did. Not till nearly six o'clock did she fall into a sleep which though full of terrifying and exhausting dreams was at least unbroken till eight, when the noise of Wilfred and George banging their way from bedroom to bathroom and from bathroom via bedroom downstairs to breakfast roused her for good. She lay for a few moments, still immobile with fear of her last dream, till returning consciousness of the difficulties of daily life drowned the terrors of the night in a wave of sick apprehension. She sometimes looked back with incredulous longing to the first year of her married life, to nights of refreshing dreamless sleep, to a waking that was a daily miracle of happiness, to days that were full of the joy and excitement of James, his friends, his writing, his delightful irresponsibility, his passionate worship of herself. After that first year darkness had fallen upon her world. James had vanished and a stranger had taken his place, unstable and unfaithful, turning his worship of her to something from the memory of which her mind shudderingly withdrew, losing friends, work, honor, self-respect.

After two years of hopeless misery, borne at first with useless tears and entreaties, then with stupefied resignation, Francis had brought her to Beechwood. Then there was nothing but a confused memory of days and weeks in the bedroom which Anna had given up to her so that she need not be moved, of the kind anxious faces of her father and mother-in-law, of glimpses of Francis, of visits from Hugh who had brought her flowers and had nothing to say, of occasional calls from Wilfred and George when, weak as she was, she could be amused by their obvious embarrassment and their ill-concealed relief when Anna or Mrs. Danvers turned them out.

Then came the tedious affair of divorce in which Caroline did as various people told her without any particular interest. It became known later that James had gone to South Africa, though whether with or without someone who appreciated him was not disclosed. And in due course Caroline was free to do exactly as she liked with herself. Mr. and Mrs. Danvers would not hear of her leaving them and she felt apathetically grateful for their kindness, so she stayed on at Beechwood, devotedly watched by Anna, and always filling Wilfred and George with a faint feeling of discomfort by her presence. They liked her, but after all she had been James's wife and one couldn't help feeling a bit awkward. He had been a jolly good chap, and if one wasn't to talk about him in front of the family just in case it upset Caroline, that was only another instance of the grinding tyranny which one had to put up with.

For the past year Caroline had not been in town except for such law business as made her presence absolutely necessary. Hugh had been away for most of the time, doing foreign correspondence for his newspaper, and Francis had been extremely busy, so she had seen little of her cousins. Life at Beechwood had flowed again in its accustomed channels and except that Mr. and Mrs. Danvers both looked older, Caroline might have been right in feeling that everything was a dream and life might go on where it had so suddenly stopped more than a year ago.

Now as autumn drew on Mr. and Mrs. Danvers were taking

Anna, Caroline and the boys to London for the winter. The large house in Cadogan Square was opened and made ready for the family. It was the thought of this change that filled Caroline with such alarm as she lay in bed at Beechwood on a sunny October morning. She had begged her mother-in-law to leave her at Beechwood where she said she would be quite happy alone, or with the Herberts and the Beatons for occasional company, but Mrs. Danvers made such a point of her coming that Caroline had to give in.

"It doesn't much matter where I am," she said wearily to Anna who came in to sit on the end of her bed before she got up.

"Don't be so silly, Caroline. I have got a kind of sister after all these years of brothers and I need you badly. We shall have my sitting room at Cadogan Square to ourselves and go to concerts and things and it will be great fun. And now Hugh is back we can make him and Francis take us about a bit."

"Is Hugh back? I didn't know."

"Didn't Francis ever tell you? He writes to you so often that I thought he would certainly have mentioned it."

"No," said Caroline, "he never told me. Perhaps it won't be so bad in town after all, Anna. Of course Hugh is never free at night because of his newspaper, but we might have lunches or Sunday evenings. Anna, why can't I help having that morbid feeling that people will say "That's the woman who was such a soft fool that she couldn't stop her husband drinking, so he ran away with someone else?"

"Because you *are* morbid, darling. I wish I could explain to you kindly enough how very little people do notice one, even if one is as lovely as you are. Truly, Caroline, neither beauty nor misfortune is an asset. What you need is a thick skin and to enjoy life as it comes. Get up now, darling, or you'll never get packed."

When Caroline came downstairs she found Colonel Beaton and his daughter Julia in the drawing room, come to say good-bye. Colonel Beaton was a tall spare man whose blue eyes, wrinkled at the corners, looked more like a sailor's than a soldier's. He had retired from the army when he inherited a small estate near Beechwood called Whitelands. Here he farmed mildly and wrote scholarly books about military matters. Julia was just what a Julia should be, with dark hair and eyes, fair skin, red lips, and pretty hands and feet. She adored her father and was perfectly content to do whatever he liked.

"Well, Caroline," said Colonel Beaton, who had got onto very friendly terms with the Beechwood family in the past year, "I am sorry you are going to town. We shall miss you and Anna."

"So shall I," said Caroline, "I mean Anna and I will miss you and Julia."

"Will you really?" said Colonel Beaton.

"Why of course we shall. I shall miss you both especially, because I have so few friends in London now. Anna has heaps."

"That's too bad," said Colonel Beaton, a remark which Caroline could not quite interpret.

"Never mind, Caroline," said Julia. "Father is going to lecture on Agrippa—oh well, Agricola then—at the end of November, and we'll be up in town for a few days. We must all go to a show then. Do you know any men in London?"

"There are my cousins Hugh Mannering and Francis Lester," said Caroline, thinking of Hugh.

"There are Caroline's cousins Francis Lester and Hugh Mannering," said Anna, thinking of Francis.

"And there are Wilfred and George," said Julia. "Oh, we shall do splendidly. I don't know your cousin Francis but I adore your cousin Hugh, Caroline. Why don't they come here oftener?"

"They are both busy and Hugh has been abroad."

"But of course, so he has. Father and I met him in Berlin last spring. We had the greatest fun. Father wanted to talk to him seriously about political situations, but I wouldn't let them, and we danced and danced and went to all the beerhalls and places. I adore anyone who dances well. You must come and dance with us, Caroline. Or don't you dance now? Perhaps I oughtn't to have asked you."

"Oh, yes, I would dance. Divorce isn't like being in mourning, if that is what you are thinking of."

"No, no, I didn't mean that. At least not quite that. I thought it might be like a kind of half mourning perhaps. We needn't go anywhere *very* smart."

Julia was then suppressed and taken away by her father, who made no effort to apologize for his silly daughter, feeling that she was her own excuse.

"Julia!" said Anna in an exclamation when they had gone.

"I know," said Caroline. "No one could mind what Julia says, but it doesn't help one to get over the morbidness, does it? Of course it is good practice to talk about divorce as if it were quite an amusing trifle, and I need some practice. Anna, I won't be morbid."

The journey to London was a short one, taking under an hour, which was why Wilfred and George were able to go up and down to work every day when they were at Beechwood. It was on this day in no way remarkable except for words between Wilfred and George, who had been given a day off from the office because their mother felt she needed them, though for no specific reason. The words were on the subject of breakfast. George said a man couldn't possibly do a decent morning's work unless he had a decent breakfast with porridge and eggs and bacon and toast and marmalade and tea. Wilfred maintained that half a grapefruit and a small cup of coffee were the only food a man could work on. Any more than that, he said, and a man was useless for the rest of the day. This led by easy stages to George comparing Wilfred with Hitler, and Wilfred drawing a trenchant parallel between George and the Ogpu, at which point Mrs. Danvers who was doing a crossword puzzle, asked for the name of a bird in three letters, only it mustn't be emu or tit.

"There is only one other bird in crossword circles," said Mr.

Danvers suddenly waking from a feigned sleep in which he was trying to ignore his sons' differences, "moa."

Mrs. Danvers thanked him, and Wilfred, who could not bear not to be of help in anything that was going on, went and sat next to his mother and annoyed her frightfully by suggesting words before she was ready for them.

"Do you know, I have never been upstairs in this house?" said Caroline to Anna who was showing her the bedroom next to her own and the bathroom they were to share. "When I used to come here to dinner with James I sometimes got as far as your mother's room to take off my coat, but never any further. I sometimes thought I'd ask your mother if I could spend the night here instead of going home, but it would have seemed too marked."

"Why?"

"It would have looked as if one wanted to get away from James, as indeed one did," said Caroline, as she took things out of her dressing case and arranged them. "Anna, I do wish there were a name to call one's husband after one has divorced him. It sounds so silly to say James to outsiders when a person is right out of one's life. Could I be continental do you think and say Danvers?"

"Well, darling, you could," said Anna, "but as father is Danvers, not to speak of Wilfred and George, and heaps of cousins and uncles that we have, I think it would be less confusing to say James."

"Yes, perhaps. All the same a name like Nemo, or The Aforesaid would be much less uncomfortable. I don't mind with you, Anna, but with anyone else it is uncomfortable past words. I wish words didn't hurt one so much."

"If you say them often enough they won't," said Anna. "It's all habit. Say your own name often enough and it sounds like gibberish. Similarly with any other name."

"Do you think so?" asked Caroline, much interested. She sat down before the mirror and looked at herself; saying "Caroline,

Caroline, Caroline." Her image in the glass blurred and faded and became clear again. From under the brim of her hat a white face looked at her with dark eyes, its lips, twisted with whimsical disbelief, making the motion of "Caroline, Caroline."

"No, it doesn't work," she said at last. "I can't get away from my own name or my own face. It's a horrid thought that one's same name and face may be waiting for one after one is dead for ever and ever. The one thing one wants to get away from one is tied to for ever and ever."

"Tonight I shall say you are tired with the journey and the way those silly boys behaved," said Anna. "Tomorrow I shall scold you if you go on like that. Go and have your bath first, because I haven't started unpacking. We haven't much time if Francis and Hugh are coming."

Caroline jumped up.

"Is Hugh coming?" she asked.

"And Francis. Didn't mother tell you there was a telephone message when we arrived?"

"She did say something," Caroline confessed, "but to be truthful, Anna, I was so busy feeling sorry for myself that I didn't listen. What a self-centered beast I am. I can't think how you can bear me."

"Nor can I. Hurry up with that bath."

When Caroline came down she found Francis and Hugh in the drawing room with Mrs. Danvers. Because she was anxious to be in the background as much as possible, she had dressed in black which didn't suit her. Hugh was very sorry to see his cousin Caroline looking so unwell and determined to be very kind to her and do his best to cheer her up. Luckily he was next to her at dinner, so he had every opportunity of carrying out his kind plan, but he found the result rather disappointing. In vain did he tell Caroline about his experiences on the Continent, the statesmen he had met, the information he had gathered, the plays and ballets he had seen. Caroline was very quiet and hardly did more than say yes or no at the right moment, or sometimes at the

wrong moment. She had a disconcerting way of suddenly looking straight into one's eyes, as if she were sending a message over
the flow of speech between her and whoever was talking to her.
More than once while he was speaking Hugh found Caroline's
eyes fixed upon him with this strange penetrating quality, as if
she were trying to see right into his mind, ignoring the obstruc-
tion of speech. Once or twice he tried to return her direct gaze,
but there was something baffling in it, as if she were prepared to
advance and yet were on the point of flight. So Hugh contented
himself with smiling kindly at her whenever their eyes met.

Presently her attention was claimed by George who wanted
her sympathy. Did she, he inquired, think there was anything
wrong in going straight to bed when one came home after a
theatre. Caroline said she thought it a reasonable thing to do.

"I thought you would. But Mother always wants us to see if
the light is on in her room and come in and say good night and
give her a chatty little account of what we've been doing. I must
say for Old Intellect that he never bothers one so long as one
doesn't slam the front door when one comes in, and turns up at
the office on time next day. If one isn't to have any freedom at
all, one might as well be in the nursery. Ask Wilfred and see
what he says."

"It is rather horrid to have to talk about plays directly you
come home," said Caroline sympathetically. "I always feel very
cross after I have seen a play I like, and hate everybody. I
remember once at a play with Hugh—"

She stopped suddenly. If she began to remember that evening
she would remember too much, she would remember how
James had looked at her when she got home, what that night
had been.

Francis, looking at her between the shaded candles from the
other side of the table, wondered what George could have said
to make her suddenly look as if she expected someone to hit her.
George was an extremely good example of a spoilt young man—
both the boys were spoilt he considered—and quite insensitive,

but not unkind. Caroline must still be very unarmed, very easy to hurt. When she came into the room before dinner he had been looking forward to resuming the companionship that the last year had interrupted, but now he hardly knew whether the old Caroline lived at all. She was not changed in any respect that he could single out, yet she was different. Something like an invisible sheet of glass was between them. He wondered uneasily if she still thought of James, if she was blaming herself for not enduring more, for having decided to break the tie between them forever. If this were so he would have to blame himself as well for the part he had taken when her divorce was under discussion. At first he had not wanted to interfere, but Caroline would not or could not express her feelings, and Mr. and Mrs. Danvers had begged him to help them in the decision. As he looked at the matter there was no doubt at all what was best for Caroline, and his advice, together with the Danvers's urgent wish to see Caroline in safety, had certainly played a part in persuading Caroline to agree. Some step had to be taken, and Caroline was so broken that she would have let things slide forever, so her nearest friends had to make her decide.

As he looked at her she turned around again to Hugh and he saw her looking into Hugh's eyes, for she was tall and their faces as they sat were almost on a level, with the curious insistence that had so often charmed and baffled him in her. Twice in her deepest need she had summoned her spirit from its unknown fastnesses to send a message to Hugh. What was the meaning of the messages, the meaning of her grave appraising gaze? Francis told himself not to be a fool and began to talk to Mrs. Danvers, who was full of plans for the winter, for committees, dinner parties, lectures, the manifold business of an idle winter in town.

"I want you to get Caroline to take more interest in things," she said in a low voice. "Dr. Herbert is fairly satisfied with her now, but she has very little life. Anna and I feel that she ought to make an effort and go about more. Partly on Cecil's account, because it makes him so unhappy to see the poor child living through each day simply to get to the end of it. You and Hugh must take her out. She looks quite happy talking to Hugh now."

"You never hear of James, I suppose?" said Francis, finding himself, much to his own annoyance, speaking of James in a hushed voice as if he were dead.

"No, never, except that his allowance is drawn regularly. It is very thoughtless of him. I sometimes feel," said Mrs. Danvers with the voice of one who has a gentle grievance, "that if Caroline had been a little firmer we should not have had all this trouble. But no one listens to me, so I say nothing."

"You don't know what she feels about it?"

"Anna may know. I don't. She doesn't tell me anything. I find it very trying not to know what is going on. The boys are just the same, or if they do tell me what they are doing it is at such awkward times. George for instance still keeps up his schoolboy habit of coming to say good night when he gets in late. I don't mean at four in the morning, but after a dinner or a play. Of course I love to see him, but so often I have just read myself into a comfortable sleepy state and the dear boy comes crashing upstairs and hangs about outside my door till I have to call him to come in, and then he gives me a long account of his evening which is, I must say, usually a complaint about how boring the play was or what a poor dinner he had, and by then I am entirely unsleepy again. And then he goes off and doesn't shut the door properly and I have to call after him. So trying."

Caroline had turned to Hugh, rather abruptly deserting her young brother-in-law's grievances, because her ears had caught a phrase passing between Hugh and her father-in-law who owing to a dearth of women were sitting next to each other.

"Oh, Father," she said breaking into their talk, for during the past year she had come to call Mr. and Mrs. Danvers by name as if they were her own parents, "Father, is Hugh really to stay in London now? What fun?"

"Not only London," said Hugh, "but no more night work except, my dear cousin, what conscience dictates. Didn't you know that I had given up my newspaper work and am editing the new monthly about international affairs?"

"No, I didn't know," said Caroline. "I mostly don't know about things. Will they pay you well?"

"Very well. I shall now be able to afford to give you champagne. Or do you fancy an oyster?"

It was at this moment that Caroline had given Hugh one of the beseeching inquiring looks which Francis had seen from the other side of the table. Her lovely generous mouth smiled the pleasure that she felt, but her look held some secret thought.

"I would adore oysters," she said. "When?"

"We must fix up an evening and get Anna and Francis to come," said Hugh enthusiastically, and then he continued his talk with Mr. Danvers about the new review. Hugh was doing what he called "picking Danvers's brains," a process that took the form of a monologue which though amusing and brilliant in itself never gave Mr. Danvers a chance to get a word in edgeways. But Mr. Danvers was quite content to be amused, though he thought Hugh would be better employed in amusing Caroline.

After dinner Francis at last found an opportunity of talking to Caroline. Hugh had swept the rest of the party into his conversational net and was finding them a better audience for his continental experiences than his cousin had been. Wilfred was anxious to be confirmed in his feeling that Soviet Russia was on the whole Antichrist and an underbred Mongol one at that, while George counted on Hugh to support him in his view of Hitler as a second Attila and Russia as a rather better version of the Millennium. Mrs. Danvers fluttered anxiously at the sound of voices in unbrotherly debate, Anna enjoyed the riot, while Mr. Danvers, amused by it all and perfectly conscious that no one would be interested in his point of view, admired the skill with which Hugh pacified and satisfied both the boys.

Francis sat by Caroline on a sofa in the back drawing room

and could think of nothing better to say than "How are you, Caroline?"

"Very well, thank you, Francis, and so pleased to see you again. And how very nice that Hugh is to be in London again. He said we could all have oysters, you both, and Anna, and I."

"And very nice too. Caroline, are you really well now? You don't look quite yourself."

"Well, you see I am not quite myself," said Caroline, giving him one of her level glances which disturbed him. "One isn't, you know."

Francis found no answer to this.

"But I have every intention of being someone, even if I'm not myself," Caroline continued, spreading her hands out between herself and the fire. "Mother—Mrs. Danvers—is full of plans for this winter and I shall try to do things to please her. They have been such darlings to me and it's the least I can do to try to please them."

"You have such lovely hands," said Francis, who did not appear to have heard what she was saying.

"Yes," said Caroline complacently. "I get a good deal of comfort from them sometimes. When I see people being very comfortable and fat and prosperous and having the pitying feeling for one which is so embarrassing, I say to myself 'Never mind, Caroline, your hands, though doubtless no index to your true inner self, bear every mark of sensitiveness and breeding.' As a matter of fact," she added, "I was showing them off to see whether I could get a compliment from my kind cousin."

"Well, you have," said Francis, "so now we can go back to talking about your winter plans. What exactly do they include?"

"I don't really know. Anna and I are to enjoy ourselves and go about a good deal, whatever that means. And we are to do some good works which I detest; teach the orphan boy to read and teach the orphan girl to sew probably. Mother manages a good deal, you know. Oh, Francis, I do so little want to do things, to do anything at all. I would so much rather just sit here with you on a sofa and do nothing, and have Hugh to come and amuse us. I did so want to stay at Beechwood. Still, if Hugh isn't doing night work any longer it will be much more fun. I do hope he will remember the oysters. Oh, and Julia will be in town in December."

"Who is Julia? Why does that sound familiar?"

"Because you are thinking of Sylvia probably. I thought you knew Julia Beaton; Hugh does. Colonel Beaton owns White-lands now. He is perfectly delightful and writes books."

"Oh, Beaton, of course I know his books. Is Mrs. Beaton a great friend of yours?"

"Mrs. Beaton? Oh, you mean Julia. She is his daughter. His wife died years ago. But he is extraordinarily young for his age. Anna and I are extremely fond of him."

Francis could not but dislike Colonel Beaton on hearing these words.

There was a great noise of laughing from the other room and George came strolling across to them looking sulky.

"I can tell you, for a man who takes the political state of Europe seriously, as I do," he said, keeping the fire off his sister-in-law and her cousin, "it's pretty ghastly to hear the way people talk. Anyone who sees behind the scenes a bit can see what's going to happen before long. And whose fault will it be?"

"Not mine, George, though by your scowling you seem to say so," said Caroline.

"It is the fault of those men," said George, leaning the weight of one foot heavily on the old brass fender so that it began to bend and crack, "who framed the Treaty of Versailles. No one thought of us younger men. It is an old man's muddle. Russia is the only country where youth has an equal claim. Here we are ciphers."

Francis and Caroline made soothing noises.

"Look at me," continued George. "Product of a rotten public school system, brought up in comfort, put into my father's business, a safe future before me, no chance of developing my own personality. Pretty foul, isn't it?"

"Well, I shouldn't call it too bad," said Francis.

"If you don't like being yourself, what would you like to be?" asked Caroline.

"A balletomane," said George with proud courage.

"There are such a lot of new states since the map of Europe got altered," sighed Caroline.

George looked with deadly scorn at his sister-in-law.

"An amateur of the ballet," he explained. "The whole future of civilization is bound up in the Russian ballet; music, drama, rhythm, miming, self-expression through discipline. That is why Russia must eventually lead the world."

"The word ballet surprises in himself," murmured Francis, and Caroline looked gratefully at him.

"But you would need some money to live on, wouldn't you?" she said doubtfully. "I mean, the ballet is frightfully expensive, and really not much fun unless you go to the good seats."

"Good seats are simply a product of capitalism," said George angrily.

"And thank God for it," said Francis, who seeing that there was no chance of continuing his conversation with Caroline, felt that at least he need not stay and listen to George's views on the world. "Let's all go to the ballet one night. Would you like it, Caroline? I'll make Hugh fix a night and we can combine it with oysters. Will that suit you, George?"

"Oh, thanks awfully," said George, suddenly becoming a nice, natural young man.

"If I take you to good seats you mustn't mind," said Francis. "I'm a bit of a capitalist. It's a point of view, you know."

George, whose outburst against good seats was chiefly a mild form of sour grapes, as he had to economize severely on his salary to afford the stalls from which alone the balletomane can do justice to his profession, considered this statement. If capitalism was a point of view and not merely a soul degrading material state, there was obviously something to be said for it.

There was a tremendous comparing of engagement books among the younger members of the party and a night in the following week was fixed for dinner and the Russian ballet. A great deal of unselfishness was shown by the men of the party. Hugh, who had a journalist's dislike to being tied down to a date, so far condescended as to say that he would of course come unless some utterly unforeseen event prevented him. George gave up a very dull evening party at which he had hoped to meet a Communist, and Wilfred ran a pencil through an entry in his diary which had read, "West Kensington Blackshirt Rally, 7:45?", while Francis was able to enjoy the spectacle of Caroline thanking Hugh for his half-promise to come. Caroline and Anna were frankly delighted and began a babbling conversation about frocks which absorbed them entirely.

Francis and Hugh decided to walk part of the way home as the night was fine and starry.

"What a different woman Caroline looks," said Hugh. "I do hope she will have a good time this winter. It is a pity those boys have to be such a bore. I had an uneasy feeling that either of them might quarrel with me for agreeing with the other, but that both would jump on me if I tried to argue seriously with either. And neither of them knew what they were talking about. I'm sorry for Caroline."

"I think most of it slips past her," said his cousin. "When George said he wanted to be a balletomane she thought it was a Balkan state."

"Bless her," cried Hugh. "I do like that woman. I hope she will find exactly the right man to marry."

"Do you suppose she will marry again?"

"Why not? Now she has got over that swine's behavior she ought to do better. I can't imagine a more delightful wife. She is so charming, not frightfully intelligent perhaps, but quite a darling. I adore the way she looks at you as if there were someone else just behind your eyes that she was trying to see. Here, Francis, I've had enough walking."

He hailed a taxi, but his cousin preferred to walk home.

"All right," said Hugh. "I was going to have treated you to this, so you've missed a free ride." And off he drove.

Walk as fast as he might Francis could not outstrip the thoughts that were racing through his head. Hugh's assumption that Caroline would marry again had startled him. The impression that she had left upon him when he had taken her to Beechwood was so strong that he had never since thought of her except as a victim, dedicated, apart. Her languor, her expressed preference for sitting still and doing nothing that evening had not altered his point of view. But Hugh evidently saw her simply as a young woman who, being free from the consequences of an unhappy marriage would be ready to try her luck again. Perhaps, thought Francis, if one didn't feel so desperately romantic about her one would also see her in that light. If she were to marry again, what guarantee could there possibly be that she would do any better? If she did marry again it must be someone who could be trusted to look after her, someone who had known her for a long time and understood how to be kind to her. And think as he would he could discover no man in his large acquaintance who would satisfy him as a husband for Caroline. Then a horrid thought intruded itself that there might be some man unknown to him who could kindle Caroline's heart to new warmth, and with that the name of Colonel Beaton whom she had known at Beechwood came to his mind—Colonel Beaton whom she had known at Beechwood and was very fond of. It was just like women, he reflected bitterly, to be very fond of a colonel. Probably a case of propinquity. He mentally endowed the colonel with every unpleasant attribute of the colonels of fiction from senility and garrulity to heavy mustaches and a vile temper. The mere thought of anyone with heavy mustaches being in a temper with Caroline so angered him that he had to imagine himself protecting her from this phantom of his imagination, and the thought of protecting her naturally leading to the vision of himself with an arm around a frightened Caroline, telling her that Colonel Beaton would never come near her again, he suddenly stopped dead.

"Of course," he said to the pillar box which stood looking at him with a gaping expression, "I love Caroline myself."

As the pillar box had nothing to say, he continued his walk, thinking the matter over in what he considered to be a cool legal way, but what was in fact a man who had never been badly in love before discovering what anyone with any experience could have told him weeks and months ago.

Hugh, reading proofs of a contributor's article for his review, looked up as his cousin came into his room.

"Hand me down the big atlas, will you?" said Hugh.

Francis took down a large book from its shelf and put it before his cousin.

"I didn't say the bound volume of Leech, you ass. I said the atlas."

"Sorry," said Francis, making the substitution. "I say, do you think I could ask Caroline to marry me?"

"Why not?" said Hugh, looking up from his proofs for a moment.

"You don't think she might think it rather soon?"

"Soon? Why? Considering her decree was made absolute about six months ago, I should say you've been a bit slow about it."

"But I didn't know till tonight."

"Didn't you? I did."

"Knew that you loved her?" asked Francis anxiously.

"Lord, no. That you did. My dear cousin, it has been extremely visible to my trained journalistic eye for a very long time, long before that pestilent fellow left her. Seriously, Francis, I rather hoped that this would happen. I am frightfully fond of Caroline and it sounds a perfect arrangement. Go ahead."

"You don't think she cares for that fellow Beaton, do you?"

"Damn," said Hugh, with his finger on a point in the Balkans, "they've altered the spelling again—I knew they would. It used to be Gratianopolis, and then we had to say Gratzenburg, and then Graziano, and now if it isn't Gsrztz. It sounds like a place in Caroline's new state of Balletomania. What did you say about Mrs. Beeton?"

"I didn't say Beeton, I said Beaton. Colonel Beaton."

"What about Colonel Beaton?"

"You might take your head out of the atlas and listen to me for a minute, Hugh. Tell me, do you think Caroline cares for that fellow Beaton?"

"I don't know. Who is he? The one that writes?"

"Yes. He lives at Whitelands now."

"By Jove, so he does. And has a very pretty daughter too. I met them both in Berlin last year. He is a delightful fellow, the very nicest army type, a specialist on his own subject and very well informed all round. Young-looking too to have a grown-up daughter."

Francis went out of the room, slamming the door. Hugh picked up his fountain pen and continued his task of substituting Gsrztz for Graziano throughout the article.

CHAPTER 3

CROSS PURPOSES

The party for the ballet was to be a joint affair. Hugh said the dinner was his because he had promised Caroline an oyster. Francis said he would get the tickets because it was he who had suggested the ballet.

When the party assembled at a restaurant, George was seen to be carrying white gloves.

"What on earth have you got those things for?" said Wilfred to his brother.

"One does, for the ballet," said George.

"Well, one looks no end of a fool," said Wilfred.

Francis pressed cocktails on them and storm was averted.

"And how do you find London again?" Hugh asked Caroline as they ate their oysters.

"Very nice, but so terribly tiring. It is so much fuller than it was a year ago. What with Welsh Miners, and little dogs on leads, and traffic lights, one doesn't seem to be able to get anywhere. Today I was trying to shop near Sloane Square and I couldn't get along at all because of young men in black shirts giving away pamphlets."

George laughed offensively and provocatively.

"That's about all they do give away," he said.

"Has that remark any meaning?" asked Wilfred.

"None at all," said the balletomane.

"But some of them looked very charming in their black blouses," continued Caroline. "In fact I went into one of their offices to ask if I could have the pattern, and they were most sympathetic."

"They are," said Wilfred.

"I think that shirt is terribly becoming to good looking young men," said Caroline, disregarding Anna's danger signals, "but I don't think the low, rather deformed looking spotty sort look so well in it. One always wonders about the washing, of course."

"No need to wonder if you've ever been within a yard of one," said George.

Hugh, used to dealing with delicate political situations, managed to switch the conversation off to less dangerous subjects and dinner proceeded normally till coffee came, when George got up.

"Will you excuse me if I go on ahead, Hugh?" he said. "You know Simonovna appears tonight, and I have promised to meet some fellows, great admirers of hers, before the show begins. I may go around to her dressing room afterwards," he added carelessly.

"Good old non-Aryan name," said Wilfred.

George glared at his brother.

"Simonovna said I could bring any friend I liked with me," he said coldly, "but of course if you feel like that we will drop the matter."

Wilfred, on whom the lure of any theatrical dressing room exercised the potent attraction which it has for the young, at once repented his unkind words and offered to accompany his brother.

"I expect she's as Christian as any of us," he said.

"As a matter of fact," said George, "she is an Old Catholic."

"There's no need to talk about them like that," said Wilfred, nervously looking around. "Or do you mean she is old herself?"

"That," said George, "just shows how appallingly insular we are. You ought to be more internationally minded. If you said that to any continental, he would simply roar with laughter."

Wilfred was on the point of saying what he thought of foreigners who roared with laughter, but he was afraid of not being taken behind the scenes, so he went off with his brother, reconciled, but still perplexed.

"I feel about a hundred and twenty-two," said Hugh, as the young men went out.

"It means nothing," said Anna wisely. "All the young men I know are violently political, but they are always interested in other people's politics, not ours, so I can't think it is frightfully important."

"A lot of James's friends used to talk like that," said Caroline, and then went quite white.

"It's too hot for you in here, my dear," said Hugh, who was next to her, looking at her with concern. "Come along and we'll get a taxi. You bring Anna, Francis, and give me our tickets."

There was the usual block of traffic which gave plenty of time for conversation.

"Caroline," said Hugh, "I'm going to do a little blundering. Do you still care for James?"

Caroline shrank from him as if he were James himself and shook her head.

"No, no," she said. "I hardly even remember him."

"But you don't like talking of him?"

Caroline put her hand on his arm.

"No, I hate it. But I feel I ought to do a kind of five finger exercises by saying his name till I can say it without making a fool of myself. Not because of hating him, because you don't hate a person that you never think of. I think I forgot all about him when I was ill, after Francis took me to Beechwood. But a person's name can suddenly hurt one so much. Do you know what I mean?"

"I do. There are some names that one can't even say in a

normal voice because they lay open some nerve. I was frightfully in love with a woman once. Her name was Susan and she came from Norwich and she lived with her husband in Ovington Square. I fell out of love with her, and I haven't seen her or heard of her for years, but if I read or hear the words Susan, or Norwich, or Ovington, I go all queer. Nearly as queer as you went just now, my poor Caroline."

"Thank you," said Caroline, edging back towards him.

"Not at all, dear cousin. I only want to show you that though I don't forget for a moment what you have been through—and probably I don't know half of it—I don't want you to think that you are alone and shut off in being self-conscious about mentioning James. The more you can mention him the better. I didn't mean discuss him, which thank heaven we needn't do, but just to be able to let his name slip out naturally. It will be easier for his people too. Do you mind my telling you this, darling?"

"No. I am really very grateful and I'll try hard. Was she very lovely, Hugh?"

"Who?"

"Susan, that you were in love with."

"I suppose she was. I really would hardly know her now."

Caroline had by now reached her normal position in the taxi so that Hugh could comfortably slip his arm through hers.

"I shall try to behave better," she announced.

"My dear, you are perfect. But I can't bear to see my cousin pale and distressed, so I had to give you good advice. Don't let yourself be too lonely. You need someone to bully you. Not really bully," he added, as he felt Caroline flinch, "only for your good. I hope some day we may be on terms that will let me bully you even more than I do. Bless you, child. How much does it say on the clock? Two and threepence? I shall give the man three shillings to mark my approval of my fellow passenger."

Francis and Anna were also beguiling the time with conversation, as their taxi moved forwards with jerks and grindings.

"How is everyone at Beechwood?" asked Francis, approaching the subject cautiously.

Anna, pleased to talk of her beloved Beechwood, said that everyone was very well. Francis inquired if a fellow called Beaton hadn't come into Whitelands. Anna said he had, adding that the society of Colonel Beaton and his daughter Julia had been the greatest pleasure and solace to herself and Caroline.

"Everyone likes Colonel Beaton," she said. "Father is so glad to have someone really clever to talk to, and Mother adores him. He has done Caroline a lot of good and really takes her out of herself."

Francis said how glad he was to hear it.

"He is working on Gustavus Adolphus at present," Anna continued. "Julia tries to do secretary for him, but she is so silly, though an adorable creature, that she isn't much good. So Caroline goes over to help sometimes. She is rather good at reading Colonel Beaton's handwriting, which is like an oriental manuscript. I hope she will go on with the secretarying when we go down to Beechwood again. It is so good for her."

Francis said with some difficulty that he was sure it was.

"Francis," said Anna, "I do hope darling Caroline will marry again. It sounds a brutal sort of thing to say after the time she had with that beast James, but she oughtn't to be hanging about as an unattached woman. She seems to have a kind of feeling that people don't want her because she hasn't a husband. It isn't true of course, but she can easily make it true by shutting herself away from people. You will do all you can to help, won't you, Francis?"

"Of course I will."

"I have sometimes had a kind of idea that she and Hugh might get married," pursued Anna, zealous for her sister-in-law's good.

Francis nearly laughed at the preposterous idea, but determined not to disabuse Anna. It would be all the more amusing for her when she found how wrong she had been.

"Do you think we are a nice family to marry into?" he asked carelessly.

"Of course I do."

"I'm glad you think so," said Francis, examining a handful of silver and coppers, "because what you think will mean a good deal to me."

Anna got out and went into the theatre while Francis paid the cab. Her mind was so whirling with the thoughts that Francis's last remark had roused that at first she hardly saw her brother George, white-gloved, the center of a group of serious young men, with Wilfred hanging about nervously at the edge of the crowd. George waved kindly to her, but she gathered that the presence of an acknowledged sister might be a blot on his evening, so she went on with Francis to the seats where Caroline and Hugh were already installed.

During the interval Francis and Hugh found themselves alone for a moment.

"I say," said Hugh, "I did some good work for you in the taxi. I hinted to Caroline that she needed someone to look after her, and she didn't seem at all displeased."

"Oh," Francis. "I say, what do you think Anna said? She has a mad kind of idea that it is you who are fond of Caroline."

"That," said Hugh, "is where her toes turn in. But seriously, Francis, you know I would be frightfully pleased to see you and Caroline happy, so go ahead. After all, why should you want me and Anna to help you, I don't know. Perhaps I'm butting in where I'm not wanted. But you aren't being very ardent, you know," said Hugh in a slightly disappointed voice.

"Ardent," said Francis with a short laugh. "Oh, well, never mind. But one daren't say too much or go too fast. She is all quivering with nerves still and I feel as if one word too much might drive her so far into herself that I couldn't get her back."

"Damn that swine James," said Hugh in a loud cheerful voice which made a young man near him, whose name happened to be through no fault of his own Henry James, give a nervous start and move hastily away. Francis heartily concurred.

When the performance was over the younger men disappeared, to continue the arduous night life of balletomanes in Simonovna's dressing room and afterwards at the Café Royal, so Francis and Hugh took the others home in a taxi.

"I would ask you to come in," said Anna at the door, "but the parents are probably asleep, and if they are asleep they will infallibly wake up and be gently reproachful tomorrow. On the other hand, if they are awake they will expect me to go and report myself, and wonder why we stayed so long downstairs. So, do you mind?"

"Good night, Caroline," said Francis, "come and have tea with us one day soon."

"Yes, do," said Hugh. "Good night, dear cousin."

"Good night, Anna," said Francis. "Take care of Caroline. I am so thankful that she has you with her."

"Of course I will," said Anna.

"And will you come to tea if Caroline comes?"

"Of course."

So Anna and Caroline went upstairs to bed. As they slept on the third floor back and Mr. and Mrs. Danvers on the second floor front, they were able to talk in safety, once they had got past the landing. But neither was very much inclined for talk, so they kissed and said good night.

Anna lay awake for some time thinking about Caroline and her cousins. If Hugh and Caroline did get married, it would be an excellent plan. Francis evidently thought so too, and Francis had said that what she thought would mean a good deal to him. It seemed to Anna that if Francis, whose image was seldom absent from her thoughts, cared so much for her opinion, he might perhaps care for her in other ways. If she had heard Hugh's conversation with Caroline, she would have appreciated what he said about the potency of names. The mere mention of the words Lincoln's Inn Fields (where Francis had his office), was enough to set her whole being madly adrift like a leaf in a gale. She was by now indulging in her favorite pastime when alone, of imagining the scene in which Francis would ask her to marry him, the extraordinary bliss it would be when he held her in his arms. Just as she was trying to make up her mind whether it would be more romantic to be proposed to on the drawing room hearth rug after dinner (her family having obligingly dematerialized), or in Francis's study when she and Caroline went to tea there, a sound from Caroline's room broke into her imaginings. She sat up in bed to listen and again heard a stifled cry. At once she got up and opened the door between their rooms. Feeling her way by the light from her own room, she turned on the reading lamp by Caroline's bed. Her sister-in-law lay looking at her with unseeing eyes and such an expression of frozen terror that Anna was almost afraid.

"Can I do anything, darling?" she asked uncertainly.

Caroline recognized her and the wild light died from her eyes.

"I am so sorry," she said apologetically. "It was a nightmare, and I didn't know where I was. I hope I didn't wake you. What time is it?"

"Only one o'clock, darling. I was still awake and you didn't wake me a bit. What was it?" she asked, sitting on the bed and holding Caroline's shaking hands.

"James," said Caroline. "I thought he was here, and then I tried to call Hugh to save me, and then I must have screamed till I woke myself up. I am so dreadfully sorry."

Anna's feelings towards her elder brother were so venomous that she could not trust herself to speak. Telling Caroline to put a shawl around her and keep warm, she padded downstairs in dressing gown and slippers and explored the kitchen regions for milk. While the milk was warming on the gas stove, she gave herself a good deal of relief by squashing two or three black beetles with a flat iron, treating each as symbolic of James. Then she took the milk upstairs. As she reached the first floor landing she heard the chink of a latch key, and Wilfred and George came in. She gathered from the muffled noises that reached her that both her brothers were taking their shoes off, less from an altruistic desire not to disturb their parents than from a wish not to be caught on the way upstairs. She ran up to her own landing, and bending over the banisters in the dark, listened. The boys had accomplished more than half their journey in safety when just outside Mrs. Danvers's room George let one of his shoes fall. Immediately a line of light appeared at Mrs. Danvers's partly open door, and Anna heard her mother's voice saying, "Is that you, boys? Come and tell me if you had a nice time."

There was a short scuffle on the landing and Wilfred appeared breathless beside her, so exalted by his back stage experiences that the sight of his sister on the landing at half past one in the morning with a glass of milk did not appear to strike him as at all unusual.

"Mother has caught George," he announced in a whisper. "I'm off to bed."

"Go quietly," said Anna. "Caroline can't sleep tonight."

"Rotten luck," said Wilfred sympathetically, and went into his room where he performed a series of ballet steps, reminiscent of Simonovna, to his own whistled accompaniment while undressing.

Anna took the milk to Caroline, sat with her while she drank it, and remained with her till George, whose pleasure had been dragged to earth by having to tell his mother about it, and even having to allude to Simonovna in so soul destroying a place as his own home, came muttering upstairs and banged his door. After this Anna went back to bed and fell asleep with Francis in her mind.

CHAPTER 4

ANNA HAS A SERIOUS TALK

Although the cousins and Anna met on various occasions, the projected tea party did not take place for some weeks. Hugh had to go abroad once or twice and Francis was away for several weekends, so it was not till near the end of November that Hugh rang Anna up one morning, inviting her and Caroline to tea on the following Saturday. Anna said they would love to come, but they were going to Colonel Beaton's lecture that afternoon at three-thirty, so might they bring him and his daughter to tea as they would be staying at Cadogan Square.

"Of course that will be splendid," said Hugh. "You know I met Beaton and Julia in Berlin and fell for them both. How is Caroline?"

"Very well. How is Francis?"

"Very fit. He'll be awfully glad to have the chance of meeting Beaton. He was asking me something about him only the other day."

Francis was standing by his study fire when his cousin broke the news to him that evening, and his pleasure took the outward and visible form of kicking a piece of coal violently and uttering a malediction on people who couldn't leave plans alone.

"Dash it all," said Hugh, not unreasonably, "why shouldn't I ask Beaton and his daughter? I know them both, and they are charming. Besides, I want to pick Beaton's brains for the review."

The whole Danvers family looked forward to the visit of the Beatons. Anna and Caroline were very fond of father and daughter, and Julia got on excellently with the boys. With Mrs. Danvers Colonel Beaton was a great favorite, while Mr. Danvers, who had talked a good deal with him at Beechwood, had a great respect for his capacity and had made certain suggestions which Colonel Beaton divulged to Anna.

The Beatons were to spend the night before the lecture at Cadogan Square. As Mr. and Mrs. Danvers were out when the Beatons arrived, Anna gave them tea in her sitting room. When Wilfred and George came in about six o'clock, they carried Julia off to hear some new gramophone records, so that Colonel Beaton and Anna were left alone.

"Anna," he said presently, "do tell me something about your young brothers. I don't know them well, and I have a rather special reason for wanting to know."

"Well, Wilfred is an English Fascist, but he can't be bothered to go to the blackshirt meetings much, because they are apt to happen on nights when he has a theater or dance, besides somehow involving him in high tea. George is very pro-Soviet and adores Russian ballet. At least that is what they have been this autumn, but really you never know. Of course it's easier for George than for Wilfred, because the ballet is so nice to go to, though expensive."

Colonel Beaton laughed.

"That's all right," he said. "All young men need a label. But I mean how do they seriously think of their lives? Do they like the business? Are they keen to get on in it and make it a success?"

"As far as I can see, and of course an elder sister, I imagine, sees less than many other people, George is keener than Wilfred. George does so love town life and being what he calls a balletomane, and he wants to get rich so that he can go about a

lot and entertain. But Wilfred loves going abroad. Sometimes
he says he will go to a friend who farms in Kenya, but we haven't
heard so much of that lately. I don't think he will stay in father's
business myself."

"That's very helpful. Now, Anna, I will tell you what is in my
mind, because you may be able to help me with a decision. Does
your father ever discuss his affairs with you?"

"Sometimes."

"He has talked about them a good deal to me and he is, like
you, not at all sure that Wilfred is fitted for his business and he
wants me to consider coming in. Now this interests me very
much. I have a pretty good knowledge of the markets your father
deals with, and I've got some capital, and I'm not entirely
without business experience. But I can't go much further in this
unless I am absolutely sure that I'm not injuring your brothers'
prospects in any way. It would hardly affect George, for he is still
so young that he couldn't possibly hold for some time to come
the kind of position your father wants me to take. But with
Wilfred I feel a certain difficulty. He is older and might resent
an outsider coming in over his head, and whatever I do I can't
possibly imperil my delightful relations with your family. No
decisions need to be made immediately but if you can, by your
clever brain and your intuition, get at what your brothers,
Wilfred in particular, feel, I shall be very grateful. Wilfred
doesn't take life as easily as George. He will expect too much
and feel rather bitter when he doesn't get what he wants. I have
seen dozens of young subalterns like him. The first time things
go wrong they want to shoot themselves; if they don't, they are
some of our best men in time. He is growing up slowly and it
hurts him. Now George is growing up quickly and easily, and no
outsider would guess that he is the younger of the two. I
wouldn't mind hurting George, because he would soon get over
it and bear no malice. Wilfred would resent the shattering of any
dream or ideal he had and never forget the humiliation. That's

why I so need your help, to prevent me from making any mistake which might be disastrous to our friendship."

Anna, immensely flattered at being treated as a grown-up person by her guest and having her opinion asked, promised to do all she could to sound her brothers without rousing their suspicions. The colonel then asked after Caroline.

"She is much better," said Anna. "I think London and seeing people are doing her good. By the way, you know her cousin Hugh Mannering, don't you? He said he met you and Julia abroad."

"Of course I do. A very intelligent and delightful fellow. And what is he doing now?"

"He is editing that international review affair. I do hope you and Julia can come and have tea with him after your lecture. He wants so much to meet you both again. And you'll like his cousin Francis too. He's a solicitor."

"We shall be delighted. I suppose, Anna, your brother, Caroline's husband, is never heard of?"

"James? No. Father pays him an allowance, and we think he is in South Africa. I hope to goodness he will never come back. Don't think me horrid, but if you had seen what Caroline used to be like—oh, it's too horrible, too unfair," said Anna, a storm of indignation suddenly rising in her as it always did at any mention of James, and tears of pity and rage coming to her eyes.

"My dear, forgive me," said Colonel Beaton. "I never meant to give you pain by asking. I only wondered. I admire Caroline so very much and I am naturally anxious for her happiness."

"How dear of you. It has been hard work for her, but I honestly think she is through the worst of it. I wish she would marry again, someone frightfully nice and kind."

"Do you think she—I don't want to pry into her affairs—but have you any idea if there is anyone?"

"Yes, I have, but I don't think I'd better tell you."

"No, much better not. Whoever he is, he is a very lucky man. And now, what about you, my dear? Are you being a good daughter, and a good sister, and a kind, protecting sister-in-law, and a charming unselfish woman as well? All those things that you always are?"

This praise to Anna, whose kindness and what one can only call dearness were accepted by her family and not perhaps much valued except by her father and Caroline, was almost too much. She colored violently and tried to laugh it off. Colonel Beaton having said his say began to talk of other things, but the memory of his words remained as a warm glow in Anna's heart. He, like Francis, had said that he wanted her help. The thought of having him as a partner and friend of her father was very reassuring, for sometimes she felt anxious on Mr. Danvers's behalf. If James had been in the business, if James had been different, her father would have had help and support. But Wilfred and George were so much younger that he would still have to shoulder his burden at an age when he ought to be taking life more easily. If James—oh, it was no use thinking about it. Rather let her think how Francis whom she loved and Colonel Beaton whom she loved too, though so differently, both wanted her help. If one could help where one loved, give with full hands, how happy one could be.

While she dressed for dinner she conversed through the doorway with Caroline and told her how anxiously Colonel Beaton had asked after her.

"Nice creature," said Caroline, "how kind of him. But he is kind. Oh, Anna, how I wish I could marry an elderly Jew."

"My dear! But why?"

"Well, Jews make such kind good husbands, and an elderly one would make one feel safer. He would be established and settled and one would only have to fit in."

"Caroline, do you really want to marry again, or are you only amusing yourself?"

"How can I tell. Do I ever mean anything I say? 'I know who I love, but the dear knows who I'll marry,'" she sang. "At least what I mean is, the dear knows who would care to marry me. People don't want secondhand goods."

Her voice suddenly became so bitter that Anna hardly recognized it. If Caroline was really feeling like that, poor, poor Caroline.

"Rubbish," said Anna, with the best air of assurance she could muster. "Anyone would marry you. Why, even an elderly man like Colonel Beaton admires you. He is always saying so."

"As I said before, he is a nice creature, though not so elderly, Anna. Only forty-nine, he told me so. Quite young for a man," said Caroline loftily from her twenty-six years as against Anna's twenty-five. "If it comes to getting married, Anna, you have far more right than I. I mean I have had a husband and you haven't, though I doubt whether you need envy me."

"But darling, James is en disponibilité now, so it isn't as if you would make the man shortage worse. Anyway this is a disgraceful conversation and thank goodness the parents can't hear it. Isn't it depressing, Caroline, to think that if mother and father heard what we have been saying, they would be shocked at our modern cynicism and wickedness, and if the boys heard it they would laugh at us for silly old frumps trying to be dashing. We come off badly, you and I, between Victorian elders and Georgian youngsters."

Caroline appeared in the doorway, dressed for dinner.

"It all matters so little," she said. "One gets through the day because there is the night to look forward to, and then one has nightmares. All my days are trances, and all my nights are dreams," she said self-mockingly, looking over Anna's shoulder into the glass. "That's a nice, useful life, isn't it?"

Anna knowing how useless it was to try to deal with Caroline in one of her sardonic, self-torturing moods, determined to talk to Colonel Beaton, upon whose quiet strength she had great reliance, and ask his advice and help. Francis—it was no good, one's thoughts came homing to him at every turn—would not be much help; Colonel Beaton would.

At this moment Julia put her head in at the other door. "All dressed?" she cried. "Heavens, I must fly. We had such a heavenly time with the gramophone. George put Russian ballet music on, and we danced a lovely ballet that we invented. George is a divine dancer and I did pirouettes and entrechats and George partnered me beautifully with that pleasant set smile they have, and then Wilfred got cross because he can't play the fool as nicely as George, so he stopped the gramophone and said Russia was a menace to the world, and he put on a record of Hitler or one of them making a speech and George said it made him sick. They are such darling boys. So then we all came up to dress. Can I use your bathroom, Anna? The boys are all over the other."

Without waiting for a reply she ran off, and coming back with an armful of clothes and towels dashed into the bathroom, where she could be heard singing at the top of her voice.

"That's a Russian song," she shouted, interrupting herself for a moment. "I'm singing it so loud to annoy Wilfred. I must learn a German song to annoy George. Caroline, I'll ask your cousin Hugh to teach me one when we go to tea. He is such a darling. Don't you adore him frightfully?"

"Yes," said Caroline.

"What is cousin Francis like?" continued Julia. "Is he a darling too?"

No one answered.

CHAPTER 5

FRANCIS MAKES A WRONG MOVE

On the appointed Saturday Colonel Beaton gave his lecture on Agricola, whom his devoted but ill-educated daughter continued to think of as Agrippa, moved thereto by recollections of Struwwelpeter. Hugh had joined Caroline, Anna and Julia in the lecture room and sat between Caroline and Julia. From time to time Caroline looked contemplatively at her cousin's profile and wondered why she liked it, because as a rule she particularly disliked men with good looking profiles. From this, still looking at Hugh, she drifted to a consideration of good looks in general. Beauty of any kind in women roused her deep pleasure and admiration. Julia's perfect, finished prettiness gave her keen satisfaction. Anna she would have loved in any case for her kindness, but it was agreeable that Anna should also have reddish lights in her brown hair, wide set brown eyes and a clear golden skin. But in men who were attractive in their looks she always felt an extreme want of interest which they had to conquer by being very charming, or clever, or simply kind. It was kindness always that disarmed her in the end. There was James—

Hugh, magnetized as one always is by a look fixed upon one,

turned towards his cousin and saw a look of terrified distress in her eyes.

"Are you all right?" he whispered.

Caroline recalled her thoughts and found Hugh looking at her with affectionate concern. So affectionate that her quick heartbeat sent the color to her face. Hugh, anxious for her, met her deep searching gaze and smiled kindly.

"Quite all right," Caroline whispered back, "but thank you for thinking about it."

The color died from her face as she retired again into her thoughts, but this time not to memories of pain. It was of Hugh's kindness that she dreamt, while Colonel Beaton's voice went on unheard by her. Hugh, relieved to find himself mistaken, settled himself again in his chair in a position which made it easier to look at Julia, the pretty, gay creature.

Francis, who had been unable to get away from work, was in the drawing room when the lecture party arrived. All afternoon he had been trying to concentrate on legal papers, but his mind had strayed again and again to a fancied image of Colonel Beaton, who was by now assuming in his mind the appearance and attributes of Mr. Murdstone. To think of Caroline being the possible prey of such a brutal and designing villain made him press on the nib of his fountain pen till it became cross-beaked, and smoke far too many cigarettes. Finally he gave up trying to work and went into the drawing room to see if the fire were bright enough and the tea sumptuous enough to do honor to Caroline. He looked long and abstractedly at a plate of sandwiches containing Gentlemen's Relish, wishing that he knew enough about poison to fill one of them with a deadly mixture whose delayed action would kill painlessly and leave no trace. But even if he had the right poison he would have to be an accomplished prestidigitateur to force the envenomed sandwich on the colonel; it would never do to kill Anna or Hugh. Then, with a great wave of nobleness and self-pity he reflected that Beaton's death might make Caroline unhappy, and anyone who made Caroline unhappy again after what that rotter James had done, would deserve flogging and branding. So thinking, he paced the room angrily, taking a sandwich mechanically whenever he passed the table, till his thoughts and his perambulation were rudely disturbed by finding that the sandwiches were finished. At the same moment he heard the front door shut and voices on the stairs, so he put the empty plate under a cake plate, hoping that Rose, the parlor maid, wouldn't see it, and prepared to be a good host.

Anna and Caroline came in with affectionate greetings, followed by Hugh, Julia and Colonel Beaton. Francis was excessively annoyed to find that his unseen enemy had the appearance of an intelligent and courteous gentleman, but choking down his righteous indignation he prepared to be deeply suspicious of one whose exterior so craftily concealed an inward depravity. Caroline was asked to pour out, and was in the middle of inquiries about milk and sugar when Hugh interrupted her by getting up and ringing the bell.

"I'm so sorry," he explained. "I told Rose to give us Patum Peperium. Why on earth she can't remember a simple thing like that—but that's the worst of faithful servants who have seen you grow up—oh, Rose, you have forgotten the Gentlemen's Relish."

"Oh, no, Mr. Hugh," said Rose. "I cut them sandwiches myself and put them on the table."

"Well, look," said Hugh.

Rose cast a trained eye over the tea table. With the certainty of a conjurer she lifted a plate of cakes and took from beneath it a plate, empty save for a few crumbs and a brown smear.

"They've been ate, Mr. Hugh," she stated. "Should I cut some more?"

"Yes. Quickly. But who ate them? Did Maud bring them up to the drawing room?"

"No, sir. I brought them up myself. They have been ate upstairs."

"All right, Rose," said Francis, "get some more quickly. I ate them myself," he added as Rose left the room. "I was thinking about poisoned sandwiches and somehow they all got ate, as Rose would say."

"But why poisoned sandwiches, Francis?" asked Caroline.

"Because I was thinking of people I'd like to poison."

"So would I," said Julia enthusiastically. "I'd like to poison my Aunt Edith, and a girl I was at school with who had a flannelette blouse with spots on it, and people who aren't kind to dogs, and that dreadful Baron we met in Berlin. Hugh, do you remember him? The one that had a sister. Father, you didn't say anything about Agrippina poisoning people in your lecture?"

As Julia appeared to have a figure in her mind composed of three or four very different personalities on each of whom she was singularly ill-informed, there was some confusion at the tea table. Her father openly renounced a daughter who could not distinguish between Agricola, Agrippa and the two Agrippinas. The ladies sycophantically sought information from the gentlemen.

"Well anyway they all end with an A," said Julia, "and that's a sign of being a poisoner, like Borgia, or else a Pope."

"And Pope and Poisoner both begin with a P," said Hugh. "Not that that leads you anywhere."

"I can't follow this intellectual conversation," said Caroline to Colonel Beaton who was next to her.

"Nor can I. I think Julia, for a really dear girl, is the silliest creature I've ever met. Perhaps it comes of having no mother."

"If you are trying to make out that it is your fault, that certainly isn't true. But Julia isn't silly, Colonel Beaton. She has a genius for a home and making people happy. She is really clever in that way, and she is good with people. She is more grown-up in that way than I shall ever be."

Colonel Beaton's face lighted up at this praise of his daughter.

"Thank you, Caroline," he said. "You are perfectly right and I am over-anxious. She *is* a kind of genius in that way. Don't you know how one kind of pride in one's belonging makes one underestimate them in public?"

"I know. Like saying something unkind about a person you are fond of, just to have the pleasure of talking about them."

"'Uritur et loquitur' wasn't written for nothing. Beware, Caroline, if you ever find yourself saying quite unkind things about a friend just for the pleasure of saying his, or her, name. That will be your fatal hour."

Tea was over and people were moving about. As he finished speaking Julia's voice could be heard saying to Hugh at her side:

"No, Hugh, don't try to confuse me. Borgias were Popes and Caesar was a Roman, and to talk of people being called Caesar Borgia is as silly as cutting a cabbage leaf to make an apple pie. Ask Father. He knows everything, besides being a darling and terribly good looking."

"Listen to Julia underestimating you in public," said Caroline to Colonel Beaton, who had to laugh.

"Did you feel faint this afternoon?" he asked.

"At the lecture? Oh, no, thank you."

"I thought I saw you looking white. Perhaps it was the faintness of boredom."

"But indeed it was not. I was entranced by your lecture. I only suddenly thought of something that frightened me."

"My poor child," said Colonel Beaton. Which remark, being overheard by Francis who was standing near them in a redistribution of groups, caused him to hate the colonel with fresh vehemence. As penance for this un-host-like thought he tried to be nice to him with such effect that Caroline, as nearly always happens when two men are with a woman, felt herself an unwanted female and went over to Anna.

"Hugh," said Anna. "What about your gramophone and a little dancing?"

"Oh, divine," cried Julia. "Quick, quick, a rumba. Hugh and I can dance a rumba. I saw it properly in Havana last winter. Have you got 'Tropical Heat Wave,' Hugh?"

"Yes, but you aren't to sing the words, Julia. This is a respectable bachelor establishment and I must draw the line somewhere. Caroline, will you dance?"

"Not a rumba. I don't know it. Ordinary dancing I'd love."

"Come on, then, Julia."

Jealousy was not in Caroline's nature. Much as she would have loved to dance with Hugh herself, she could only admire the grace with which Julia swayed to his guiding, the unison of their steps in the intricate rhythm, Julia laughing up to him as she softly sang the words and made him laugh too. Perhaps Hugh would dance with her presently. Colonel Beaton and Anna joined the dancers with a discreet non-committal step. Caroline found Francis by her side.

"Shall we dance?" he asked.

Caroline, watching Hugh's head bend to Julia's pretty face, suddenly felt such a pang as made her hold Francis's arm for support. Not jealousy, no not jealousy of that lovely happy child, only a rending devastating wish that she still had a careless gaiety, a thoughtless grace, so that Hugh would look at her and love her without care; so that she could talk and laugh with Hugh without a heartbeat that stunned and bruised her, making speech a noisy troubling stream running shallow over stones, silence a thundercloud with menace in its heavy folds.

"Do you think we needn't dance, perhaps?" she asked. "The gramophone makes such a noise."

Without a word Francis opened the door by which they were standing and led her to his study, behind the drawing room. Here a fire and the reading lamp on his table made warmth and a peaceful light. Caroline sat down gratefully.

"Don't bother about me, Francis," she said. "I can be quiet by myself quite happily. You go and help the others to dance."

Francis said he would like to be quiet too. Caroline took off her hat and lay back in her chair, while Francis watched her from the other side of the fire. The dance music from the next room made a sentimental background for firelit talk.

"Do you think I ought to work?" said Caroline, breaking a silence of some minutes.

"What at?"

"Oh, anything. Mr. and Mrs. Danvers are so good to me, but after all I'm only living on their kindness. My own money is only enough for pocket money."

Francis, who knew well that James had helped himself to most of his wife's money, sometimes by bullying, sometimes by appeals to her generosity, said nothing for fear of saying too much.

"I thought," Caroline went on, "that if I could have a job it would be good for me and make me self-reliant and independent. Only I don't quite know what sort of job. I don't think I could do much unless I took little dogs out for walks, or went as under-nurse to very small children. I'm fairly good with children. I often think it is quite a pity that my own baby came to nothing. I would have liked it a good deal. Still, perhaps as things are it is better. I would have been even more of a nuisance than I am if the Danverses had had to take in a baby as well. But I do think it is a pity that James couldn't have been more kind," she added in a weary matter of fact voice.

There was another long pause, while Francis, his heart torn by Caroline's unresisting acceptance of sorrow, did his best to choke down his natural wish to utter maledictions upon James. It was her childlike submission to a cruelty that she couldn't understand which most moved him. Never once, since that day he took her to Beechwood, had he seen her otherwise than quiet, anxiously polite, trying to behave well in the middle of bewilderment.

"It is frightfully difficult to talk about it at all," he said at last. "You see, it's no good pretending that I don't hate James, but I don't know what you feel about him, and I wouldn't for the world say anything that could give you the slightest pain. Do you mind?"

"I don't think I mind anything, at least not anything about

James," said Caroline, thinking how deeply she would mind if Hugh didn't presently come in and ask her to dance. "I can even say his name now quite comfortably. I don't want my feelings to be an embarrassment to you, Francis, dear. I don't particularly want to talk about James, but if there is anything you want to ask, don't feel that I should be hurt. It is so impossible to express anything that one means. Hurt is a bad word, because it means too much. One is hurt by almost anything that people do or say, because one is stupidly reminded of things. A flower, or a piece of music, or the smell of tobacco, or the name of the newspaper James used to be on, they all press a nerve that runs right back to something happy or horrible that once happened. Even sausages and mashed potatoes are simply more than I can bear sometimes, because we had a joke about them when we were first married. Don't laugh. I may laugh at myself, and I will. But you mustn't laugh at me—not yet."

"I don't want to laugh in the least," Francis assured her.

"That kind of hurt is something that suddenly goes through you like a sword and can't be helped," Caroline went on. "But I don't have the kind of hurt that means being offended, at least I hope I don't. And in any case, dear Francis, you couldn't give me either kind of hurt—chiefly because you wouldn't."

She turned her face from the fire at which she had been gazing while she spoke and looked straight at Francis with such candor and affection that he could hardly sustain her glance.

"But if it doesn't bore you too much to talk about me," she went on, "do you think I ought to have a job? I mean legally, economically, quite apart from being a cousin or an old friend."

No, was Francis's immediate reaction, but the common sense part of his mind told him to consider the matter and reflect whether a young woman with health and strength wouldn't bury an unhappy experience better by doing regular work than by living in great comfort where the ghost of the past would be before her at every turn. Another question then rose: had she really the strength for it.

"How are you now, Caroline?" he asked.

"How am I? Oh, quite well, thank you."

"No, honestly. Suppose you had a nine to six job every day, could you do it?"

Caroline's face clouded.

"That's what I don't know," she said. "Dr. Herbert talks about not overdoing it and taking things easily, but I'm not sure if it wouldn't be a better plan to work very hard and take the consequences. If one bursts, one bursts, and that's all. Francis, I am so tired of being tired that I don't know what to do. Do you think being dead is less tiring than being alive?"

To this question Francis could not give an answer.

Hugh came in looking for cigarettes.

"Don't you want to dance?" he asked his cousin. "Poor darling, you are tired. That comes of gadding about to lectures. Never mind, you rest comfortably and Francis will look after you. Julia and I did a superb tango and now we are going to do the rumba again, only drawing the line at the place where you put your foreheads together. She is the best dancer I ever met, and such fun."

"She is a darling," said Caroline, "so is her father. I don't know what Anna and I would do without them at Beechwood."

Hugh had now found his cigarettes. All unconsciously he had further depressed his cousin's low spirits by praising that pretty young Julia, while Caroline, trying to be generous, had no less unconsciously wounded Francis by her mention of Colonel Beaton as an indispensable darling. Hugh merely conscious of having done a kind action in encouraging Caroline to stay with Francis, returned to the drawing room where Colonel Beaton and Anna were comfortably conversing over the gramophone while Julia practiced steps by herself. As he shut the drawing room door behind him she swirled up into his arms and they moved away together.

"I suppose you see quite a lot of the Beatons," said Francis when he and Caroline were alone again, miserably unable to keep away from the horrid subject.

"Oh, yes, at Beechwood we do. I used to go long walks with Colonel Beaton at Beechwood and I miss them so in London."

"I expect he is very interesting," said Francis, determined to be fair.

"I expect so, but he doesn't talk to me. We just walk along very fast and I feel much better afterwards."

This evidence of a silent communion was even more exacerbating to Francis than the thought of his rival imparting useful information.

"And Julia is a darling," said Caroline again, anxious to persuade herself that her heart was not aching for Hugh. "But however nice one's friends are, Francis, it doesn't prevent one being lonely—oh, always unspeakably lonely."

"Poor Caroline."

"Not that I miss James," Caroline went on, more interested in trying to explain herself to herself than in talking to Francis, "because I don't. I think I had stopped loving him long before I knew I had. But just desperately lonely."

"Have you ever thought about marrying again?" said Francis. "You see I am taking you at your word about asking questions."

To his surprise Caroline's face flamed darkly as she said:

"Oh, yes. I suppose people always think about that."

Francis, who could not know that the words Hugh had spoken to her in the taxi were responsible for her unashamed confession, felt a stirring of hope.

"You have tremendous courage," he said.

"Courage? I don't think so. One doesn't need courage with you, Francis, you are so safe. Do you think we ought to go and dance now?"

But Francis, desperate at the thought of an indispensable Colonel Beaton waiting in the next room, would not be denied.

"Darling Caroline, I love you more than anything in the world," he said. "I adore your lovely hands and your courage and the way you look straight into my eyes and make my heart turn over like a pancake. Could you, dearest, think of marrying me?"

Caroline sat up in her chair and looked at him in astonishment and terror.

"I don't mean now, this very moment," said Francis, alarmed by his cousin's panic stricken face. "I mean in a year, in two years, a lifetime, whenever you like."

Still Caroline said nothing, wrapped in fear and amazement. Francis came and knelt down beside her.

"If I have frightened you, my darling, I am more sorry than I can say. Can't you say one word?"

"I am so cold," said Caroline in a small remote voice.

Francis took her hands, which were indeed ice cold. She made no effort to withdraw them, seeming to find a kind of comfort in the warmth of his own. Francis was content to remain by her side and would have been all too happy for this firelit moment to last forever. He was entirely at a loss to understand what had happened, unless it was that the very thought of marriage after her unlucky venture was enough to freeze her into dumb terror. Yet she had admitted that the thought was not strange to her. He could only humbly fear that while she could entertain an abstract idea of a second husband, she had some feeling against himself, or some stronger feeling for another man—he would not allow himself even to think the name Beaton—which made his suit an outrage to her too sensitive mind. When she had said that she felt safe with him, this dependence had touched him to the quick. Now perhaps he had destroyed this confidence for ever. Sick at heart he bowed his head over her cold hands, lifting them to his lips. Caroline still made no attempt to release herself, but her hands trembled so that Francis could do nothing but let them go. They both stood up and Caroline said with the polite voice of the Caroline he had taken to Beechwood on the day when her life's foundations were destroyed:

"I think we might see what the others are doing. Anna and I mustn't be late, because there are people to dinner."

She put on her hat before a mirror over the fireplace. Francis, looking at her reflection, his heart torn by the sight of her adored face strained and harassed as he had hoped never to see it again, blaming himself for his haste, his swift unprepared proposal of marriage, suddenly felt an insane desire to force her to drop the mask of an indifferent courtesy, to penetrate her frozen armor and wring some kind of feeling from her.

"Who is it then, Caroline?" he asked her reflection.

"I don't quite understand," said the too polite voice.

"Is there another man that you love?" said Francis, furious with himself, pulling Caroline around by the arm.

She looked at him steadily till he released her and then said, "Yes."

Hugh was delighted to see his cousin Caroline looking more rested. She said she and Anna ought to be getting home, but Hugh begged her to dance once with him. Julia insisted on dragging her father through some new steps, so Francis went to talk to Anna who was changing the records.

"Have you been thinking again about our plan for Caroline marrying into your family?" she said, hunting among a pile of disks.

"Yes," said Francis truthfully.

"Well, I still think it's a nice family to marry into," said Anna, and then wondered if she had said too much. But she need not have wondered, for Francis could hardly hear what she said, even with the well-trained social part of his mind. Caroline's frank avowal, for that was what it came to, of her preference for Colonel Beaton, had almost stunned him. To feel that he had frightened and bullied his cousin was far from pleasant. When he thought of Caroline's terrified immobility, her abandonment of her cold hands to the caress which she could not feel, he saw no reason to think himself better than James. A last glimpse of her sitting huddled in a corner of the taxi, white-faced and forlorn, while Anna and the Beatons said their good-byes, was of little comfort. Before he could collect his wits he found himself embroiled in dining with Hugh and the Beatons, who were returning to Beechwood that night, and then dancing. Or rather, in watching Hugh and Julia dance while he talked to Colonel Beaton and had to admit, reluctantly and dejectedly, that Caroline couldn't have made a better choice.

If he could have seen Caroline he would have been even less comforted. She had moved through the evening as best she might, conscious that Anna's loving eyes were uneasily following her, and praying that no one else was noticing her.

The dinner guests stayed late and the last of them had not been long gone when Wilfred and George came in.

"Where have you been, darlings?" said Mrs. Danvers.

Both darlings, determined that this sort of thing must be put down with a firm hand, ignored their mother's question, bursting though they were to talk of their evening. But there are other ways to approach a subject besides the direct.

"Julia Beaton is quite a possible woman," said George to Anna.

"Of course she is," said Anna, who found her youngest brother's present affectation of calling all girls women inexplicably annoying.

"Not bad for a kid," continued George, feeling all the superiority that twenty-two has over twenty.

"What made you think of Julia?" said Anna.

"We were dining with some people at the Legation Club," said George, "and who should be there but old Beaton with Hugh and Francis and Julia. Gosh, that woman dances well. Wilfred tried to get her to dance with him and got turned down. Julia wasn't dancing with anyone but Hugh. It looked like a case, didn't it, Wilfred?"

"That's about enough about that," said Wilfred, on whom the rejection of his advances appeared to be preying. "All right, all right, George, you needn't wink like that. That Russian girl you were dancing with wasn't much class anyway, and she was as Red as they make them. I danced with her once, and I put her in her place pretty strongly."

"If your place was with your great feet walking all over hers," said George, "I expect you did. By what she told me, Julia did the wise thing in turning you down. She couldn't have driven her father down to Beechwood tonight with two smashed feet. I say, mother, we saw one of Wilfred's blackshirt friends making a row tonight outside the Legation, and he was carried away kicking by two policemen. It was frightfully funny."

"Oh, frightfully," said Wilfred bitterly, and would have said more, but was interrupted by his mother who said with much dignity that she would go up to bed and not keep them from their talk. Caroline followed her, and Anna only waited long enough to see Wilfred and George reconciled over a new jazz record. She feared to guess what was wrong with Caroline, but if, as she thought, Caroline was unhappy about Hugh and Julia, her heart ached for her ill-starred sister-in-law. Caroline, she hoped, was tormenting herself quite unnecessarily. If Hugh had danced with Julia that afternoon it was because Caroline was in the study with Francis. She couldn't have both her cousins at once. And if Hugh had danced again with Julia that night, what else could he do? It was George who was to blame for talking such conceited nonsense.

Full of foreboding she turned on the light in her own room and looked through into Caroline's. Even as she had feared, Caroline, self-control thrown to the winds, was lying on her bed, still fully dressed, shaken with sobs from head to foot. Anna approached her with every endearment her affection could devise, asked no questions and persuaded her to undress and get into bed. But all the time Caroline's tear were flowing freely and Anna had to get her three clean pocket handkerchiefs to cry into.

"Now," she said when Caroline was safely in bed, a miserable tear-drenched sight, "what is it all about?"

To her immense surprise Caroline answered in a choked voice, "Francis."

Anna conceived that Caroline had taken leave of her senses and must mean Hugh.

"But Francis didn't dance with Julia," she said.

"Why should he? It wouldn't matter if he did. It was what he said. Anna, Anna, I can't bear it."

"But, darling, what did Francis say? Something about Hugh and you? There is nothing dreadful in that."

"Hugh? Why should Francis say anything about Hugh? Hugh doesn't care if I am dead or alive. Francis asked me to marry him. I could die of shame that he could do such a thing. Francis, whom I always trusted. And then he asked me if I cared for anyone else. Oh, how could he? But I told him the truth, I said yes. I hope it hurt him as much as it hurt me."

At these words Anna knew, fatally, that her own hurt would be before long almost unbearable. Francis, Francis, rose like a cry in her heart. But knowing that her fiercest grief would not reach her till her numbed senses began to live again, she turned to her task of comforting Caroline. Ever since the day that Francis had brought Caroline to Beechwood, since she had learnt the depths of her brother's infamy, she had appointed herself Caroline's guardian sister. Even her parents did not feel more keenly than she the disgrace that James had brought to them all by his callous unkindness to so gentle a creature as Caroline, and very strong in her was the feeling that atonement could be made in some measure by a devotion of herself to her sister-in-law. In the nights when she sat by Caroline's bed, in the days when she had tried to bring Caroline's remote mind back to the quiet comfort of daily life, she had come to love her as a generous nature must always love the object of its generosity. That Francis had given Caroline into her hands in that dark hour was an additional reason for cherishing her. Without her help Caroline would hardly have been recalled to life. It was she who had gently forced Caroline to take her place in family life, to make friends with the Beatons, to walk the hills with Colonel Beaton. And if truth were known her parents' plan to spend the winter in London was more than half her doing. Here, she thought, Caroline would find old friends again and discover how little people were thinking about her. Now she trembled to think of the harm she might have done. She had hoped that Caroline, taking up a busier life again in London, would see more of Hugh. Caroline must not be hurried. Any sign of interference would, Anna knew, drive her into her cold fastnesses again, but with time surely Hugh, for whom Caroline had again and again betrayed to Anna her deep diffident affection, would help his cousin to forget the past, would make her life revive. Anna had not consciously looked forward very far, but if she could plan for Hugh to refashion Caroline's life, could she prevent herself from imagining sometimes what might be her own fate? Was it not possible that Francis, grateful for her care of his cousin, would see that she too would be glad of help, glad to lay down the burden, dear though it was, of sustaining Caroline, and make her own happiness his care?

Now she must never think more of this, must put every thought of herself aside till Caroline could rest. Never, never could she grudge Caroline a possible happiness, but for a moment she suffered a bitter pang. With what gratitude, with what silent awe would Anna have stretched out her hands to receive the gift from which Caroline averted her gaze in fear and horror.

The abandonment of what Anna knew to be an intensely proud and reserved nature was painful to see, difficult to soothe. Caroline, fighting herself at every step, had succeeded in mastering her hysteria, only from time to time she let the name of Hugh escape on a sobbing sigh. Anna longed to tell her that all would be well, that Hugh could not help caring for her, but she was afraid to treat so dangerous and comforting a hope as fact. It was impossible for her to tell whether Hugh cared for Caroline, or for Julia, or indeed for anyone at all, and to tell a kindly lie to Caroline now might mean more unhappiness later. So she soothed her sister-in-law as best she might till Caroline was able to drink a glass of water and dry her eyes for the last time.

"I am very, very sorry, Anna," said Caroline. "Poor Francis had just thoroughly upset me and I was hateful not to be more patient with him. I do love him, Anna, but because he is my cousin and I have always known him. But to be touched, to be anyone's property again—oh, horrible, unless one loved a man quite unbearably. Forgive me, my darling. Go to bed and sleep. I won't cry again and tomorrow it will all be forgotten. Thank heaven we go to Beechwood for Christmas. There one can breathe and be oneself again and walk on the hills. Good night, Anna dear."

She put up her face to be kissed, and Anna as she bent down to her took up her burden of responsibility again silently and with love.

Caroline slept an exhausted sleep, but it was a poor night for Anna, who saw no light at all. If Francis loved Caroline, he must have her. If Caroline loved Hugh, she must have him. How could these claims be reconciled? And where, as an afterthought, did she herself come in? One thing was clear, she could not face this problem by herself. Sometimes she thought of speaking to Hugh, sometimes to Francis, but to do the first would be to betray Caroline's heart, to do the second might betray her own. Morning found her still undecided.

Caroline was not down to breakfast. Mrs. Danvers went up to her room to ask her about some plan and found her looking so unwell that she ordered her to stay in bed. Caroline was quite glad to obey her mother-in-law, who enjoyed having invalids and reading aloud to them. Her own children all hated to be read to, but Caroline liked it and found Mrs. Danvers's voice very soothing.

The day was wet and dark. Anna felt disinclined to go out alone so she took some embroidery down to her father's study, knowing that he liked to have her near him while he worked. Since James had become a stranger to his family, Mr. Danvers had turned more and more to his only daughter, who was in many ways nearer to him than his wife. As a young man he would willingly have devoted himself to the humanities and could have made a high place for himself among scholars, but his father had begged him, an only son, to come into the family business and help him. Seeing this as a duty he renounced his books and brought to affairs the persistence and occasional genius which he had shown in other fields. In worldly matters he prospered, he married well and happily, but his heart was never more at rest than in his library. Here he worked at night, producing at long intervals one of those books which make English amateur scholarship one of England's glories. Here, as he was able to let the ties of his business slacken, he lived with his oldest and dearest friends, whether tasting honey of Hymettus, olives from a Sabine farm, or a halfpenny worth of bread with two gallons of sack. He had hoped for a son to share these gifts with him. James had such gifts as he himself had possessed, but James wished to write, to create, not to accept the wisdom of others, so his father, remembering the sacrifice of his own youth, made a fresh sacrifice of his riper years that James might do as he wished, and allowed him to choose his own path. That James had done brilliantly and gave promise of more solid achievement to come was Mr. Danvers's reward. In face of his son's downfall he bowed his head and sought an anodyne among his books. Wilfred and George had a certain respect for their father's attainments, but no wish to emulate them, so Anna, who could enjoy the sack and bread, though the olives hung almost too high for her to reach and the honey was stored for her in vain, became his chosen companion in his leisure hours.

When Anna came in he was sitting at his table. His daughter kissed the top of his head and sat down near the fire, while a sooty rain fell outside and the house was silent.

Mr. Danvers asked Anna where her mother was.

"With Caroline, Father. Caroline isn't very well today, so Mother is keeping her in bed."

Mr. Danvers looked up with the face of gray anxiety that Anna knew too well. She knew that he was taking on himself the responsibility for anything that happened to Caroline, because it was his eldest son who had betrayed her, and her heart grieved for her father's unhappiness.

"Don't worry, darling," she said. "She isn't really ill, only tired. She gets easily tired, you know. Dr. Herbert said she wasn't to do too much and we have rather racketed lately."

"Not enough for the change I have been seeing in Caroline," said Mr. Danvers, laying down his pen. "Anna, do you think it was really a good plan to bring her to London this winter?"

As this was exactly what Anna had been asking herself, and as she felt partly responsible for the plan, she answered with rather forced cheerfulness, that she thought it ought to do Caroline good.

"Doubtless it ought to, but has it? Of late, Anna, I have seen Caroline looking driven and anxious as she did in those first dreadful days. Ought we to have persuaded her to come to town? Do you think she was happier at Beechwood?"

"She does love Beechwood, of course. And she liked the Beatons so much. But she will soon be all right."

"Yes," said Mr. Danvers musingly. "Beaton is an excellent man, one in whom one could place implicit trust. You don't think she misses him, Anna? I have sometimes wondered a little. But then she has seen him in town during the last few days and doesn't seem any happier. I did think that being near Hugh and Francis would be an interest, a stimulus for her, but it seems to be quite the opposite. Anna, if Caroline gets ill again I don't know how to face it."

"Darling Father," said Anna, stretching out a hand and stroking his coat sleeve, "you mustn't worry so much. I know what you are thinking, that if you had beaten James when he was little all this wouldn't have happened. But it would. I mean James is James and there it is."

"We are what we are," said Mr. Danvers, finding comfort in

the familiar words. "But that doesn't make me feel less responsible, Anna, for Caroline's disappointing lack of progress. I fear she isn't happy, and I don't know what to do."

"Father, I simply can't bear you to be so anxious. Caroline is unhappy, I know she is, but it isn't your fault or anyone's fault."

"Tell me what it is—unless it is a secret," he added quickly.

"No, Father, not a secret, exactly, because Caroline hadn't quite told me herself, but I know about it. You see, Father, Caroline was always very fond of Francis and Hugh. Then James quarreled with them and she missed them dreadfully. I think she was thinking about them when James was unkind. Then there was the time when she was so very ill at Beechwood. You remember when she was so ill that she hardly knew where she was, but one name she did remember all through that time, and that was Hugh's. He did come down and see her, you remember, and though he could only sit and look charming and had nothing to say, that gave her strength to go on."

"Do you mean, Anna, that she has been building up her life again with Hugh Mannering in her mind?"

"Father, you wouldn't mind, would you? One can't expect her to go on caring for James, and after all it is a long time ago now, more than a year since she first came to Beechwood. You don't blame her, do you?"

"Blame her?" said Mr. Danvers. "You couldn't really think that of me, Anna. No, I would rejoice if in any way that poor child could be happy again. But Hugh. I like him, Anna, I like them both. But Hugh isn't the man Francis is. Francis isn't as brilliant as Hugh, perhaps not even fundamentally as clever, but he has a more tempered nature. A woman like Caroline could put her trust safely in him, but she would have to support Hugh, and she isn't strong enough. She can endure—and God knows the child has endured—but to deal with Hugh one must be more vital. He needs bullying," said Mr. Danvers almost unkindly.

This praise of Francis turned the knife in Anna's heart and

she did not speak. Even to hear him spoken ill of would have been a pleasure. To hear her beloved father speak so well of him pierced and rejoiced her.

"But Anna," Mr. Danvers went on, "have you any reason to think that Hugh knows her feelings? Or that she hopes he may? My dear, I don't want to ask indiscreet questions, but you know how anxious I am for her happiness. Don't answer if I am pressing to know too much."

"Oh, Father, I wish I knew," said Anna, fearing that her breaking point might come, yet unwilling to loose this precious chance of disburdening herself in some measure to her father. "I don't think Hugh has the slightest idea. And I rather agree with what you say about him, though I'm very fond of him. But there is something else which I'm not quite sure if I ought to tell you but it is too much for me to deal with alone and I have dreadfully wanted to have some good advice about it. Father, Francis has asked Caroline to marry him and she says she can't. She was frightened. She said to me last night that she could never think of a man again unless she loved him unbearably, and there is only one man that she cares for like that, Hugh"

"It would appear to be," said Mr. Danvers, "a case of Ein Jüngling liebt ein Mädchen, allowing of course for slight differences."

Anna knew that this rather aloof and sententious manner of her father's always meant that he was more moved than he would admit and, moved herself, tried to answer him in his own vein.

"At least we haven't got as far as den ersten besten Mann," she said lightly. "Caroline isn't likely to throw herself into, say Colonel Beaton's arms, because Hugh doesn't care for her as much as she cares for him."

"One sometimes wonders whether that story was really as bad as Heine pretended," continued Mr. Danvers, seeking refuge from himself in words. "Perhaps the girl really went back to the youth in the end. Or perhaps," he added, looking at Anna and yet past her, "there was still another personage in that unfortunate and really rather unnecessary entanglement; someone unmentioned who loved the youth and with whom he was very happy when they had all got over having broken hearts. But this history does not relate."

Anna nearly jumped at this. Whether it was a shot in the dark or a piece of her father's disconcerting insight, she could not be sure. Dearly would she like to think that Francis's bruised heart might at her hands receive peace and healing, but to think of Francis seemed to her disloyal to Caroline. Caroline, for the first time, fell ever so slightly in Anna's estimation because she could not see the worth of what Francis offered. Then Anna blamed herself for judging Caroline. Was she not in the same case as her sister-in-law, loving where she was not loved? But Caroline at least had Francis's love if she wanted it. For Anna no fond heart waited, and her path must be lonely between warring loyalties.

"Father," she said, "do you think it would be very unfair to wish that a person one liked didn't care for a person that didn't care for them?"

"Owing to your indeterminate use of indefinite and plural pronouns, a course doubtless dictated by delicacy," said her father, "I find it difficult to give any judgment on this point. And in any case wishing won't help whatever it is. These things will come; they will come."

Presently Anna put her work into her bag and went away. Mr. Danvers remained alone, disquieted by what he had heard. Anna's well meant efforts to cheer him by explaining that Caroline was unhappy from causes beyond his control had not been very successful. It was cruel enough that his own son should be the cause of Caroline's misery, but if her cousins were now going to add to her troubles, there seemed to be no end to them. He could only hope that Anna's account of Caroline's feeling for Hugh was exaggerated. Girls did so love a romance that she was perhaps magnifying a cousinly affection to something warmer. As for Francis, that was more serious. If he had actually asked Caroline to marry him, that was a solid fact, and Mr. Danvers found himself wishing that he had the right to speak to Caroline a few words for her good, for he had sometimes felt uneasily that the child was becoming too absorbed in her own position, feeling more pity for herself than was good for her. But he hadn't, nor perhaps the courage. It was a kind of comfort to reflect that Anna at least was not involved in any of these emotional tangles. That she would marry he could not but hope, but not yet, not till her fate sent her unmistakably to the right man, a straightforward happy love affair such as his and Evelyn's had been. If only James had not been as he was. Oh, if only it had been so.

CHAPTER 6

A WALK AND A TEA-PARTY

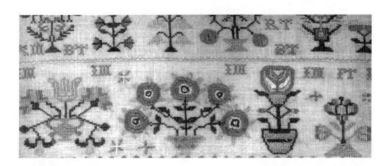

A t Christmas the Danvers family went down to Beechwood
for ten days. Hugh and Francis were going to stay with
the Beatons, so there would be dinner parties and a constant
coming and going.

"I hand it to Julia," said George admiringly as the younger
members of the Beechwood party sat on after breakfast on
Christmas Eve. "Two eligible young men in the house at once.
She is some go-getter, that girl."

George's family were not unaware, partly from the style,
partly from the substance of his conversation, that the Russian
ballet was at the moment in peril, its ascendancy threatened by
what is called, though only in newspapers, the silver screen. It
was not always easy to foretell whether George would be a
balletomane or a film fan at any given period, and any mistake
on his hearers' part gave great offense.

"And why shouldn't Julia have Francis and Hugh to stay?"
demanded Wilfred. "This is a free country, it isn't Russia."

"You're telling me," observed his brother, which apparently
harmless remark caused Wilfred's resentment to rise again.

"I am," said Wilfred. "I say, this isn't Russia. Why Julia
shouldn't have Hugh and Francis for Christmas in her father's

house, and both of them old enough to be her father, even your arguments fail to explain."

"But Wilfred," said Anna, "you can't call them old enough to be anybody's father. Francis can't be more than thirty-two and Hugh is a bit younger."

"If I weren't old enough to be someone's father by thirty-two, I'd feel a frightful fool," said George frankly.

"You don't need to be thirty-two to feel that," said Wilfred.

"You're telling me," responded George.

"Francis is thirty-three and Hugh thirty-one," said Caroline. "Hugh is five years older than I am except in January. Then he is six years older than I am just for a month."

This, George said, was due to relativity. Wilfred remarked that Einstein was a poisonous little Jew. George said that say what he liked, the film world would be absolutely nowhere without the money and the artistic sense of the Jewish race. Wilfred said that if George didn't know the difference between Einstein and Eisenstein he couldn't be much good at his own rotten subject. George said in a loud rude voice, "Hitler, Goebbels and Goering. My God!" and went defiantly but quickly from the room.

"I say, Anna," said Wilfred, "can't you stop George being so infernally impertinent? I'll lose my temper and go for him one of these days. It's like this cheek to criticize Julia. Go-getter indeed. She is worth a million of him. As a matter of fact," he added quite unnecessarily, "I'm going to play golf with her this afternoon. And by Jove, George has got my clubs."

Upon which Wilfred also precipitated himself from the room.

Anna and Caroline looked at each other and laughed.

"Thank heaven," said Caroline, "the boys' barks are worse than their bites. At least their barks are very trying in family life, but I notice that they never bite each other really. Is Whitelands, or are Whitelands, coming over today?"

"No, but Colonel Beaton wants to know if we will go for a

walk with him this afternoon, him and Francis, and then all go back there to tea. Is that all right?"

"Perfect."

"I mean, you won't mind?"

"About Francis? No, darling, that's all over and done with, and I'm very much ashamed of myself and I love Francis very much, and I love walking with him. Besides, the minute one is at Beechwood one isn't half so silly. It's rather priggish to talk about Nature being the great healer, but I am six times less stupid and annoying here than I am in London. When once I get upon the hills I am almost good enough even for you, Anna."

But when the walking party set out, it was Colonel Beaton who took his place by Caroline's side, at Francis's previous request. The cousins had met several times since the fatal tea-party, and though the good breeding and the real affection of both had made things as smooth as possible, Francis still found it difficult to be with Caroline. Therefore he hinted to Colonel Beaton as they walked up to Beechwood that he would like if possible to attach himself to Anna. Colonel Beaton who was fond of both the young women was quite contented to walk with Caroline, whose long swift step matched his own, though he did wonder for a moment whether Francis had any special reason for wanting to talk to that delightful Anna Danvers.

As they went up the hollow road to the high lands, Colonel Beaton and Caroline drew away from the other two, not from any wish to be alone, but from pure selfishness. To the real walker it is agony to walk at any pace but his own. If he has to accommodate himself to a slower step he forges ahead, stops and waits, apologizes, rushes ahead again, and either goes mad and disappears over the horizon, or, walking with ostentatious slowness beside his companion, becomes a prey to sulky melancholy. It is far better for him to indulge in his innocent excesses and throw courtesy to the winds.

In silence they pulled up the last steep half-mile of the ascent and stood on the ridge to breathe. To the north fields and heath stretched away to the distant hills. Southwards the high table land on which they stood lay between them and the sea. To east and west one could walk for hours on springy turf, looking down steeply onto the bare crowns of the beech trees that grew up the escarpment of the hills. They turned to the west. The path they took ran for miles among scattered juniper bushes which had the shape of pygmy armies, or birds and animals. Both walkers felt the higher air in their blood, and they pressed forward in silent emulation. Caroline could outwalk most men in speed, if not in ultimate endurance, but with Colonel Beaton she was hard put to it to hold her own. After the first mile she had blissfully lost consciousness of herself and sped onward, rejoicing in the rhythm of footsteps, the sense of mastering the earth at each stride, the physical joy of swift movement in the thin pure winter air.

Colonel Beaton, remembering the pale harassed Caroline that he had seen in town that autumn, was amazed and delighted at the change which a few days at Beechwood had made in her. Her face which had been so haggard and drawn after the lecture tea-party was quite vulgarly cheerful and carefree. She walked with the assurance of a creature that takes strength from the earth with each fresh step. For an hour they never slackened their pace till they stood on an old earthwork overlooking a gap in the hills through which a river flowed southward to the sea. Here by silent consent they stopped. The sun was not far from setting. From the villages in the plain below rose thin curls of smoke, scattered noises of road and farmyard.

"I suppose Francis and Anna are miles behind," said Caroline. "We shall meet them on the way back. Oh, this heavenly, heavenly walk."

"I didn't think you were in such form," said Colonel Beaton. "We were doing four miles an hour easily. You couldn't have done that a month ago, Caroline."

"No, I couldn't. Oh, but you mustn't judge me by the days you were in town for your lecture. And at any rate one can't help being well here. Always when I am among the hills I can do anything. I feel I don't really know any friend with whom I haven't walked. Unfortunately one can't live on the top of a hill forever."

"You might want to come down if you did."

"Oh, no, I think not," said Caroline, as if a hilltop where no one could reach one might be the happiest place in the world. "It would be nice to be where no one could ever get at one. Then one wouldn't be frightened."

"But what would you be frightened of?"

"Oh, I don't know. Remembering things, seeing people, having demands made on one."

"You wouldn't like it. You would really be wretched if demands weren't made on you. In fact you would be a good deal happier now if more demands were made on you. You need to give and you are having to take. It's all wrong."

Colonel Beaton then looked at the dusky valley, at the red westering sun, at the path by which they came, and Caroline said nothing. Finally, looking at the turf, he said:

"I haven't ever presumed to talk to you about your marriage, Caroline. I needn't say that Anna has told me about it, and Mr. and Mrs. Danvers have spoken of it sometimes. I have admired what I have heard of you, and I admire exceedingly what I know of you. Courage among other things. But don't let that courage wear itself thin and fade, Caroline. One has to shut oneself away sometimes after a great grief, but there does come a time when it is cowardice not to take one's place in the world again. Am I offending you?" he asked, raising his eyes and looking at her.

Caroline's face was all in flame, whether from her thoughts or from the low winter sun, he was not sure. She gave him one of her long steady looks and answered:

"No, not offending. Being kind on the whole. Colonel Beaton, I'm only too ready to think myself a coward, and it may be good for me to be told I really am one. Then out of spite perhaps I'll think I'm not."

"A muddled kind of truthfulness appears to be another of

your virtues, though I'm not sure if you don't enjoy running yourself down. And by the way, is Colonel Beaton necessary? I would like to think that you and Anna didn't look upon me as the kind of person you have to be respectful to."

"William is rather an awkward name," said Caroline cautiously.

"I'm sorry," said Colonel Beaton seriously. "But I have never been Willy or Bill, so William it has to be. To go back to what I was saying—"

"Must you?" cried Caroline, anxious-eyed.

"Yes, I think so. I wouldn't have the impertinence to talk to you about your attitude to life, only I know a bit about it. When my wife died I thought my private world had come to an end. I only wanted to get away alone into myself. But I had two things to help me that you haven't got, so I didn't have so much excuse for avoiding life."

Caroline looked a question.

"My work in the army and Julia. Something to do and something to love. Also, which is not unimportant, I am pretty well off and that necessarily makes an enormous difference in one's attitude to life."

The low sun threw such a glow on Caroline's face that she looked younger than Colonel Beaton had ever seen her.

"I have nothing to do," she said in half humorous self-depreciation. "I can't very well do the housekeeping when it isn't my house, and I hate the poor, and I haven't any gifts. I was rather good at having a husband and a home, but I'm out of work now."

"But you have people to love."

This time there was no mistaking the flame that sprang to Caroline's face, nor the appeal of her eyes.

"I mean all your in-laws, and I hope Julia, and your cousins," said Colonel Beaton, making matters worse.

"Has Anna told you then?" asked Caroline in a breathless voice, protecting herself by a backward step.

"No, no. Anna had told me nothing," said Colonel Beaton, quite at a loss and annoyed with himself for having, he didn't know how, embarrassed Caroline. "I'm a bungling meddler, and that I'm well-meaning perhaps only makes things worse. Let's start back and we will pick up the others on the way."

Accordingly they set off at their usual speed and said nothing till Caroline, given courage by their rapid motion and the growing dusk of the evening said:

"You were quite right about loving people. But please don't think about it, or even guess."

"Of course I won't, my dear. And I may say that I haven't the faintest idea what you are talking about."

"Oh, thank you," said Caroline, with what seemed to him disproportionate rapture. It did occur to him that she might be caring for some man, and high time too, he thought, that she found someone to be fond of after the hideous uprooting of her affections. But he knew none of her friends except their own Beechwood circle, so it was no use guessing.

While Anna and Francis walked at their less headstrong pace, Anna had the pleasure of watching Francis bury his head in the sand and walk around and around himself. Caroline was quite obviously the center of his thoughts, and he was obviously wanting to talk about her. So he did, and though again and again he sheered away from the subject, it was only to return fascinated. Anna, who was still able to be amused by what she knew would fill her with sadness later on, realized what he wanted to talk about, realized that he thought he was cleverly concealing his own wishes, and unkindly didn't give him any help. Therefore Francis floundered about, now talking of Caroline's health, now her money affairs, now of her plans for the rest of the winter till Anna, rather fatigued by so much sympathetic listening, stopped beside a half-used haystack just under the ridge of the downs.

"Let's get out of the wind here," she said, leaning up against the sheltered side. "I haven't enough breath to walk and listen, Francis. Listening uses up nearly as much breath as talking."

"I have never seen anyone respond to the hills as Caroline does," said Francis, leaning against the hay beside her. "You don't look half as well as she does, Anna. You thrive better in London, don't you?"

Anna was wondering how much more she could stand. It appalled her to think that Francis could be so utterly unmoved by her proximity as he obviously was, and even worse, to think that this might go on forever and ever. Also her feeling for him was at the moment so mixed with exasperation that she felt she might burst. Having paid this debt to politeness, if politeness it could be called, Francis went on with extremely wearisome stumblings and haltings to explain to Anna what she already knew, and to ask her if she thought she could put in a kind word for him with Caroline.

"That, Francis, is about the silliest thing you have said yet. How on earth could I attempt to persuade her? No one who had any sense would press her on the subject of marriage," said Anna coldly. "You can't expect her to be in a hurry to marry again after James, can you?"

Francis's silence confirmed his unwilling conviction of this.

"I can always wait," he said at last. "And you will always be there, Anna."

"Oh, shall I?" snapped Anna. "I might get married myself."

"Yes, I beg your pardon, you might. But I could count on you as a kind of link between me and Caroline, couldn't I? I daren't say anything to her now. I can't forget how frightened she looked. Anna, you don't know what it is to care for anyone as much as I do for Caroline and have so little hope."

Anna knew quite well. She could have hit Francis with all her strength, or she could have said: "Caroline loves Hugh. Take me for next best." But these were not things to say or do. There was silence for a time as they both took the path again.

"It will be a most enormous relief to have you to talk to," said

Francis with fine self-absorption. "And perhaps Caroline may sometimes talk about me to you. If she does—"

But now Anna was tried beyond endurance. Suddenly her loyalty to Caroline, the loving loyalty which made her keep silence and never raise a finger to beckon Francis lest she might be spoiling some ultimate happiness for her sister-in-law, was submerged. All the jealousy she might have felt but couldn't feel rose up in an intense shrewish anger against the man she loved who could so brutally wound her. Yielding to a savage desire to hurt and destroy she said coolly:

"But Caroline wouldn't talk about you. If she talked of anyone it certainly wouldn't be of you. There are other people in the world."

The meaning in her voice so startled Francis that he stopped. They were now on the top of the hill, following the path by which their companions had preceded them. Francis turned and faced Anna, his form black against the winter sunset at his back.

"Do you mean other people that she cares for?"

"Why not?"

"Any person specially?"

"Why not?"

"Who?"

Anna now began to feel repentant and afraid. Mischief she had undoubtedly done, but more she would not do. It would do Francis no harm to be unhappy, she angrily told herself, but Caroline was not to be harmed. She alone knew what Caroline felt for Hugh and secret it should remain. Her father she could trust.

"My dear Francis, you can't expect me to tell you that," she said.

Francis stood irresolute, his whole figure suddenly looking as if life had been withdrawn from it. Anna wanted to hold him, to give him strength again, even if it was only to feel justified in bludgeoning him yet further, but these also are things one cannot do. As they stood they heard the steps of the returning walkers and Colonel Beaton and Caroline swung down upon them, almost charging into them in the half-light.

"Such a walk," called Caroline, checking her pace. "William and I have tired the sun with walking and sent him down the sky. What were you two doing?"

"Walking and talking," said Anna. "When did this William-ness happen? Am I allowed to say it too?"

"Of course," said Colonel Beaton. "I hate being on these formal terms with either of you. Caroline has taken to it nicely and you must too."

"William is a highly agreeable name," cried Caroline, drunken with the hills and the thin clear evening air. "We must make Hugh come up here, Anna, mustn't we? I have been thinking about him so much. He would adore it."

Without waiting for an answer she raced on again, half running down the hollow lane, followed by Colonel Beaton calling warnings against stumbling in the dark.

As the others also passed down into the gloom, Francis said to Anna, "You needn't tell me who it is, Anna. I see there isn't much chance for me. I didn't believe it till just now."

Caroline's gaiety so unexpectedly returned, her new and friendly use of Beaton's name, her evident joy in his company, these told him all he cared to know, and he set himself to wishing her all the happiness from Beaton that she would not take from him. What better fate could Caroline have than a man of his age and experience, a soldier, a gentleman, with brains and money and a certain position in the learned world. All the Beechwood circle would approve and he must approve too. God knew he wanted Caroline more than anything else in the world, but now he must want her happiness instead. He sighed in the darkness.

So Francis had guessed, was Anna's silent thought. Caroline, in spite of her newly restored lightheartedness could not keep her voice from softening on Hugh's name. For the cousins to be rivals would be so terrible that Anna felt the only safety was never to speak of it again till matters were more settled and could be openly discussed. Her heart, sore for herself, ached again for Francis when he saw his cousin Hugh where he would so willingly have been. Under pretext of a rough path in the gloom she slipped her arm through Francis's. They were near White-lands now. The lighted windows could be seen through the trees, but the path was still deep in the shadow of the high banks.

"Francis, if I can help you at all, ever," she said diffidently, "I'm always here. I didn't mean to be cross just now. I'd do anything for you. I am so very fond of you."

"Bless you, my dear," he said, grateful to her for trying to comfort him by an affection which she couldn't really feel. "But there isn't any help for me. It is simply Caroline for now and always. I've given my heart and there it is. I won't bother you again with my troubles."

The light from the front door now shone on their faces. Anna released Francis's arm with a lingering touch and went before him into the house. Here they found Julia entertaining Hugh, Wilfred and George.

"Come in," cried Julia. "Come in, Father, and everyone. Thousands of crumpets by the fire."

"And what have you done?" asked her father.

"I was going to play golf with Wilfred, but George had the clubs, so he came too, and then Hugh said he would come too, so that was a foursome. George and I won. Wilfred was quite off his game and Hugh was too."

"I don't know what I was thinking about," said Hugh. "I was chiefly looking at Julia's very peculiar game and it made me laugh so that I couldn't hit the ball."

"I don't see anything funny about Julia's game," said Wilfred belligerently. "She plays all right when we play together. I expect George put her off her stroke. It's enough to put anyone off their game to come out for a quiet round and find it's a foursome."

"Well, I apologize," said Hugh. "Come and dance a tango, Julia."

"No, let's do a golf pas de deux," said George, quickly putting on a dance record, after which he and Julia improvised what can only be called a golf cancan so funnily and gracefully that their audience laughed to crying point. All except Wilfred, who sat gloomily apart, being misunderstood. It was sickening enough, he reflected, to have one's afternoon with Julia spoilt without having young George make an ass of himself. Resentment and envy mingled in his breast as he watched his brother dancing with entire abandon, partnering Julia to perfection with a gauche elegance very attractive to a stranger's eye, revolting to a brother's. Finally it became more than he could bear. He stood up and surveyed the room with Satanic scorn, but as no one was looking at him he went home, wondering whether Julia would mind if she heard that he had gone to Kenya overnight.

When Julia had collapsed, breathless and laughing, on to the sofa by Caroline, George and Hugh took it upon them to perform a rumba so foolishly that Caroline longed for death to stop her laughter.

"But Hugh, you are divine," cried Julia, springing up. "I never knew you could be so silly, at least not quite so silly. You must dance the rumba every night with George. George is divine too. Can we dance a rumba on Christmas Day, Father, or would the servants mind?"

"I'm afraid our servants would mind dreadfully," said Anna, "so for goodness' sake don't dance a rumba when you come to Christmas dinner tomorrow. I hardly think the parents would appreciate it either. Come along, Caroline, we really must go back."

Wilfred's absence was then noticed for the first time, but it roused neither interest nor anxiety. When the Beechwood party got home, Caroline went to the library to look for a book. Turning on a light she threw off her coat and was beginning to hunt in the shelves when a hollow groan made her jump. The groan proceeded from Wilfred, who was sitting Byronically in the most comfortable armchair with his hair a good deal ruffled.

"Good gracious, Wilfred, how you startled me," said Caroline. "Have you been asleep?"

"Asleep!" said Wilfred, repeating his groan.

"Or ill?" asked Caroline. "Is it influenza? There's lots about. Shall I ring up Dr. Herbert?"

"Never mind me," said Wilfred.

"I don't. But it is so very frightening for people if you sit in the dark and roar at them."

"I could talk to you, Caroline," said Wilfred. "You know what life is and the damned rotten deal it gives one."

Caroline looked at the clock, saw that she needn't think of dressing for a quarter of an hour, and sat down near Wilfred, expressing her willingness to be talked to as much as he liked.

"I suppose you have noticed that Julia is very attractive," he began.

"I have."

"What about the old colonel? You get on with him all right. Would he put a spoke in one's wheel, do you think?"

Caroline said she didn't know, and with great truth, for what spoke he would be likely to put into what wheel of Wilfred's she couldn't conceive.

"Well, I know he's frightfully rich and all that," continued Wilfred, "but, hang it all, that's not everything. In Germany marriage is encouraged, however poor you are. Why should I have to wait for years because of a rotten, capitalist system that only allows eldest sons to marry? Oh, I say, I'm sorry, Caroline."

"It's quite all right," said Caroline, in whom perplexity was beginning to give way to pity and amusement.

"Well, there you are, you see. I mean, without being conceited I can say I'm a better member of society than poor old James; but can I marry?"

As Caroline only looked at him inquiringly, he had to supply his own answer, a violent negative.

"Were you thinking of Julia?" she asked.

"Thinking! You don't know what it means, Caroline, to care for anyone as frightfully as I do for Julia. Of course I know you must have been fond of James, but dash it all," said Wilfred, who felt the vague sense of repugnance that we all experience at the idea of physical passion among our near relatives, "you were married. And here are Julia and I, absolutely the sort that any decent state would want, and where are we?"

At the end of this impassioned and rather muddled outbreak, Wilfred hit his head fairly hard with both his fists.

"Does Julia know?" said Caroline.

"She ought to, but women are such damned coquettes. You're not, Caroline: no one would think of trying to make love to you. I made my attitude to the Reds and the Communists pretty clear to her and she agreed with every word. A brain, that girl. But like all the rest she prefers the frivolous side of life. When I saw George making such a fool of himself with her after tea I couldn't stand it. God, what would Hitler have thought of it. He'd have had them all in a labor camp within twenty-four hours."

Caroline hardly saw how this would further Wilfred's plans, but knowing well that whatever she said would be treated as evidence of a capitalist or communist mentality, she only said mildly:

"Well, Julia was only doing it for fun. And she didn't dance the rumba. That was George and Hugh."

"Fiddling while Rome is burning," said Wilfred bitterly. "But look here, Caroline, you'll stand by me, won't you. I dare say James was a bit unsympathetic. I usedn't to think so, but loving a girl does open your eyes to some things. If anyone tried any rough stuff on Julia, I'd kill him with my bare fists. You'll help me, won't you, Caroline?"

"To kill people?"

"No, no. To get a chance alone with Julia tomorrow evening.

Oh, Caroline, you haven't the faintest idea what really caring for a person means."

"Well, I'll try to imagine, and I'll do what I can, but don't expect too much, Wilfred dear. She is a bit young to know her own mind."

"Never has youth been so strong, so certain as it is today," said Wilfred. "By Jove, I must hurry up. I want to get that bath before George."

He dashed upstairs, leaving Caroline to reflect that youth certainly knew what it wanted and usually got it; but in this case Wilfred cannot have been quite young enough, for as she passed the corridor where the boys slept, she heard George loudly singing the International in his bath, while Wilfred banged furiously at the door. During the evening Wilfred showed a deference and courtesy to her which delighted his parents, mystified Anna, and seriously alarmed his brother George.

CHAPTER 7

CHRISTMAS DAY

C hristmas Day began at breakfast with the usual medley of presents, wanted and unwanted. Mr. Danvers pleased everyone with generous checks. Wilfred and George bestowed chocolates upon the female members of their family. Wilfred gave George a book about the ballet by an author whose views George found altogether unsound and retrograde, while George gave Wilfred a translation of Hitler's *Mein Kampf* which Wilfred had already perused, with no little ostentation, in its original tongue. But both were fine gestures and the brothers were much moved. Equally were both disgusted at receiving Book Tokens from some of their female admirers.

"That's a rotten kind of present," said Wilfred, holding up a Token between his thumb and finger with every sign of repugnance. "Does the woman think I'm going to spend my time hunting around booksellers' shops? If she wants to give me a book, let her *give* me a book, something like that one you gave me, George, but not a soup ticket."

"And anyway," said George, "what do you do if you want a book that costs more than the ticket, or if you want a book that costs seven and six and your ticket is worth ten shillings? The bookseller isn't going to shell out half a crown."

Anna suggested that another book, costing the exact sum specified might solve the difficulty.

"Yes, but hang it, I mightn't want a half-crown book," said George. "It's just what Wilfred said, like having a food ticket, like the Germans. I bet a German would be sick if you sent him a Book Token when he wanted a food ticket."

"At least food tickets mean that everyone gets a fair share," said Wilfred. "If we were in Germany you wouldn't be eating sausage and bacon and tomatoes and toast and butter while millions were starving."

"Well, I jolly well wish we were in Germany," answered George, who was rummaging among the dishes on the sideboard, "and then you wouldn't be able to take the last sausage. I had my eye on that fellow; a nice little one with a good frizzly skin."

"That's just too bad," said Wilfred in a strong American accent, which showed that he also was at the moment a film fan and did not propose to be drawn by his brother on the subject of Germany.

"Hullo," said George, ripping open the last of his letters, "here's a Christmas card from James. I say, I clean forgot to send him one. If I bought one tomorrow, or dash it all the village shop will be shut won't it, or if I could find one that hasn't got my name written on it, I could get it to him in time for the New Year, couldn't I? I don't know where he is, but I dare say his bank would forward it. Anyone else have one?"

Mr. and Mrs. Danvers and Anna, who had all had cards from James, looked up apprehensively. Caroline said, "I'm afraid it takes about three weeks to South Africa, George, but you could try air mail."

Wilfred, whose newfound chivalry to his sister-in-law had inspired him to hide his own card, made such hideous faces at his brother that George, not to speak of everyone else at the table, realized that he had been far from tactful. Mumbling something about getting ready for church, George left the room. Caroline was too much occupied by her own feelings to notice this by-play. When George first spoke her old sense of unreasoning terror had made her faint and dizzy for a moment. But before he had finished speaking she had realized with grateful surprise that this reaction was only automatic, that her deep self was untouched and even amused. She saw her relations' apprehensions, rallied every force to combat them, and was able to say quite easily the few words that she thought would best meet the situation.

"I'm very glad James thought of you all," she said, getting up, "and I think it was very nice of him not to think of me. I'll be ready for church about a quarter to eleven, Mother, shall I?"

When she had gone the four others sat in silence, consumed by various and tumultuous feelings. Mr. and Mrs. Danvers were full of joy that their graceless son had not forgotten them, though to see his writing was a pang in their hearts when he was so far. After a few words about arrangements for the day, Mrs. Danvers got up and went to the library, followed by her husband. Left alone, Anna and Wilfred looked at each other.

"Wilfred," said Anna, "did you happen to look at the stamp on your card from James?"

"No."

"Then do."

Wilfred looked among his letters and drew out James's envelope.

"By Jove," he said, "a French stamp."

Anna nodded.

"And why on earth no one noticed it, I can't think," she said. "It was the first thing I saw, and I was hoping Mother and Father wouldn't. I didn't dare to look at it for fear they should begin thinking. Wilfred, the postmark is Paris. What on earth is James doing in Paris?"

"Staying there, I suppose."

"Of course. But does it mean he is coming home?" And if so,

how? And will he be—oh, it's all very disconcerting. What can we do?"

"I don't see that you can do anything. There's no earthly reason why James shouldn't come to England, or to Beechwood, if he wants to. I must say I'd hate Caroline to be upset. She has had about enough of that kind of thing. Look here, Anna, find the envelopes and burn them. Here's George's. Then if he goes back to South Africa or doesn't come to England no one need be upset. And I'll tell Hugh. He has scouts out all over the place abroad through his newspaper friends, and I expect he could find out what's happening. Have you found the parents' envelopes? That's right, now yours and mine and I'll burn the lot. Now forget it, sister," said Wilfred, relapsing from the man of action to the gangster.

Anna patted his shoulder gratefully. The immediate danger was averted, but a depression lay on the conspirators' spirits which they found it difficult to shake off.

Dr. and Mrs. Herbert came up for dinner, making with the Beatons, and Hugh and Francis a party of twelve. The Herberts were a middle-aged couple without children who had been established at Beechwood for some years. Dr. Herbert was physician in ordinary to the Danvers family and much loved by them. His wife, who had been an actress before she married him, wrote stories for twopenny magazines under her stage name of Pearl Trotter. But she was not puffed up, looking upon Pearl Trotter as a mere matter of business, and never expected her friends to have read or even heard of her works. The fact that quantities of shop girls, domestic servants and young men about to be married wrote to her for advice on life and conduct, gave her great pleasure. Her one regret was that the great and honorable class of barmaids appeared to be untouched by her literary compositions. Never had one of them appealed to her for help. The Danvers family called her Pearl, because her name was Oenone Crystal.

"A Christmas dinner without children is a sad thing indeed," said Mrs. Herbert in a deep resonant voice as they all sat down to turkey and champagne, not to speak of soup, fish, chestnut stuffing, bread sauce, sausages, plum pudding, mince pies, fruit, port, chocolates and everything else.

"My dear Pearl," said Mrs. Danvers, "there aren't any children, so don't be unreasonable. And in any case they would certainly not be allowed to stay up till half-past eight. When all my children were small we used to have a big family lunch for them on Christmas Day, but never dinner."

"I think it is lovely to have children for Christmas," said Julia, "only not at dinner do you think, Mrs. Herbert? We had a divine Christmas tree for the Whitelands children this afternoon with tea and cakes and crackers and we enjoyed it frightfully, and Hugh was Father Christmas. But that is quite enough. Really, not at dinner too do you think, Mrs. Herbert?"

Mrs. Herbert at once gave in to Julia's pleading.

"Perhaps you are right, my dear," she said tragically. "Youth is often right."

"What I always think," said Julia fixing her large velvet eyes on Mrs. Danvers, "is that children are an awful nuisance, the darlings, but one would feel an awful fool if one hadn't got any. I shall have heaps."

Luckily this confession of faith was not heard by Mrs. Herbert who had begun to discuss village matters with Mr. Danvers. Caroline heard it and felt a momentary pang. It wasn't one's own fault always if one hadn't got children. Colonel Beaton who was next her said apologetically that he was in no way responsible for his daughter. Wilfred on her other side gazed ecstatically at a woman whose ideas were sometimes so near his own. Mrs. Danvers also approved the sentiment, though she felt that Julia was not the one to make it.

Julia and the young men now raised conversation to such a riot that private talk became impossible. Foolish jokes produced an inordinate amount of mirth and the noise was deafening, when suddenly a dreadful thing happened. Mrs. Danvers had for some time been showing symptoms of wanting to make a speech. Her family and friends kindly hushed themselves, and in the silence which ensued she pronounced the following words, uncomfortable enough at any time, but doubly so at the present moment.

"There is one toast that we all ought to drink: Absent Friends."

Her audience, cowed and flattened, lifted their glasses, murmuring in varied tones "Absent Friends". George, who had just made and placed in his mouth a complete set of orange-peel teeth, forgot that he was wearing them, tried to drink through them, choked, and let them fall out on to his plate. Anna was thankful that the servants were not in the room. Caroline knew that her mother-in-law was thinking of James, but could well have dispensed with Wilfred's sotto voce remarks, "And may they never come back." Mrs. Danvers then cried gently and sat down.

Mrs. Herbert gallantly took up her cue.

"Curiously enough," she said, gathering all the table on her as if they were a packed house on a first night, "*Absent Friends* is the title I have chosen for Pearl Trotter's next book. The Friends in this case are Maisie Watson and Frank Trevor, who were brought up in the same village, but in the battle of life they are separated. After many trials and temptations, both male and female, Maisie and Frank meet again in the cinema where they had first avowed their love."

"And may we venture to conclude," said Francis, seconding her nobly, "that in their case friendship will ripen to something warmer and deeper?"

"You may," said Mrs. Herbert graciously.

"It sounds divine," said Julia. "When will it be out?"

"The opening chapters will appear in a weekly periodical called *Cissie's Companion* early in January," said Mrs. Herbert, who preserved such a sphinx-like attitude towards her work that no one had ever discovered whether she was laughing at it or not.

"I know what," said Julia in a peacock shriek of excitement, "we'll act it after dinner. Oh, could we, Mrs. Danvers? You'll tell us the plot as we go along, Mrs. Herbert, won't you? It would be too divine."

Mrs. Danvers, her attention thus happily distracted, gave permission, and dessert was finished in a babel of plans.

The host and hostess, Dr. Herbert and Colonel Beaton were made into permanent audience. Julia was universally cast as Maisie Watson, but over Frank Trevor there were difficulties. Francis said Frank was too like his own name and made him uncomfortable. George said he must insist on being the villain who makes advances to Maisie at the Saturday night social. Wilfred, who was longing to do hero to Julia's heroine, but was too stiff with self-consciousness to ask for it, was cast for a policeman. Mrs. Herbert took for herself the part of the wicked Madame Isabelle in whose beauty parlor Maisie was to be offered worse than death by the villain during a manicure, while Anna, Caroline and Francis were general utility.

From that moment the audience was as if it had not existed in the eyes of the performers. Such in fact was the laughing and shrieking, such the length of the intervals, that Mrs. Danvers suggested bridge in the library. If the absence of the audience was occasionally noticed by the performers, it made no differ-ence to their pleasure in their own acting. Mrs. Herbert supplied a scenario step by step, and enjoyed herself tremendously as Madame Isabelle, Purveyor under the disguise of manicure, of Young Girls to Roués. She it was who, knowing Maisie to be an heiress, a fact ignored by all the other characters, spurred on the wicked nephew to meet Maisie at the social. Here George, his parents being happily no longer present, insisted on a rumba, token, as he explained, of a depraved nature. Just as he was making dishonorable proposals to Maisie in the beauty parlor next day, Hugh, who as Frank Trevor was hiding behind a curtain the more fully to foil the villain's plans, said:

"Mrs. Herbert, may I interrupt?"

"Certainly."

"Wouldn't it be better if George offered her marriage? She is supposed, I understand, to be an heiress, but I can't help feeling that his chances of getting at her money would be much better if he married her. You see, taking a girl to Southend, which appears to be the villain's dashing and ingenuous—I mean ingenious idea, won't give him any particular claim on her property."

"Right, perfectly right," said Mrs. Herbert who had been listening attentively, "that is an extremely practical suggestion, though," she added wistfully, "Southend is a very good selling proposition. But I will consider it and am truly grateful to you. Go on, George."

Hugh put his head back behind the curtain and the plan proceeded. The dénouement was highly successful and when Wilfred had taken George into custody and Madame Isabelle, now a reformed character, had adopted Caroline the orphan flower-seller and Anna the comic charwoman, there was nothing left but for Francis to come forward as Frank's rich uncle with a check for ten thousand pounds, and for Julia to fall into Hugh's arms, which she did most engagingly.

Wilfred, who had much embarrassed Caroline during the evening by sticking to her like a burr, except when either of them was momentarily required on the stage, and throwing out dark hints and confidential glances, now approached his sister-in-law.

"I say, Caroline, be an angel and help me now," he said urgently. "Look, there she is with Hugh, near the door. Could you possibly get Hugh away so that I could take Julia into the hall?"

Caroline did not at all enjoy the thought of interfering, but she was sorry for Wilfred, so she walked over to the hero and heroine.

"Hugh," she said, "Mrs. Herbert would be so grateful if you would just go over your idea of changing the Southend plan again."

"Of course," said Hugh, and went over to Mrs. Herbert who was only too enchanted to discuss her work.

Wilfred then strolled carelessly up.

"It's frightfully hot here," he said to Julia, wasting no time on his approaches. "Come into the hall and I'll get you a drink."

"Oh, I'd love a drink," said Julia. "I'm frightfully thirsty. Wilfred, you were divine as a policeman. I could quite imagine you in uniform."

"You may yet see me in a uniform. I can't find the things in the dark. Oh, here they are. I do think Mother's economy of hall lights is too ridiculous. Barley water, whisky, what?"

"Barley water, please. Why uniform?"

"It all depends on you," said Wilfred, sitting on the fender of the big hall fire, while Julia flounced herself gracefully on to a cushion.

"Are you really going to join the police? What fun!" said Julia with an innocent rapture most annoying to Wilfred, who had hoped and expected that she would say "Why?"

"I don't know. I might do anything."

"That's just like Father. He is never happy unless he is dashing about somewhere giving lectures or writing books."

Wilfred felt that another avenue of approach which did not entail comparisons between oneself and other people's fathers might be more profitable.

"You are a marvelous actress, Julia," he said.

"I did a lot of acting in India when Father was there. I love it. But the others were divine. George was too divine as the villain and Hugh was divine too."

"In fact everybody was divine," said Wilfred with a bitterness that was entirely lost upon Julia.

"Will you do something for me?" asked Julia, raising her large eyes.

"Anything," said Wilfred jumping to his feet.

"Some more barely water, please," said Julia, holding out her glass.

Gently disappointed Wilfred refilled it and returned it to her. Their fingers touched. Encouraged by this Wilfred established himself on the fender again and said, "I have thought a good deal about marriage."

"So have I," said Julia with much interest. "I have had eleven proposals, eight in India and three here. Some of them were quite divine. But the Baron we met in Berlin, the one who had a sister you know, was horrid. He was quite angry when I said I couldn't marry him."

"Weren't the others angry?" asked Wilfred, seeking a guide to conduct in the improbable case of his sharing their fate.

"Of course not. They were all divine. They are all married now, all except poor Jack Harvey who went mad."

"I shall go mad soon, like Jack Harvey," said Wilfred.

"You ought to fly to Paris by the first plane tomorrow morning and go straight to the Pasteur Institute then."

"Why?"

"If poor Jack Harvey could have been treated at the Pasteur Institute he wouldn't have died raving mad, but of course up near the frontier it was impossible. They shot the dog, a divine dog it was and would never have gone mad if that brute Major Berkeley hadn't left it chained up in the sun while he was proposing to me, but of course it was too late."

"But I haven't been bitten by a mad dog."

"Then you won't go mad," said Julia, nodding her pretty head with an air of finality.

"Julia," said Wilfred.

"Yes."

"Julia."

"Well?"

"Oh, Julia."

Julia had by now not the slightest doubt of what was coming. She got up and came over to Wilfred.

"Dear boy," she said with an oddly maternal air, laying her hand on his shoulder, "don't say what you were going to say. Forget all about it. We will have divine times together and play golf."

Wilfred turned an agonized face up to her.

"Oh, Julia, I must. Hang it, I *won't* be stopped. Julia, I do love you so frightfully. I don't suppose anyone has ever loved anyone so much as I love you. It just gets worse and worse. Julia, I'm only earning three hundred a year at present, but it's bound to be more later, or we could go to Kenya and I'd slave for you. I can't go on bearing it any longer. Oh, Julia, Julia."

Julia was extremely sorry for Wilfred. Of all her rejected admirers few had been so inarticulate and none so stricken. She had no fear that he would pine for more than a few days, or that he would blow his brains out, but the sight of his troubled young face with a flicker of firelight on it touched her strangely. Putting her hands over his mouth she murmered, "Don't say any more. It's all impossible. But ever the best of friends. Can you say yes to that?"

Wilfred, only conscious of her nearness and her warmth, was safe for a moment from all harm. He pressed her hand against his eyes and she could feel that his eyes were wet. Then without a word he left her and going blindly into the drawing room luckily walked straight into Caroline who was tidying away some of the débris of the theatricals.

"Wilfred," she exclaimed, shocked at his appearance.

"Are you alone?"

"All the others have gone into the library except Hugh. He's somewhere about. My dear, what has happened?"

"She turned me down."

Caroline could think of no words of help. She had felt the hopelessness of Wilfred's suit from the beginning. She poured out all the endearing and comforting words she could think of, but it was impossible to add to them a word of hope. Wilfred listened in silence, holding on to her hand tightly as if for safety. When her consolations had died away into murmurings of affectionate concern he took out a handkerchief and blew his nose violently.

"I'm off now," he said. "I may go to bed, or I may walk all night, but I'll be back for breakfast. Don't worry about me, Caroline. You've been an angel and I'll never forget it."

Just as he got to the foot of the staircase he met Hugh and a thought struck him.

"I say, Hugh," he began, glad now of his mother's parsimony in the matter of staircase lights, "I want a word with you and this will do as well as any other time. Did you know that all the family except Caroline had Christmas cards from James."

"Like his blasted impertinence," said Hugh.

"And the postmark was Paris."

"My God. What did they all say?"

"Well, by the special mercy of providence Anna was the only one who had the wits to notice it. She told me, and collected all the envelopes and burned them. If he comes here it can't be helped, but Anna and I thought if you could get any news of him we would know what to prepare for. Do you think you could find out anything?"

"I'll do my best. I know James's favorite bars and I'll put a couple of newspaper men on to the job."

"It would be rotten if he came worrying Caroline," said Wilfred. "She is so jolly decent."

"So you've found that out, have you? Where is she, do you know?"

"In the drawing room. But you'll not say anything about it, will you."

"Not a word."

Wilfred went upstairs to his room and changed into walking

clothes, faintly comforted by the thought that he hadn't forgotten to do his best for Caroline.

Hugh found his cousin still tidying chairs and cushions.

"Don't knock yourself up, Caroline," he said kindly. "You are always the Martha."

"Not a bit. Anna is the Martha. I really enjoy being domestic."

"I believe you do. I'll get a drink and come back to you."

He went into the hall where the fire still gave enough light for him to get a whisky and soda. Then by the fire he saw Julia sitting quietly on a cushion, her skirts billowing about her.

"Hullo, Julia," he said, "all alone?"

"Yes," said she in a voice so unlike her own that he hardly knew it. "All alone and a little sad."

"Why sad?"

"I don't know."

"I expect you do, but you won't tell me."

"No, I won't."

"Could I cure it?"

"Do you think you could?" she asked, still in the sad voice of a disappointed child.

"Certainly. This is the first time I have ever seen you in low spirits, and I just can't bear it. Can I give you a sun, a moon, a star, to make you happy?"

He held out his hand to her. She took it and rose to her feet.

"I feel George would do this better than I can," said Hugh, suddenly finding it difficult to speak. "He could hold you while you pirouetted twenty times and then fell into his arms."

"But I needn't pirouette," said Julia with great simplicity.

"Come then," said Hugh, who was still holding her at arms' length. She let go his hand and with a child's gravity walked up to him and raised her face. Hugh bent to her and kissed her hair.

"You are so little," he remarked, "that I shall never get down to your face."

Julia begged him to wait, and fetching a footstool she stood upon it and kissed him heartily.

"Well, my precious love," said Hugh, lifting her down and making room for her beside him in a large chair, "I don't suppose this is exactly a surprise to either of us, is it?"

"Not a bit. Oh, Hugh, you are divine. Have you had heaps of love affairs?"

"Have you?"

"Only seven," said Julia modestly, "at least really twelve, but that would make you thirteenth, so I won't count the twelfth one, poor thing. But what about you? I asked first."

"One rather bad one called Susan, and millions and millions of small ones that didn't count."

"I hate them all," said Julia indolently.

"That's all right. Do you realize, my lovely adored Julia, that we are engaged and going to be married."

"Of course. What did you think I thought?"

"Well, I never saw anyone take being proposed to as calmly as you did."

"If it comes to that, I have never seen anyone propose as calmly as you did. Oh, Hugh, it's divine. Of course we mustn't tell anyone till we've told Father."

"And I must tell Francis."

"Darling Francis, I adore him. Hugh, you haven't lots of relations, have you?"

"Not many. But there is Rose the parlormaid. She is equal to several relations."

"Never mind, she'll like me. Hugh, that is twelve o'clock striking. I must find Father or he will think I am dead. Help me up," she cried, giving Hugh both her hands. Hugh swung her to her feet and into his embrace. Caroline standing in the drawing room door saw the lovers in the light of the dying fire. Julia looking around saw Caroline outlined against the light room and slipping from Hugh's side sped across the hall.

"Darling Caroline, we're engaged, isn't it divine," she cried, throwing her arms around Caroline, "and you are the very first

to know, only you mustn't tell anyone because of Father. I must
tell him first. Are you pleased?"

"Caroline, dear, please congratulate," said Hugh coming up.
"Just at the moment I feel as confused as a bad channel crossing,
but everything is perfect and I am going to marry Julia. Are you
pleased?

"I hope you will both be happy," said Caroline. "I hope you
will be as happy as I once was—I can't wish you better—and
never know anything else."

Kissing Julia she gently released herself and said, "I'm going
to bed now, so good night darling Julia and darling Hugh. I
think it was so dear of you to tell me first."

She stopped half-way across the hall to look back. Julia and
Hugh were standing where she had left them, transfixed with
love, living in each other's eyes and names. She knew it all so
well, and her deepest feeling was thankfulness that her own
story had only been her peculiar misfortune, that young love and
happiness were to be found everywhere, and here among those
her heart most dwelt on. They moved away and she went on. On
her way up she knocked at Wilfred's door. As there was no
answer, she went in. His evening clothes lay in confusion about
the room and his bed was untouched, so it was evident that he
had gone off walking. Willingly would she have followed him,
but she dared not. If Anna or Mrs. Danvers came to her door to
say good night, there would be a fright, a scurry, a rousing and
questioning of servants, and explanations next day. There were
still a good many things women couldn't do. And for some
reason consideration for others was expected from them when
no one expected it from men. As she lay awake she deliberately
set herself to forget the sight of Hugh and Julia in mutual adora-
tion, and all night she walked in spirit upon the frosty downs,
under the cold stars, hoping that the darkness would never lift.

Of all the parties interested, George Danvers perhaps got the
purest enjoyment from the engagement. Had he not said in

November that it looked like a case? It was his first plunge into the matrimonial stock exchange and he was intoxicated by the success of his prophetic powers.

"I say, Caroline," he remarked to his sister-in-law as she came into the breakfast room next morning, "do you remember me saying that Julia and Hugh looked like a case? After Colonel Beaton's lecture it was."

Caroline remembered well.

"I was quite right," said George negligently. "They got engaged last night. All the rest of us were in the library when those two came walking in and by Jove, I spotted it at once. You can't keep a thing like that from me. Old Intellect was a bit surprised and so was the maternal parent, but I wasn't."

"What about Colonel Beaton?"

"He was surprised all right, but he seemed quite pleased once the idea had got into his head. So he ought to be, getting Julia off with a fellow like Hugh."

Caroline agreed.

"Well, Caroline," said Mrs. Danvers, coming into the room, "I suppose George has told you the news. I had no idea anything was going on, but when the young people came into the library one couldn't help guessing. I must think about wedding presents. You and Anna must help me."

"Are they to be married soon then?" asked Caroline.

"Before Easter I think. Where are Wilfred and Anna?"

"They've had their breakfast," said George, "and gone off somewhere. Wilfred looked as if he were in for flu. Never saw him look so rotten."

This put Mrs. Danvers into a fine maternal ferment, which was only allayed by George offering to state on oath that though Wilfred looked rotten, he was sure he hadn't got a temperature.

"Did you feel his forehead?" asked their mother.

"Oh, I say, Mother, I couldn't do that. But I'll swear he's all right."

Mr. Danvers then joined them and Caroline heard for the

third time the story of the engagement. She listened pleasantly, and then on the pretext of wanting Anna went into the hall. Anna was not in the hall, but glancing into the drawing room, Caroline saw Anna and Wilfred talking together by the fire. She went into the room, shutting the door behind her.

"Good morning, Anna," she said. "Are you all right, Wilfred?"

"Yes. Look here, Caroline, do tell Anna not to fuss. Just because I went for a walk last night she thinks I'm in a melancholy decline."

"It was the most sensible thing he could do," said Caroline with a fury that surprised her hearers and herself, "and I wish to God I could have gone too and walked myself to death."

Wilfred stared, uncomprehending. Anna did not dare to offer sympathy while Wilfred was there.

"I mean, I had a bad night," said Caroline, "and I might have slept better if I'd had a walk before I went to bed."

"Bad luck," said Wilfred. "Look here, Caroline, what can I do? I know Hugh's a decent fellow and has heaps of brains, but when Anna told me this morning what had happened, I thought I'd go mad. It was hard luck to be turned down last night, but I didn't think she was waiting for Hugh. I don't blame her, but it's enough to make a chap a bit queer, and now we've got a week more at Beechwood with fussing and congratulating. I can't bear it. I'll go up to town and find some fellows and have a burst."

"No, don't," said Caroline. "It will upset your people frightfully if you leave them for no reason. If I promise to arrange some way of your getting away tomorrow, will you promise not to go today?"

"All right."

"There's that hockey match this afternoon," said Anna, "and the parents are dining with the Dean of Barchester tonight, so we can be quite to ourselves. I'll get you sandwiches if you want to cut lunch."

"Thanks awfully, both of you," said Wilfred, a little cheered.

"What can I say, darling?" asked Anna when Wilfred had left them.

"Say? That it serves me right for being forward and loving without encouragement. One shouldn't, you know."

"When they came into the library last night I knew at once what had happened and I was wretched for you. I went up to your room to see you, but I thought you would hate me, so I came away." Caroline was thankful that she had not gone out onto the hills. If Anna had come in, what infinite worry there would have been.

"I didn't hear you," she said. "But I wouldn't hate you, Anna, however often you came to see me. Oh, it's no good pretending that I didn't feel mortally wounded. You see, I saw Hugh and Julia together last night before they went to the library and they told me. Anna, I can truly say that I was glad. No one could envy Julia anything. Pretty creature, she is meant to have what she wants. She ought never to have troubles and I don't suppose she will. There are people like that. And as for Hugh—why I naturally want him to have what he wants. If I had happened to be the object—" she said with a wry smile, "but I wasn't. And I can't imagine a better object for either of them than the other. Grief seems to be affecting my grammar a bit, but you know what I mean. I wouldn't really have done for Hugh. He needs someone who is young and alive and can respond to all his restless ways. I am a tired, stupid woman, Anna, and I couldn't dance and dine and visit and travel. Julia can do everything. Anna, you have been so dear to me, and we won't talk about it ever again. Now I am going to see what I can do for Wilfred. Did you know he cared so much for Julia? I didn't till two days ago."

"No, I knew nothing. But this morning I went to his room about half-past seven to ask him about that awful girl of the butcher's to fill up the hockey team, and he was sitting there in his clothes looking quite worn out. He was too tired to keep his secret, poor boy. So I got breakfast hurried up and fed him."

"You bear everybody's burdens as usual," said Caroline, "but you shan't bear mine anymore. I won't have any. You know I'm not playing hockey? Dr. Herbert was slightly disagreeable about it, so I said I wouldn't."

"Yes, I know. He told me. That's why I wanted the butcher's dreadful daughter."

But when Caroline had gone Anna sat thinking. Her first thought when Hugh and Julia had come in, bursting with love and secrecy, had been of such pure compassion for Caroline that she had not considered the effect on herself. Now she began to wonder how Caroline would feel about Francis. As long as Hugh was free Caroline might dream and hope, but Anna knew that her sister-in-law would never allow herself to dream any dream that might bring hurt to Hugh or Julia. Therefore, she argued, determined to face the worst, Caroline, subduing her thoughts as far as lay in her power, might as time passed turn to Francis for comfort. And to be comforted was Caroline's right. I don't really deserve it, was Anna's thought, because I have never had that happiness to lose. If Caroline could master her heart and only wish good to Hugh and Julia, surely she also could master her heart and only wish good to Francis and Caroline. It was Francis who gave Caroline to her care. To go on helping Caroline would be a way of showing love for Francis.

She looked up, and saw to her surprise that it was nearly eleven. "I must have been thinking too much," she said aloud, and hurried off to grapple with the butcher's undesirable daughter. It did not occur to her that her silent renunciation of Francis had anything unselfish about it; it was merely a question of playing fair.

Caroline had promised Colonel Beaton to go over and do a little secretary work that morning. As she walked, having re-fused her mother-in-law's offer of the car and thankful for the chance of being alone, she allowed her thoughts to come down from the hills and take up their heavy way through the valleys.

To examine her thoughts was like stalking wild animals. Round and round them she circled, catching a glimpse of a claw or a fang, mistrustful of her power to fight and subdue. Of Julia she could honestly say that she felt no envy. There are some blessed beings to whom happiness comes as a birthright. One can no more envy them that than any other natural gift. One may wish a little wistfully that one were of their company, but the longing holds no bitterness, no wish to hurt or belittle. Her thoughts of Hugh were less easy to explore. Pride had sustained her so far. It is easy enough to bear any mortal blow with pride at one's side, but to live with an ever-open wound needs more than pride. If she had thought of Hugh last night she would have gone mad. Today she could think of a future in which Hugh had no share with a less tormented mind. Her spirit, fortified by its vigil under a dark sky, on darker hills, had returned to her with a help that pride could not give. She knew now that she would never think of Hugh with love again. The image of one whom she had loved might wring her heart, fill her blood with hot shame, for weeks, for months, how long, but Hugh himself had become a stranger to her with the look that he gave to Julia. One's pride would never let one die of love for any man, but to cherish the memory of an illusion could harm no one. It did not come into her mind that Francis bore an equal wound, though helped by his love for her more than by his own pride.

"And I dare say by the end of a year I'll have forgotten even Hugh, just as I can mercifully forget James," she said to herself sardonically as she opened Whitelands side door which was always kept unlocked.

Colonel Beaton was not in his room, so she took off her outdoor things and set herself to transcribe some notes from his curious calligraphy. She worked quietly and methodically till he came in.

"Well, Caroline, what do you think of the news?" was his greeting. "Julia and Hugh are like creatures demented, and I have come to you for a little peace. I am almost angry with you. Julia told you before she told me."

"You didn't mind really? You see I saw them looking like the Black Brunswicker, so I couldn't but suspect something and they had to tell me. I think it is all perfect."

"So does Julia. I feel a bit out of it. I think I shall build a grotto in the garden and become a hermit. I'm glad we are to be connections."

"I never thought of that," said Caroline, interested. "Of course you will be a kind of ninth cousin of mine. How truly delightful. Oh, William, there is something I very much want to ask you. Wilfred has a very special reason for wanting to get away to town as soon as possible, but he doesn't like to go on his own for fear of upsetting his people, because he had promised to stay the week. Do you think you could possibly invent something for him to do so that it will seem to Mr. and Mrs. Danvers as if they were doing you a favor in letting him go? It all sounds rather complicated, but I can't explain. Only it would be terribly kind of you. Anna and I are so worried about him."

"Is there a lady involved?"

"Well, in a sort of way, but not anything I can tell you about. Will you take my word?"

"Certainly. And I think Hugh and I can find some kind of job between us."

"Oh, I don't think Wilfred will want a job from Hugh—" Caroline began, and then pulled herself up, annoyed at her indiscretion.

"Did Wilfred have a feeling for Julia?"

Caroline nodded.

"You haven't given him away. It was that young George Danvers who became so extremely we-could-an-if-we-would last night that his meaning penetrated even my thick wits. I can quite understand the poor boy not wanting to stay on here, and I'll arrange it for you, Caroline. It isn't the first time I have had to give sulbalterns leave to go tiger shooting to repair the ravages made by my irresponsible daughter. I hope Hugh will beat her."

"I think he will keep her so busy that she won't have much time to be irresponsible. You see, I've known him all my life. He is such a restless person, always on the move, never happy to settle, longing for excitement all the time, adoring lots of ladies, though of course he won't do that now, a frightfully difficult person to be with unless you are up to your best—but so kind and such a dear," added Caroline hastily, seeing the colonel's eyes fixed curiously on her and remembering what he had said about speaking ill of those you love.

After a discussion of the hockey team in which Francis, Hugh and Julia were playing, Caroline began to get ready to go, singing idly in a soft voice as she arranged the papers for next day.

"What's that you are singing?" asked Colonel Beaton suddenly.

"Strauss. Rosenkavalier."

"A charming affair. I have the music here. Do sing what you were singing."

Hating to disoblige, Caroline politely sat down to the piano and turning to the end of the last act sang with a silver thread of a voice:

"Hab' mir's gelobt, ihn lieb zu haben in der richtigen
   Weis', dass ich selbst sein Lieb' zu einer andern
   noch lieb hab'.
Hab mir freilich nicht gedacht—'

Her voice failed and she let her hands fall from the keys.

"I can't go on," she said. "It goes into three voices, and not being a female Cerberus I can't do justice to them."

She got up and put on her gloves.

"The Marchallin's words, I think," said Colonel Beaton looking over the music and then looking at Caroline. "I find them moving."

"Oh, William," said Caroline, anxious to change the subject at any cost, afraid that he had guessed, terrified that he might tell her so, "as you aren't playing hockey can you take me for a long silent walk, very quickly, this afternoon. There is only a week more here, and I pine to walk."

Colonel Beaton immediately consented and Caroline went home to lunch.

CHAPTER 8

WILFRED FINDS HIS FEET

The hockey match was like all other Boxing Day hockey matches. The butler's daughter had been approached by Anna, and after saying that she didn't seem to fancy it, had been brought to the stage at which she said she didn't mind if she did.

"You are center forward," said Anna to Wilfred who had arrived just as the game was going to begin, "and I'm afraid you'll have to have Dolly Brush for left wing. I know she can run, because I saw her at the sports at the flower show last year. Otherwise I know nothing."

This, reflected Wilfred, looking at Miss Brush's inelegant form, as she put her pads on, was just another of the blows that fate gives a man. But Miss Brush could not only run, she could pass a ball and hit it. Wilfred's spirits rose a little. Against the opposing team which consisted of two angry female semi-professionals and the usual country players who get five or six games a season, he and Miss Brush had it all their own way. Julia, who had never played before and had offered her services partly to be with Hugh, partly to fill a gap, was away somewhere at the back where Wilfred never needed to look at her. After a brilliant attack, during which Wilfred and Miss Brush poached shamelessly all over the field, Beechwood won by ten goals to one.

"Jolly good, Miss Brush," said Wilfred, shaking his left wing warmly by the hand.

"That's all right," said Miss Brush.

"You'll come up and have some tea, won't you?" said Wilfred.

"Thanks," said Miss Brush, "but Dad would go off quite a treat if I wasn't in to give him his tea."

"Oh, well, if you must," said Wilfred, secretly relieved.

"That's all right," said Miss Brush and departed.

Caroline and Colonel Beaton, striding down from the hills, met the hockey players on their way home. Colonel Beaton attached himself to Wilfred and asked after the game.

"We won," said Wilfred. "The others hadn't a chance. The butcher's daughter, Miss Brush, was the making of our side. A haughty woman, but runs like a hare. Not a bit grateful to the Young Squire for asking her up to tea either. I'd fall on anyone's neck who asked me out to tea in this god forsaken place."

"If you talk like that about Beechwood, it makes it easier for me to make a suggestion. I rather need someone to go to Paris and look up some papers for me. I'm doing an article for Hugh's paper and I meant to go over myself and take Julia, but this engagement has turned everything upside down. If you haven't any special plans could you go over, say tomorrow? It wouldn't take you long and you could be back at work just as soon as you meant to."

Wilfred's heart bounded. To get away. To go to Paris which he knew fairly well and adored. To be considered grown-up enough to go and look up papers for a celebrated chap like Beaton.

"I'd love to, if you think I'm really good enough," he said. "I could leave early tomorrow morning and be in Paris tomorrow night."

"Good. Come over after dinner and I'll show you exactly what

I want. I shall be alone, as Francis and Hugh and Julia are going to the Herberts. Of course I pay all expenses."

"Thanks awfully, sir. By the way, I haven't spoken to Julia to congratulate her yet," said Wilfred. "I went to bed early last night, and then I was out for lunch today and didn't get to the hockey field till the game was beginning. Will you give her a message from me and say I hope she'll be jolly happy and all that sort of thing."

"You wouldn't like to speak to her yourself? She is somewhere behind with Francis."

"Thanks awfully, sir, but I must simply dash off," said Wilfred, unable to invent a reason for not delivering the message to Julia himself. "I'll be around after dinner."

He sprinted away down the lane. As he turned off by a field path to Beechwood, a dark figure came out of the obscurity.

"That you, Wilfred?" said Hugh's voice.

"Yes," said Wilfred with an inward curse.

"I want to talk to you. Only a moment. Did Beaton ask you to go to Paris for him?"

"Yes."

"Then look here," said Hugh, taking no notice of Wilfred's curt replies, "if I tell you where you are most likely to find James, will you have a look around in your spare time? It would be a relief to know what he is doing and we must do what we can for poor little Caroline. Francis was awfully keen on someone going and he can't get away, nor can I just now."

"Of course I will," said Wilfred in a more human voice. "Oh, and I say, Hugh, congratulations and all. I'd gone to bed last night when the great news came out, or I'd have said it sooner. I hope you'll both be awfully happy and all that."

"Thanks ever so much," said Hugh, grasping Wilfred warmly by the hand, much to that forlorn swain's embarrassment. "Here's a list of James's usual bars that I made out, and you might get in touch with a couple of newspaper men I've mentioned."

Wilfred took the note and sprinted away again in the dark, while Hugh rejoined the Whitelands party. Anna was delighted when she heard the news. Caroline pretended her surprise well enough to deceive Wilfred, but not Anna, who guessed what had happened.

"But it was nothing," said Caroline. "I asked Colonel Beaton, I mean William, this morning, and this afternoon he told me what he meant to do. He said he was only too glad to help any of this family and would do all he could for a brother of yours. Otherwise we didn't talk at all which is so restful. I think I'll have dinner in bed tonight if you don't mind, darling, I feel so tired. Not walk-tired, just tired."

When Mr. and Mrs. Danvers came down to breakfast next morning they found an affectionate little note from Wilfred telling them that he had left by the early train to go to Paris on work for Colonel Beaton, but would be back at the office at the time arranged. His parents, though sorry to lose their son, were glad that he had the chance of going abroad and suspected nothing.

"Was it a nice dinner party at the Deanery?" asked Anna.

"Very nice," said Mr. Danvers. "Some of those young Grantlys—some kind of connection of the Dean's they are—were there, very pleasant young people. Mrs. Crawley tried to explain the connection to me, but I can't understand other people's families. I think the Dean's aunt married a Grantly—but no matter."

"I'll tell you who *was* there," said Mrs. Danvers, thus wiping out anyone mentioned by her husband, "that Mrs. Morland who writes books. I must say she wasn't at all what I expected. Not at all attractive. Her hair all coming down and talking about nothing but her children, and how her youngest boy had passed an entrance examination to a public school. Nothing to boast about."

"Well, darling, every one isn't as clever as your sons," said

George. "I used to get the scripture and drawing prize every term, and I bet you told everyone about it."

"I must say, Evelyn, I don't agree with you about Mrs. Morland," said Mr. Danvers. "I found her very agreeable and we should have had a really interesting talk after dinner if it hadn't been for that intolerable bore Knox."

"Do you mean George Knox, Father?" said Anna. "The one that writes biographies? I adore his books."

"So you may, my dear," said her father. "They are written with ease and fluency and have a well-deserved popularity. Nor is the man entirely without scholarship. But he talks—!"

"I know what happened," said George. "Father wanted to talk to Mrs. Morland and this Mr. Knox got in first. Is that so, Intellect?"

Intellect sank behind the *Times* in offended silence.

The rest of the week passed peacefully. Caroline worked for Colonel Beaton, Anna did village jobs and Francis went back to town. Hugh and Julia were so entirely absorbed in each other that they were almost invisible, but whenever they emerged from their golden trance they were very sweet and loving to everyone.

On the day before the Danverses were to return to London Wilfred suddenly appeared late in the afternoon. He had to bear as well as he could the questions his parents saw fit to put about his time in Paris. From the unwilling answers that he gave, any listener might have gathered that he spent his entire time either at his place of work, or at the quiet hotel where he put up. But if parents will ask questions, they bring the answers upon themselves.

Anna, Caroline and George were privileged to hear a rather less expurgated account of Wilfred's adventures, and George for once felt some faint respect for his elder brother as a Dog who had Seen Life.

"Did you go to the Caveau d'Ali Baba?" asked Caroline.

"James used to go there quite a lot, but it didn't sound frightfully attractive."

Wilfred, who secretly admired the way Caroline was able to mention James as if he had never happened, said he had been there. It was, he added, far from attractive and he had not repeated his visit. He had however met a very possible sort of woman, sister of one of Hugh's newspaper friends, and had had altogether a delightful time."

"Poor woman," said George with a loud sigh.

"And why?" said his brother.

"I know what your idea of amusing a woman is. Telling her all about the Saar."

"She happened to be remarkably well informed about that question and I learnt a good deal from her."

"Oh, my hat," said George and strolled out of the room.

Wilfred thought of following him and having a bear-fight, but remembering that he was now a man of importance who went to Paris on confidential errands, he smiled contemptuously, which gave him deep satisfaction though none of his relations saw it and they would have been entirely unable to account for it if they had. He then rang up Whitelands to report himself to Colonel Beaton who asked him to dinner, adding that Julia and Hugh would be very glad to see him.

Wilfred dressed for dinner with considerable palpitation, not knowing how the sight of Julia would affect him. He had thought of her a good deal when he was in Paris and had had moments of acute and satisfactory suffering, but his work by day and his dissipations by night had certainly helped him to forget. Also there was that quite possible woman, sister of Hugh's friend, a woman who had lived in Germany and really understood the anti-communist point of view. Even so, when you are to meet the girl who turned you down not more than a week ago, you may be excused for feeling perturbed.

But when he walked into the drawing room at Whitelands

and Julia came flying to meet him and Hugh shook him by the hand as an ally, his heart gave one leap and then settled down in its place forever as far as Julia was concerned. She was prettier than ever, kinder, gentler, but not, Wilfred realized, the kind of woman that would have satisfied both heart and brain. More than once during dinner, when Julia showed an ignorance and levity about world problems which he found lamentable, did he think with affection of that really brainy woman, Hugh's friend's sister. Now there was a woman with looks and brains. Both Hugh and Colonel Beaton treated him subtly as an equal in a way they had never done before, and Wilfred sunned himself as a man in the regard of men. After dinner there was music and talk, and then Julia went off to bed early, kissing everyone on the top of the head with complete impartiality. Wilfred mechanically put up his hand and smoothed his well-pomaded hair. One had to care for a woman really deeply before one could stand her interfering with one's hair. After all Julia was only a child.

"Now," said Colonel Beaton, "my business can wait. I got your letters, Wilfred, and they told me pretty well all I wanted to know. A very good bit of research, I may say. But Hugh and I both want to know what you saw or heard of James, as I must call your brother, though I don't know him. Perhaps it was as well that you didn't write about it. Julia might have seen the letters. She is very apt to go through my correspondence."

"Well," said Wilfred, "I got on to your friends, Hugh, and they had met James. They used to know him before he was married. I suppose on a newspaper."

Hugh nodded.

"But they didn't know his address. They said he had been going the pace a bit and told me the likely places to find him. It wasn't till last night at a place called Ali Baba that I found him. That friend of yours, Hugh, took us there."

"Who was us?" said Hugh.

"His sister, of course," said Wilfred sulkily, but suddenly remembering that he was a man of the world and as such liable to be chaffed, on quite an equal footing, by other men of the world, he smiled kindly at Hugh and continued his story.

"It's sort of dancing place and they drink a lot, and your friend said there was probably a lot of cocaine and stuff changing hands, but we weren't having any, so that didn't matter. And then I had the shock of my life, because I saw James sitting on a high stool at the bar. He had two or three women with him, and he looked ghastly. His face had gone sort of flabby and it looked as if someone had put a sponge over it and made his features all run into each other."

"I recognize your description perfectly," said Hugh. "I have more than once had the pleasure of seeing James looking like that, and knowing that he was going home to Caroline. Go on."

"Well, I felt sorry for old James, but I couldn't exactly go up and claim him as a long lost brother with that nice sister of your friend's with me. So presently your friend got one of the girls that he knew a bit to come to our table, and she said James had been in there most of the week standing drinks to everyone and telling them how his wife had bolted with another man who wouldn't marry her. My God, sir, though James is my brother I felt pretty sick when I heard that. I used to think Caroline was a bit hard on James, but since I've seen him and heard the sort of lies he tells, I see she was right. No decent woman could stay with him. The girl said she thought he was drugging too, but that may be an exaggeration. Anyway I gave her a hundred francs and my address, and she said she'd let me know if James left Paris. She said he talked a lot of hot air about a fortune in South Africa, but no one believed him, and the last two days he had been cadging drinks instead of standing them, so she thought he was on the rocks."

"It's an ugly story," said Colonel Beaton, "and you deserve all our thanks, Wilfred. Have a drink."

"Thanks, sir. Oh, I can't tell you what a brute I felt," said Wilfred walking about with his glass in his hand. "You know, sir, James is the eldest, and I've always thought a lot of him. One does with one's elder brother, you know. He is seven older than I am—there is Anna in between and another sister that died— and I thought he was the biggest hero in the world. He used to be awfully decent to me when I was a kid and let me oil his bat and things like that. So when he began all this drink business I just didn't believe it. I often saw him a bit above himself, but I thought it rather a joke. I thought Caroline was making a fuss about nothing. But now I've seen what he can be like I really don't want to set my eyes upon him again. To talk of Caroline like that. Why she never looked at another man in her life. Oh, I'm thoroughly ashamed."

"It's not your fault," said Hugh, catching him by the arm and making him sit down. "All Caroline's friends know she couldn't do such a thing to save her life. I've known her ever since we were children and I'm pretty sure she would have told me or Francis if she ever had any feeling for anyone. She adored James and he broke her heart, and that's the end of it."

Colonel Beaton said nothing, but thought that he was on the whole thankful for a certain want of perspicacity in his future son-in-law. If he and Caroline kept silence, there would be no chance of Julia's light heart being even for a moment made heavy, as it undoubtedly would if she guessed that Caroline had been unhappy. He did wonder for a moment if Anna knew anything, but knowing Anna's steadfast loyalty, he was able to dismiss the shadow at once.

"Beaton," said Hugh, interrupting his thoughts, "after all what is it we are frightened of? We all want to save Caroline, but from what? James can't touch her now. The Danverses will take care of her, and if he did want to come home as the prodigal son, she could always go to friends for a bit. Julia and I would love to have her as soon as we've settled about a house. And if I know

James he would soon get sick of being at home and go off again on the loose. Aren't we exciting ourselves about nothing?"

"I have asked myself that question," said Colonel Beaton, "and I confess it puzzles me. Not knowing James Danvers, it is more difficult for me to form a judgment. I have never heard any good of him. Even your parents, Wilfred, who adore him, can only speak of him with pain. On the other hand his friends may have a very different story. What do you think, Wilfred?"

Wilfred, pleased and flattered by the question, wrinkled his forehead and made several false starts in the immense difficulty of putting his thoughts into words.

"Well, sir," he said at last, "I dare say what I'm trying to say will sound a bit dippy to you, but it's the best I can do. If you think of the awful amount of trouble James has made, nearly killing Caroline, pretty well breaking the parents' hearts, giving our name a thoroughly unpleasant sound, leaving debts all over the place, telling whacking lies about his own wife, what guarantee have we got that he won't do it again? It sounds pretty rotten to say this, I know, especially as he has had a thin time since then and after all he never did anything to me. But if you'd seen him as I did, with those cheap women, all filled up with drink and dope, you wouldn't like the idea of his coming barging into your family again, quite apart from Caroline. You see, sir, I know James a bit and I can tell you this, that even in his worst times he can pull up a few days and anyone who met him would think he was a misunderstood angel. You know, Hugh."

"I do," said Hugh. "And it is just then that he is most dangerous. But I still wonder if we aren't making too much fuss."

"We shall probably know that sooner than we like," said Colonel Beaton. "We rely on you, Wilfred, to keep us posted. And thank you very much for what you have done. As for your work for me it was excellent. Evidently Paris suits you to work in. By the way, did I give you enough money?"

"Oh, rather, sir. I've got a lot of change for you," said Wilfred taking an envelope out of his pocket and handing it to the colonel. "And here's a list of my expenses. I hope you won't think it's too much."

Colonel Beaton looked at the list while Hugh and Wilfred talked. He saw that Wilfred had stayed at a cheap hotel and evidently done his best to spare his employer's pocket as much as possible. The bills for his evening meals could not possibly include the night clubs and bars which he mentioned. Rather touched by this honesty, his first impulse was to ask Wilfred to keep the change as if he were a schoolboy being tipped. But on consideration he thought it would hurt the boy's feelings. This adventure seemed to have put him on his feet again after his young sorrow over Julia and he had earned the right to be treated as a man.

"Thanks, Wilfred," he said. "That's quite all right. But next time you go on business for me, you must treat yourself better. My representative must cut a bit of a dash when he goes abroad."

Wilfred went red in the face and gobbled.

"By the way," said Hugh, "that hundred francs you gave to James's lady friend—I asked you to do that job and it's up to me to pay the expenses for the pub-crawling. James doesn't go to cheap places, I know of old."

That temptation was considerable. Paris had made a hole in Wilfred's private purse, a hole which would have to be filled by having lunch at tea shops and averting his thoughts from Paris till his wages next fell due. But it couldn't be done.

"Thanks awfully, Hugh," he said, reddening again but speaking with a certainty which surprised his hearers and himself, "but James is my brother. This is a family affair."

Wilfred's homeward path was cheered by the thought that old Beaton had not misplaced his confidence. It had been a jolly lucky thing for Beaton that he had happened to be free, thought Wilfred rather conceitedly, little knowing what pains Caroline had taken for him. Before going to bed he gave himself a little pleasant self-torture by saying aloud, "To think of Julia in

Hugh's arms," though his boy's modest mind gave no particular interpretation to the words, which were in the nature of a sacrifice to the Proprieties from a rejected lover. But when he was in bed his mind turned, not unpleasantly, to that sister of Hugh's friend. Some girl that girl.

CHAPTER 9

FAMILY COUNCIL

The question now was, should Francis give up the house to Hugh and Julia, or should Hugh and Julia find a home for themselves and leave Francis in possession. The house had been left to Francis by his parents, but he and Hugh had shared every expense since Francis's parents had died, a good many years ago. A great deal of self-sacrifice was shown on both sides, and no one would speak the truth. Julia, whom love had deprived of the few wits she possessed except on the subject of clothes, said she didn't care where she lived so long as Hugh was there. Hugh said it didn't seem fair to turn old Francis out and probably Julia would like something more up to date. Francis said he wouldn't care to stay on alone in a house that size, and he could easily find a flat for himself so long as there was one room big enough to hold his books.

Anna and Caroline who were having dinner with Francis and Hugh before going to a cinema, agreed that it was a very difficult question.

"I suppose," said Anna, "whoever keeps the house keeps Rose."

Both men looked at her in terror and admiration.

"By Jove, Anna, you are right," said Hugh. "That settles it.

Francis, you stay on. I wouldn't let Rose get at Julia for words. Julia wouldn't be able to call her soul her own."

"That's not fair," said Francis indignantly. "Just because I'm not going to be married you propose to hand me over to Rose. No, Hugh. You and Julia, who is capable of managing any number of parlormaids, keep on the house. I shall go to the club for a bit till I find a flat."

"But need either of you live there?" asked Caroline.

Again her cousins stared, but this time in admiration unmixed with terror.

"Why don't you sell it," continued Caroline, "and have a nice new flat each? If you don't, one of you will get stuck in that house forever and ever, and Rose will close your eyes when you die"

"She would," said Hugh with much feeling. "Francis, can you remember a single day in our lives that hasn't been blighted by Rose?"

"I like her," said Anna. "When I set up house on my own I'll have Rose to look after me. When do the Beatons come up?"

"Tomorrow," said Hugh. "Julia says she needs three weeks to her get clothes, though what she wants with clothes—"

"Yes, Hugh, we all know you would take her in her shift," said Caroline, "but one doesn't say it. When is the wedding exactly?"

"Fourteenth of February, St. Valentine's Day," said Hugh with revolting sentiment. "It's to be in London, you know after all, and very quiet because of some dead aunt of Julia's. Francis will have to be best man."

"All right, if I must, I must," said his cousin.

"You can always kiss Anna, you know," said Hugh, not noticing how embarrassed Anna looked.

"Don't be coarse, Hugh," said Caroline.

"Course? My dear Caroline, who is coarse? It was not I who used the word shift, and it is the best man's privilege, nay his dismal duty, to kiss the bridesmaids. Why aren't you being a bridesmaid, Caroline?"

"Could I?" said Caroline, looking away.

Francis kicked Hugh hard under the table and Anna made a face at him, by which means he was brought to understand that he had not shown tact.

"One bridesmaid is quite enough," said Anna, "for the wedding of a dead aunt. And Julia is showing great sense, considering how cold February can be, in having a coat and skirt wedding."

"Well, now it is quite settled that you sell the house and Rose, isn't it," said Caroline, "and both find charming new abodes. I'll come and help you with curtains and things, Francis, when you move. Heavens, we'll be late."

The film had just begun when they got to the cinema and they had to push to their seats in the dark. Hugh went in first to find their places, then came Caroline, then Francis and at the end Anna. Each was affected in his or her way by the romantic atmosphere of film-land, the wailing and throbbing of canned music, and the occasional sounds of the electric organ when its deep toned voice faltered. Hugh, to do him justice, thought chiefly of Julia, though he was pleased to have his cousin Caroline next to him and had been delighted to find in her at dinner some flashes of the impudence that used to amuse him in old days. Her plan of selling the house—and Rose—was masterly. If only that blighter James would keep away. He also wondered vaguely how Francis was getting on, but as Francis had said nothing lately of his feeling for Caroline, Hugh had not cared to press him.

To Caroline, seated between her cousins, it seemed as if time had rolled back and she was a girl again, or happy with them in the days before James became possessed by evil. It was impossible not to be conscious of Hugh by her side. For many months, numbed and sickened by fear of James, she had let her thoughts turn to Hugh as a refuge, first as the dear cousin and friend of her youth, then, when James had left her and her life became of no account, with increasingly deep affection. She recognized it as one of the inevitable follies of her sex that she had loved without return and fed her love upon her own imagination, but her need to love was urgent beyond all reasoning. She had never even got so far as to hope for anything definite. A ceaseless immolation of herself upon the altar of a god of her own creating had been enough to fill her days. She had never written to Hugh, unless perhaps a note on business or an invitation to the Danverses, but everything that happened to her, everything she saw and thought, had been phrased in her mind as part of a long eternal letter to Hugh. Even now she found herself mentally writing to him exactly what she felt about his engagement to Julia, quoting with some pleasure the words she had sung to Colonel Beaton.

Then, while the film melted from bad to worse and the luscious canned music spilled its syrup upon the audience, Caroline suddenly, with a wave of sick shame, saw herself from outside as an enemy might see her. An idle, selfish woman who because she had once had a husband that was not kind felt rather too good for this world; who fed herself on the honeydew of self-delusion; who wantonly imagined a lover that had never existed; who had in her cowardice and egoism allowed her husband's name to be tacitly ignored in his own parents' house; who had used and profited by Anna's affectionate devotion. She was bitterly hard on herself in this moment of vision. She did not count her joy in Hugh and Julia's happiness as a sign of grace, but smiled sardonically at the weak fool who could, unloved, find joy in the happiness of the beloved, thus making herself the heroine of a fine if hackneyed dramatic situation. Like most dramatic self-torturers she forgot or omitted the one thing in which she had been cruel beyond any need, her want of self-control over Francis's proposal. If she had thought of this she would have explained it away to herself, perhaps not unjustly as the cruelty born of fear. There are natures that can be generous and forgiving under slights, neglect, privation, but if once terrified, physically or mentally, the wound to their inner self, the degradation of the immortal being, is such that they will be cold and implacable to the offender forever. They will never seek revenge, nor speak bitter words, but their lives will run frozen over black depths where past cruelties lie. Such, for right or wrong, were Caroline's feelings for James, if ever he came to her mind. Such might have been her feelings for Francis had not some unwilling recognition of his sincerity, some far echo of his pain, pierced her frozen thoughts once and again.

But Francis was not in her mind, and thinking as she did of Hugh, she began to wonder why she should suddenly be so clear-sighted about what had been till now a glorious rose tinted muddle of emotion. At what moment had she begun to see clearly? She could only imagine that the mere fact of Hugh's engagement to Julia had so removed him that she could for the first time contemplate him in perspective. She still cared for her cousin with the old affection, but there had been lately things that ruffled, that even offended her sensibilities. When Hugh had asked her at dinner why she wasn't a bridesmaid, she had shrunk back inwardly as if from a blow. Hugh might have meant it in joke, kindly, but nonetheless had he made her shrink at the thought of what she was. "Neither wife nor maid," she quoted savagely for her own benefit, and then had to laugh at the misapplication of the words to herself and her perpetual inability to avoid making a tragi-comedy of her feelings for her own pleasure.

Francis hearing her laugh looked at her with satisfaction. The film did not seem to him particularly funny, but if it amused Caroline it was well worth while. Caroline, who felt his glance rather than saw it, looked up, and with her own amusement at herself still in her mind, gave Francis such a piercing smile that all in a moment hope made his heart hit him and take his breath away. Luckily it was not necessary to talk while the film was going on, so he smiled back and grappled with the problem of normal breathing. All at once the film appeared to him extraordinarily funny and Francis, who like most scholarly men laughed with difficulty, gave vent to several loud, distinct Ha-ha's which amused his neighbors and made Caroline lay her hand on his arm.

Anna, overjoyed to hear Francis and Caroline laughing, did not trouble to tell herself what a fine fellow she was being, how selfless in her enjoyment of their pleasure. Simpler than Caroline, naturally kind and generous, her happiness was perfectly honest. She only regretted that she could not, as most young women would have done, slip her arm through Francis's to show that she shared his mirth, and she sighed, but no one heard.

It was the last performance of the evening and the audience were so packed that they could hardly move out, the more especially as the pavement outside was already choked by the crowds pouring out of other places of amusement. Hugh had got a little ahead with Caroline, while Francis and Anna were trying to work their way past a solid group of film fans, any one of whom might have been George, but wasn't. Suddenly Francis heard Anna's voice at his ear saying urgently, "Quick, quick, Francis, we must get out of this."

Francis, thinking that she felt faint in the stuffy smoky air, took her arm, wedged himself into the film fans, and split their ranks, dragging Anna after him. At the door he paused to see if she was all right, but she pushed him out into the street in a hurried anxious way, following the other two. Just as they were nearing Hugh and Caroline, Anna said to her escort:

"I saw James. On the other side of the hall as we were coming out. That's why I couldn't tell you what it was. But it wasn't James, it was a nightmare of him."

Francis stopped and dropped her arm.

"So he is here," he said, half to himself.

"Of course. I tell you I saw him. Caroline mustn't know. Let's all go and get a cab quickly."

The hurried on and caught the others up. Anna said that she was worn out and hailed a taxi in which they all drove back to Cadogan Square. Francis and Anna were longing to talk to Hugh, who in his turn was very sleepy and wanted to go home.

If Caroline would have gone to bed it would have been easier, but she wanted to talk about the cinema, and her new found gaiety so infected them that they sat on laughing and talking till nearly twelve, when Wilfred came in, looking impatient and worried.

Caroline then at last said she was tired and must go to bed. As soon as she had gone Wilfred shut the door behind her.

"I say," he said, "James has left Paris. I had a note from his little friend."

"I know," said Francis. "Anna saw him at the cinema to-night."

"I've been all up and down the Fleet Street bars to get news of him," said Wilfred, "but no one knows where he is."

"I'll get some fellows on him tomorrow," said Hugh, who had so far been too much surprised to speak.

After this display of manliness they all had drinks and then looked blankly at one another. Anna, feeling that the moment to disturb their self-satisfaction had not yet come, said nothing.

"Well," said Hugh, voicing the general feeling, "we are all very clever, but what do we do now?"

There was a silence.

"I can only see one thing," said Wilfred, "and that is to tell the parents. I don't want Old Intellect to have a fit, nor the Female Parent, and that's what they will have if James suddenly turns up looking like an uncooked sausage, which was what he was like when I saw him in Paris."

"And who is to tell them?" asked Francis.

After another silence Wilfred said, "Anna."

"What a courageous lot we are," said Hugh rather bitterly. "And will Anna tell Caroline too?"

"We are all putting quite enough on Anna," said Francis decisively, "I will tell Caroline myself."

Anna, who by all the rules should have been deeply touched by Francis's thoughtfulness, felt instead a small pang of jealousy that Caroline was to be removed from her watchful care. But knowing that men do so really do what they think best, however mistakenly and with whatever unfortunate results, she only said thank you, and suggested that they should get it all over as soon as possible. She would find a suitable moment, though unsuitable would be a better word, to let her parents know that the prodigal had returned. As Francis was giving Caroline lunch on the following day he could, she said, indulge his fancy of breaking the news to her himself.

"One thing I'm sure of," she said. "James is sure to turn up somewhere soon to ask for money. Father gives him five hundred a year, but he has never yet lived on his income. We all know that he took everything he could get from Caroline before he left her. I don't think you'll have to wait very long for news."

Just then the click of a latch-key was heard and George entered, his soft felt hat pulled rakishly forward and sideways over his brow, his coat collar well turned up, a muffler around his neck, and giving a curious impression of having rather a dirty face.

"Well, boys, how's things?" he remarked in a ventriloquial voice, speaking out of one side of his mouth.

"Rotten," said Hugh. "What have you got on your mouth, George? Hurt yourself?"

George looked with steel-glinting eyes at his questioner, and his mouth set like a trap. At least this was what he meant.

Wilfred laughed unpleasantly.

"What has he got on his mouth? You may well ask," he said scornfully. "He thinks it's a moustache. He's being William Powell, silly young ass."

George-William Danvers-Powell bestowed a glance of tolerant amusement upon his elder brother. Did he worry his head about youngsters? Aw, beat it, you make him tired.

"When you talk about mustaches," he said, speaking with his whole mouth to be better understood, "you don't mention the King-Moustache. Dear little Hitler's penny moustache stuck on upside down with glue. Oh, boy, you make me laff."

"At any rate Hitler can grow a mustache, which seems to be more than you can," said Wilfred. "Just a dirty black smudge."

"Better than a dirty brown shirt," said George, unwinding himself from the muffler and taking off his hat and coat.

This conversation, conducted at lightning speed, had paralyzed the audience, but Anna took up her usual role of peacemaker.

"Leave the shirts alone for a minute, George," she said. "Wilfred is rather worried and so are we all. James is back in London."

"Well," said George, "who's afraid of the Big Bad Wolf? Good old James. Time he came back. He's had a poor deal and it's up to us to give him a good time."

It now became lamentably clear that George, as some of his friends had already suspected, was slightly exhilarated. Wilfred, forgetting his own wrongs, took George's arm and shook him.

"Listen," he said. "If you don't take your shoes off and go straight up to bed as quietly as you can, you know what will happen. The Female Parent will haul you into the Spider's Den," for so had Wilfred and George irreverently named their mother's bedroom, "and you'll have to tell her exactly how you have been spending your evening."

The horror of this thought appeared to have a sobering effect on George, who thanked Wilfred for the timely warning and began to take his shoes off.

"He'll be out of the house before the others are up," said Wilfred pointing to his brother, "and besides I don't suppose he'll remember a thing. No, George, give me your shoes. If you carry them up yourself you're bound to drop them and there you'll be. You remember what happened last time. And mind you don't repeat a word of what you have heard this evening."

George relinquished the shoes and tiptoed upstairs. The others listened anxiously till the noise of a slamming door was heard, and then dispersed.

*   *   *

In justice to George Danvers it must be said that he was but rarely exhilarated. A small salary, combined with a naturally abstemious temperament, does not lead to alcoholic excess. But on this particular night there had been good reason. He and a band of devoted film fans had been attending what is known as a World Première of an English film about Lord Byron. George and his friends had followed it all with deep attention and then adjourned to a cheap drinking club of which one of them was a member. Here George had discussed at great length the theory of film aesthetic with his host, who said that he himself always found films rather an anodyne than an anesthetic and then began to cry. After this George had wisely come home, but the combined effects of romance, beer and intellectual discussion had so muddled his mind that the events of the evening were not very clear. He awoke next morning alert and refreshed, and with a vivid remembrance that old James was coming back and how glad the parents would be.

He and Wilfred usually breakfasted at a quarter-past eight so that they could get to work in time, while the rest of the family drifted down or had breakfast in bed as they felt disposed. On this morning George, who was rather late, found Wilfred already gone. Just as he was finishing a hurried breakfast, Mrs. Danvers came in.

"Were you late last night, darling?" said his mother.

"About the usual,"

"I heard you all talking downstairs," said Mrs. Danvers in a voice carefully denuded of any shade of reproach.

"We were talking about James," said George pushing his chair back. "Good-bye, Mother, I must be off."

"Stop a moment, darling. What about James? No trouble, I hope."

"Good Lord, no. He's not exactly on the waterwagon, they say, but he's all right. You trust James, Mother."

"What about James?" inquired Mr. Danvers appearing in the doorway just as George was trying to get out.

"He's here, sir, all right, but I don't know where," said George. "They were all talking about him last night. Well, I must be off, sir. Afraid I'm a bit late as it is."

"Stay here and sit down," said his father. George to his own astonishment and annoyance immediately obeyed.

"What is all this about James, Cecil?" implored Mrs. Danvers.

"I don't know, my dear, but I propose to find out. George, what is this story about James?"

"Well, sir, I don't really know," said George, who was beginning to feel very uncomfortable. "The others know, you'd better ask them. Ask Anna," he added as his sister came into the room.

"Anna," said her father looking appealingly at her, "what is George saying about James?"

"Look here, Anna," said the aggrieved George, "what's all the mystery? I come in last night, perhaps a shade squiffy but that was the fault of the beer, and find you all talking about James being here, and then you make me take my shoes off and hustle me upstairs, and now Father and Mother come down on me like a ton of bricks."

Anna saw her parents' anxious faces. Willingly could she have boxed her young brother's ears.

"I think, Father," she said, "George had better go off to work. He is late already and he doesn't know what he is talking about. Go along, George."

George, at most times very ready to resent female domination, was only too thankful to be released and slipped sulkily out, shutting the door behind him, while Anna continued:

"Sit down darlings and I'll give you some more coffee. And don't be upset. Last night at the cinema I did see James, but Hugh and Francis and I didn't want to tell you so late at night. I said I would tell you about it today. Then George came in and we told him, and asked him to say nothing till I could see you, but he was a bit excited and I expect he forgot. I am so sorry."

"Then you have only known of James's arrival since last night?" said her father.

Anna was thankful to be able to say "yes" with truth.

"We must have James here," said Mrs. Danvers. "He will need looking after if he has come all the way from South Africa. We haven't a spare room now, but I could put Wilfred and George together, or, Anna, you and Caroline—"

She stopped and repeated "Caroline" in a frightened voice.

"Yes; Caroline," said her husband. "How much we see of James must depend to some degree upon her feelings. Anna, does Caroline know?"

"Do I know what?" said Caroline, who to complete the nightmare came into the room at the moment. No one answered. She looked from face to face, her uneasiness growing in their silence.

"Has anything happened?" she asked. "Not Francis or Hugh?"

"Sit down, darling, here's your coffee," said Anna. "What has happened is that James is back in London. Not very surprising and nothing to worry about really, because you are with us."

"But," said Caroline, looking at her father- and mother-in-law and speaking slowly "you will want to have James here. And you ought to. I must go."

"My dear child," said Mr. Danvers, "you know we love James, but you are as dear as a daughter to us, and you mustn't think of going. We must see our son, but your peace and privacy shall be scrupulously respected."

"Where is he?" asked Caroline, speaking to the room at large. Mr. Danvers looked at Anna.

"No one knows," she said. "But Hugh was going to try to find out through his newspaper friends. If he knows anything he'll ring up. Or Francis may know by lunch time and be able to tell you, Caroline. You are lunching with him, aren't you?"

"I suppose so. Why didn't you tell me about James before, Anna?"

"I didn't see him till last night," said Anna, speaking the bare truth. "Then after you had gone to bed we talked about him and I said I would tell Father and Mother. Francis said he wanted to tell you himself at lunch. I wanted to tell you but he asked me not to."

"How very obliging and meddling of Francis," said Caroline. "But we can discuss that at lunch. Do you mind if I don't finish my breakfast? Please don't worry about me, Mother and Father. If James wants to come here I can go to friends. Besides one must want to see one's own child. Oh, heavens, I wanted to see mine, and it must be far worse when you have a child and lose him. Now he is back you must have him again. Forgive me."

"There is nothing to forgive her for, poor child," said Mr. Danvers when the door had closed behind his daughter-in-law. "No, Evelyn, don't go after her, she won't be able to bear anyone just now. I only hope that Francis will be able to help her."

"William Beaton comes to town today," said Anna. "He will know all there is to know, because of Hugh and Julia. He will be the greatest help. He is such a good friend and makes one feel so safe. I will ring up their hotel."

"Yes, do," said her father. "There is no one I would rather have to consult than Beaton. I wish I could make him decide to come into the business. He won't give me a definite answer yet. Yes, Anna, find out if he and Julia can come and see us today."

"Darling Father," said Anna, rubbing her cheek on his head.

"Well, well, everything has to be left to time," he said, getting up. "James and the business and Caroline and the whole world. I must go to the office now."

The rest of Anna's morning was spent in comforting her mother and trying to persuade her that it was not necessary to move all the beds in the house on the off chance of James coming for the night, and that George, whose unlucky use of the word squiffy had really frightened his mother, was not following

in James's footsteps. In restraining her mother's tearful excitement her time was fully occupied. She went up once to Caroline's room, but the door was locked and Caroline's voice said: "I
love you, darling, but please go away."

CHAPTER 10

FRANCIS MOVES AGAIN

Caroline spent her morning partly in abject panic, partly in telling herself not to be a fool. Hundreds of women divorced their husbands or men their wives, and met them again without the faintest embarrassment. Yet there was a difference between a divorce which took place because one or other had fallen in love elsewhere, and a divorce which was bound up with days and nights of terror. She knew husbands and wives who had divorced or been divorced and yet still cared for the creature to whom they gave freedom to bind itself again: though time or a happier union often destroyed that tenuous emotional form of romance. But there must be some kind of courtesy, of consideration, a gentlemanliness of behavior on both sides. Where the man was possessed by the beast, divorce was simply a human being striking out wildly and savagely in self defense. As this passed the anger engendered by fear might die, might give way to compassion, but the old fear could never be killed. So long as there was a chance of meeting James, so long her fear would live, beyond reasoning, beyond common sense. Knowing James to be in South Africa she had forgotten her fear. Now it came back through every nerve, vague, overpowering. She looked as deeply as she dared into her own heart, and there she saw all her own weakness, and did not feel proud of what she saw.

Finally she decided to walk as far as the restaurant where she was to lunch with Francis, hoping to calm herself, but as she walked her eyes were nervously searching and yet avoiding the faces of passers by. More than once she felt sick with fright when a man with a walk or a way of holding his head that reminded her of James crossed her path. She invented imaginary meetings at which, by a well directed look or a politely scornful word she annihilated James, knowing well all the time that she would be tongue-tied and terrified by the sight of him. So hard did she invent and imagine that she lost her way in Soho, a feat now, alas, only possible to those laboring under extreme mental distraction, and arrived a few minute late to find Francis established on a red plush seat in a corner. She slipped in beside him. Francis thought that his cousin seemed abstracted, but he accepted all her moods gratefully, accompanied as they were by her adored self. The lunch was quickly ordered. Francis asked Caroline what she would drink.

"Nothing, thank you. Coffee afterwards. Francis, I'm too stupid to drink at all today. I would lose my head altogether if I did."

"I am sorry about that, because I wanted to talk to you about something rather worrying."

Francis's idea of a tactful beginning was not well received.

"Worrying?" said his cousin. "I have been doing nothing else since breakfast. Francis, how could you, how could you know that James was in London and not tell me? Not let Anna tell me?"

"But Caroline—"

"I didn't think you could be so cruel. To let me hear it just by chance."

"But I was going to tell you myself. Anna saw him after the cinema and told me, but we couldn't stop and discuss it in the street. Our one idea was to get you away safely. We wanted to talk over what we were going to do, but we couldn't till you had gone to bed. Then Anna said—but didn't she tell you?"

"That doesn't matter. Who were 'we?'"

"Hugh and Anna and I," said Francis patiently. "Then Wilfred came in and we wanted to talk it over with him too."

"But why did Wilfred know? He wasn't at the cinema."

"He had got the news from Paris."

"But why Paris? Francis, what *are* you talking about?"

Falling from depth to depth of discomfort, Francis was finally obliged to tell the whole story of the Christmas cards, of the conspiracy, of Wilfred's visit to Paris.

"We did so hope, Caroline, that he would go back to South Africa. Then you need never have known."

"I suppose it didn't occur to you," said Caroline angrily eating an omelet, "that there was a chance of his coming over suddenly and my meeting him?"

"We thought we knew all about his movements."

"Is there anyone who didn't know all about him?" cried Caroline in exasperation. "You and Hugh and Anna and Wilfred and George—"

"George?"

"Of course. It was like Russian scandal all over the house today. George telling his father and mother and they letting it out to me and no one knowing who knew anything. Oh, my goodness!"

"I would like to thrash George. He came in last night rather full of beer and heard something of what we were saying, and he promised he wouldn't say a word."

"Oh, my goodness, how can people be so silly? The solidarity of men accounts for half the trouble in the world. Just because George is a man you trusted him. I'd have locked him into his room, anything, sooner than run the risk of his talking. He gave his parents a frightful shock. They are longing to see James of course, but they don't know where he is. Where is he?"

"My dear, I wish we knew. Hugh is our best link with James's world and he is trying to find out. He might be anywhere. He might be that man who has just come in, over there, hanging his coat up."

The man who had just come in was quite sufficiently like James from behind. Caroline, only saved by the breeding that teaches one never to be conspicuous in public, did not faint, but she clutched Francis's arm, murmuring unreasonably, "Hide me." The man, who was by no means James from the front, passed to his seat. Francis, feeling Caroline's hand slipping limply from his arm called a waiter and ordered brandy at once. When it came Caroline had recovered herself enough to drink it and be grateful.

"I am very sorry, Francis," she said in her polite child's voice. "I didn't mean to."

"My poor child, it was my fault. I was a fool. I didn't consider you. What a brute I am."

"Men do so enjoy saying that," murmured Caroline.

"You don't think much of men, do you?"

"Do you mean I don't think much of men, or I don't think much of them?"

"I mean—you know very well what I mean, Caroline."

"Well, in that sense, why should I? Look at you and Hugh and Wilfred all making a conspiracy as if I were a fool, and then not having the wits to keep it a secret but letting George know so that he can frighten his father and mother to pieces and me too. Oh, Francis, I didn't think you could. Hugh and Wilfred are rather thoughtless, but I thought you had some kindness."

"So I have. More than you know. More than you'll let me tell you. More than you have for me. If I made a mistake in trying to keep James's return from you, I'm sorry. But I still believe I was right. Caroline, we all did it for you. Are you going to hate all of us? And Anna too?"

Caroline dipped her sugar into her coffee and watched the brown stain rise. Then she ate the sugar and at last looked at Francis with her deep gaze.

"No. I'm going to hate none of you and certainly not Anna. I have been ungrateful and foolish and lost my temper as usual. I'm sick of thinking about myself; why can't I stop? If you all try to be so kind to me I might at least show a little gratitude by sitting back and not worrying. Francis, let me talk a little about myself. I don't often do it, do I?"

"Would you like some more coffee while you talk?"

"Please. Francis, I don't know why you should be kind to me. I was quite brutal to you, and I haven't forgotten it and I'm still ashamed of it. It wasn't myself, it was the fear in me. You see," she said slowly, stirring her coffee round and round and looking downwards all the time, "if you have been badly married you have rather a fear of men. You know that some of them are kind, but something in you won't let you believe it. That's why I wasn't at all charming to you that day, after William's lecture. It was not you, dear cousin Francis, that I wanted to hurt, it was just men in the lump or abstract, and you happened to be handy. And if one ever gets over that, I don't know. Also it doesn't matter for me now."

"Do you think you could make an effort, Caroline?"

"Of course. I make one every day to go on with life at all."

"I'd shake you if we weren't lunching in public," said Francis. "You are sick with self-pity, Caroline. God knows you have had enough to bear, but that gives you no right to go on being as sorry for yourself as you are. You have got to make an effort and get out of this business of pretending that you don't care if you live or die. And you have got to listen to me when I tell you again that you are my dearest love forever, even if I have to wait for you to stop being silly, which may be a very long time. Is that clear?"

Caroline, who shared her sex's intense enjoyment of being scolded by an admirer, looked hopefully at him, expecting more enchanting revelations about herself, but Francis had finished.

"That is just what William said," she remarked with the voice of a cat purring in the sun. "Thank goodness he comes to town today."

"William?"

"Colonel Beaton, as you very well know or you would have asked me that before when I mentioned him."

To her great satisfaction Francis flushed angrily.

"He is a very safe person," she continued. "He will be able to tell me what to do."

Ravaged by jealousy, Francis turned on Caroline.

"You needn't ask Beaton," he said. "He is in the conspiracy too. He cares for you enough to worry about your peace of mind like the rest of us. If you want to know what to do, ask me, not Beaton. The only thing is that if you do decide to see James, or he makes a fuss and forces you to, get Beaton to be there."

"But Francis, I thought you—"

"Never mind what I thought. But if I saw James with you I'd kill him. Beaton would behave like a civilized man and a man of the world. If James needs killing, just let me know, but I am not much use in a drawing room."

"I expect we are all fusing about nothing," said Caroline with an intolerable affectation of calm, while Francis fumed at the muddle he had made of what he wanted to say. "Thank you for a delicious lunch."

She could not forbid Francis to hold her coat up for her, nor could she prevent the very lingering way in which he put it on, letting his hands rest for a moment on her shoulders; nor did she wish to.

"Will you forgive me for being hateful and stupid, which is just being myself," she said as they parted outside the restaurant. "I will try to be good and, Francis, you make me feel rather ashamed of myself. I think I could face more things since you scolded me."

"I should like to scold you every day and if you aren't careful I shall kiss you just here in the middle of the street. Caroline, may I ask one thing?"

"I can't stop you. You have me at a disadvantage on the public pavement."

"Caroline, when I was rather a bore in my study the day of Beaton's lecture, I very rudely and impertinently asked you a question about your caring for anyone. Could I ask it again without offending you?"

"Do you mean if I cared for anyone?"

"Do you care, not for me, I won't ask you that, but for any other man?"

Caroline looked at him and through him to some place of safety of her own, her head a little on one side as if she were listening. A faint color spread over her face. Then she withdrew her gaze from that remote region and Francis found her eyes looking into his.

"Truthfully," she said in a low voice, "there is no man that I care for as you mean it."

"Is that all you can say?"

"If ever I do, you shall be the first to know. But I think I am meant to be alone."

"Bless you. And remember to let me know if you want me at any time, night or day."

Caroline laughed and left him, but her heart was singing. The weeks of semi-alienation from Francis had hurt her far more deeply than she would confess and it was bliss to have said she was sorry and for all to be well again. With Francis to guard one and William not so far away, one need not fear very much. When she got home she sought Anna and hugged her very heartily, so without any words there was affection between them again.

Julia Beaton came to tea, with word that her father would look in shortly. She soon made Caroline take her up to her sitting room to have a delicious talk about clothes. Julia intended to get all her spring things in Paris where she and Hugh would have to go on business later, but even so her lists of London shopping seemed endless.

"We are to be married in London after all, you know," said Julia, "for no particular reason that I can see and have a week in

Devonshire and then we go straight to the flat. Oh, haven't you seen Hugh's new flat? Of course you couldn't, he only took it yesterday. It is furnished of course and we only stay there till we go to Paris and then anything may happen. It's all divine. Oh, Caroline, isn't Hugh divine?"

"Well, he is my cousin, so it's difficult to say, but I think he is very clever and very lucky to have found you."

"I can't think why he didn't marry you," said Julia. "You would have looked divine together."

Caroline felt no pain as she answered:

"Lots of reasons. To begin with I was married. And then just about the time I began to get unmarried, you turned up. Also, Hugh never asked me."

"And you don't mind?"

"I think it is perfect as it is." Julia had not said, "You didn't mind."

Julia appeared to grapple for a moment with the problem of someone who didn't mind if Hugh didn't marry her.

"Well, Caroline, that is all too divine," she said. "And I am furious about your horrible James coming back. Just trying to spoil our wedding. Hugh saw him today and I believe he is coming to call here, but you mustn't mind. I do hope he is reformed. I would hate to have an unreformed person at my wedding. Do you think we ought to invite him? I would so much rather not. You don't mind my talking about him like this, do you, but I do dislike him so excessively on your account."

Caroline found that she didn't mind, and was quite grateful to her foolish young friend for her championship. But that James might call at Cadogan Square was a bewildering thought.

Julia continued her chattering and was enchanted by a Spanish shawl that Caroline gave her, improvising a Spanish dance in its honor. In the middle of the dance a knock was heard at the door and Colonel Beaton came in.

"William! I am so pleased to see you," cried Caroline.

"I am pleased to see you, my dear. Has my silly daughter been bothering you?"

"Of course I haven't, Father," said Julia. "I simply kept Caroline amused until that horrid James had gone."

Caroline looked apprehensively at Colonel Beaton, but she was not sorry for herself, she was anxious about Mr. and Mrs. Danvers.

"I gather from Anna," said Colonel Beaton sitting down, "that an attempt to keep the news of James's arrival from you was a failure. Perhaps it was as well. There are nasty places that one has to face in this world and it's no good shirking them. Would you like me to go on, Caroline?"

Caroline nodded. Julia composed herself to temporary silence.

"Hugh found James this morning. At least James walked into his office and tried to borrow money. Hugh, and quite rightly as I think, said he wouldn't do anything for him until the Danvers knew about the situation. So he gave him lunch and brought him around to me with instructions to keep an eye on him. James wanted to see his parents, so we came too."

"How is he?" asked Caroline, not so sorry for herself as for Colonel Beaton.

"Quite well. In fact surprisingly well for a man who has led his kind of life. You see Caroline I'm talking to you as man to man—it's the only way I can talk. James is a very charming man. He has his father's manners and his mother's looks, and you were quite right to marry him, quite right. Only an older and more experienced person could have guessed the weakness in him. I know his type. He can fill himself up with drink and remain charming for hours and days, and then there will be a very nasty collapse. I needn't tell you about that, Caroline. Anna," he said as she came in, "I am telling Caroline about James's visit. I think it was a success with your people, wasn't it?"

Anna looked at her sister-in-law.

"I would prefer to hear it all," said Caroline.

"Mother and Father were overjoyed," said Anna. "How James manages to look so young and well today after the face we saw last night, I can't think. But he does."

"One day he will have that face once too often, and that will be the end," said Colonel Beaton.

"He was very nice to them," Anna continued, "and very friendly to me. William was too noble for words and kept conversation going. Hugh has just been in and taken him off to Francis's house."

"Oh, Father, Hugh promised—" Julia began.

"Be quiet," said her father. "If you weren't going to be married in a fortnight I'd turn you out of the room."

"Did he mention me?" asked Caroline.

"He said he often thought of you and how sorry he was," said Anna.

"How horrid of him," said Julia.

"Yes, it was," said Caroline slowly, "but very clever."

"You are clever to know that it was clever," said Colonel Beaton. "You are a diplomat, Caroline."

"I am a diplomat, too, Father," said Julia. "It was my idea to take Caroline upstairs and keep her amused till that horrid James had gone. You didn't suspect anything, did you, Caroline?"

"Be quiet, Julia," said her father. "Now, my dear," he continued, resuming his conversation with Caroline, "I don't want to alarm you, but be prepared for his cleverness. For some reason—it may be to get money, to get sympathy, I don't know what—he is being very charming to everyone, saying in his charming disarming way how bitterly he regrets his behavior to you all and how he has thought of you as a guiding star ever since. The minute I hear a man being sentimental about a woman that he hasn't treated well, I know exactly what to think of him. Julia, I want to talk to Caroline alone."

Julia made a whirlwind curtsy with her Spanish shawl, kissed Caroline and ran out of the room.

"Shall I go?" asked Anna.

"No. I want to talk to you too. I want to explain my own selfishness."

Both young women protested loudly against this self-accusation.

"Thank you both," said Colonel Beaton, "but it is selfishness not entirely for me, but for Julia. I do want to keep things smooth, at least on the surface, till my Julia is married. I have my hands and my heart pretty full just now, but after St. Valentine's Day I shall be only too glad of occupation, and I will keep Master James under observation and try to find him a job in South America where I can pull some strings."

"Thank you," said Caroline, but so half-heartedly that Colonel Beaton had to ask what she meant.

"You are an angel, William," she said, "but have you thought that James probably won't want to go to South America. He likes London very much."

"I had thought of it. But it is no good worrying ahead."

"And till the wedding we will all do our best," said Anna. "Francis and Wilfred will help. George won't be much good, but I can always be a stopgap. Let me know if I can take James on. He is my brother after all, you know," she said apologetically to Caroline.

"It's very good of Francis to have him to stay," said Colonel Beaton, getting up to go.

"I didn't know," said Caroline faintly. "Francis didn't tell me."

"They only decided it this afternoon. Hugh wants to move into his flat at once so that he can get his work arranged before the wedding. So Francis has asked James to stay with him for the present. Well, we shall be meeting again soon, so it isn't good-bye."

Anna went downstairs with Colonel Beaton. While Julia was saying her good-byes and collecting her gloves, hat, coat, and bag which were strewn about all over the house, Colonel Beaton spoke to Anna as they stood waiting in the hall.

"You are still the mainspring and the mainstay of everything," he said. "If anyone can help James, you will, you and Francis. But don't try yourself too much. Your youth mustn't be used by James who is, I fear, in spite of all his charm as selfish and impossible as they make them."

He took her hand and kissed it.

Anna couldn't help being amused in a wry kind of way as she went upstairs by the chance which brought her and Francis together again to defend Caroline. But Colonel Beaton's praise had given her such a glow of pleasure that the thought of Francis was not too painful.

CHAPTER **II**

MISCHIEF AT WORK

How often in the fortnight that followed Francis was to regret his offer of hospitality to James Danvers cannot be guessed. When he got back to his rooms after giving Caroline lunch, Hugh rang him up.

"You sound very cheerful," said Hugh. "I am now going to do my best to depress you. Who do you think turned up at my office this morning?"

"James, I suppose."

"He did. He began by asking for five pounds, so I took him out to lunch instead. He simply massacred the whisky but he didn't seem any the worse for it. His plan was to go down Fleet Street and see the boys, and then go to tea with his people. I hardly thought a walk down Fleet Street would be a good preparation for having tea at Cadogan Square and anyway I was very busy, so I took him around to Beaton's hotel. I explained the situation to him, and as he and Julia were going to tea with the Danverses he said they would take James with them."

"Do you mean to say you let James loose on Julia?"

"Who talked about letting loose? James isn't an outcast just because Caroline divorced him. And I may say he spoke of her with very nice feeling. He said he had never got over the shock of her divorcing him, poor chap."

"I don't suppose Caroline has got over the shock of having to divorce him so easily, either."

"Sorry, Francis, I'd forgotten your feelings. But do you think I'd run the risk of Julia being frightened? Good lord, man, James was as sober as you or I. He oughtn't to have been after all the whisky he drank, but he was."

"Where is he staying?"

"That's the trouble. He seems to have run through his money in Paris and doesn't want to ask his father for any more, so he is trying to get a job. Newspaper work. He is living in some kind of cheap pub with temptation on the ground floor."

Francis made no answer. He was thinking hard.

"Are you there?" continued Hugh's voice. "Oh, I thought you were dead. Well, I would have James at the flat if I could, but what with being married in a fortnight and one thing and another, I can't very well. Have you any suggestions? We must keep him respectable till after the wedding. He's quite all right if someone keeps an eye on him, and excellent company."

"I think," said Francis with intense annoyance, "he had better come here, at any rate till you are married. Rose shall bully him and we may keep him straight for a bit. I suppose you are bound to be trailing after Julia to Cadogan Square. Bring James here when you leave and I'll give Rose instructions about him and I'll be back to dinner myself."

He hung the receiver up in the middle of Hugh's thanks and protestations and immediately began to repent his offer. But what else could he do? James in one of his moods of sodden devilry would be capable of breaking his parents' hearts for good, of making himself an extremely undesirable addition to Hugh's wedding and, worst of all, terrifying Caroline, who in spite of what she had said about feeling brave did not look equal to supporting much more anxiety. If he had James under his roof he and Rose could at least exercise some authority.

On the other hand there was the possibility that Caroline might think he was taking sides with James by sheltering him. Francis had no wish to lose the confidence he had so lately regained. What Caroline had meant by her last words he could not guess. Her avowal that she cared for no man had relieved him of a great weight, though what she meant by saying "There is no man I care for as you mean it," he did not understand. No longer need he harbor unkind feeling against Beaton, whom he liked so very much when he was not feeling it his duty to hate him. This was going to make his task easier, for he and Beaton could work together for Caroline. And then Caroline had made no sign of reconsidering her rejection of his suit. She had said that she was meant to be alone. The words pierced him. Caroline was the last woman on earth who should live unloved. He thought back over the years of youth and childhood. Caroline had always been the same, capable of deep hidden affections, very polite, often aloof, except when strongly moved, or on the rare occasions when her temper got beyond her control. He had seen her as a schoolgirl trying to kill Hugh with a cricket bat and nearly succeeding because he had teased her about trying to play boys' games. He had seen her as a young girl transfigured with love for James. He had seen her as a married woman, polite again and aloof, rigidly controlled. Now that she was free to make her life again Francis wanted to be with her. A solitary heart seemed to him a useless thing, better shared than kept to itself.

Then he angrily rang for his head clerk and set about his business, trying to drive Caroline and her affairs out of his head. So fiercely did he work that it was eight o'clock before he got home. As he opened the door Rose emerged from the downstair regions and advanced towards him.

"Mr. Danvers is come," she announced. "Mr. Hugh left him here about an hour ago."

"All right, Rose. Did you get his room ready? I told my secretary to telephone to you."

"Yes, Mr. Francis, and I locked up the cupboard in the dining room where the wine and the whisky is. I'll keep the key. As for the wine cellar you can do as you like, but no bottles come out while Mr. Danvers is here."

"Don't bully me, Rose."

"I say it's not respectable for you to have Mr. Danvers here, Mr. Francis. I remember his goings on when poor Miss Caroline was married to him. Any of his ways and off I go."

"Be sensible, Rose. Don't you see we are helping Mrs. Danvers? If you and I keep an eye on Mr. Danvers, he won't give so much trouble. And we must think of Miss Beaton too. We don't want Mr. Danvers to upset the wedding. Is he in to dinner?"

Rose assumed a reserved expression.

"Mr. Danvers arrived about seven o'clock, sir. He asked me for some whisky, so I said the cupboard was locked and you had the key."

"So what did he do?" said Francis, interested.

"Sat down on the stairs and began to cry, and told me what a good wife Mrs. Danvers had been and how he worshipped the ground she trod on till she run away and left him."

"Did you—"

"Did I believe him, Mr. Francis? Of course not. I've seen gentlemen drunk before now. Mrs. Danvers is a perfect lady, and it's a pity some people don't notice it. So I took him upstairs and laid out his evening clothes."

"Thank you, Rose. If he comes down before I'm dressed, tell him I'm looking for the keys."

Quite early next morning Anna appeared on Francis's front doorstep.

"How is everything going?" she asked Rose who opened the door.

"Mr. Francis is gone to work, and Mr. Danvers has just gone off to sleep, miss."

"To sleep?"

"Yes, miss. He was quite put out by the amount of whisky Mr. Francis gave him, the small amount you'll understand, miss, and spoke quite unpleasant about it. So about ten o'clock he used some strong language and off he went. I heard a noise in the street about six o'clock this morning, so down I come in my dressing gown and come into the hall just as he was opening the door with the key Mr. Francis lent him. He skreeked like as if—"

"What did he do, Rose?"

"Gave one skreek, miss, like as if he saw a ghost. So I got him upstairs and helped him into bed and gave him a nice cup of tea and left him nice and comfortable. He said he was going to pray for Miss Caroline, but that doesn't mean nothing."

"Shall I go and see him?" asked Anna.

"No, miss. He's not a nice sight for a young lady. I'll manage him all right. He mayn't wake till lord knows when."

"Well, when he does wake, Rose, will you give him my love and say I've gone to help Miss Beaton with her shopping. And my father and mother are expecting him to lunch."

"I'll tell him, miss, and I'll see he goes out to lunch nicely, if it means Epsom salts."

Anna with a sinking heart then turned her steps to the Beatons' hotel. Here she found Colonel Beaton and Julia in their sitting room and poured out to them the story of James's misdeeds the night before.

"What Francis can do short of locking him up, I don't see," said Colonel Beaton. "I don't like the idea of his lunching alone with your people today, but we can't interfere. I must say he was perfectly well behaved yesterday or I wouldn't have allowed him to come with Julia and me, but I could see the state he was in. If he could have chosen any other time to turn up."

"William," said Anna, "did he say anything about if he had married again? Because when he left Caroline he said he had found someone that really understood him.

"As far as I can make out the lady's understanding was not all that he expected. No, he hasn't married unless he is lying more freely than usual. In fact he makes this another grievance against Caroline, saying that the thought of her makes it impossible for him to look at another woman. I'm sorry, Anna, I am always forgetting that he is your brother. How is Caroline?"

"She is behaving like an angel. But you will see her at lunch. She talked over the subject of James with Father and Mother last night perfectly calmly. She said she didn't feel she could see him, but she didn't want to interfere with their happiness. Julia, she sent you a special message. She says will you think it hateful of her if she perhaps doesn't come to your wedding. If things get too uncomfortable at Cadogan Square she will go down to Beechwood. We keep a kind of skeleton staff there. It will leave Father and Mother more free to see James. And we count on you to ship poor James off to South America, William."

"As I said, I will do my best. Provided he will go."

"Oh, oh," cried Julia, "how hateful your brother James is, Anna. To spoil my wedding by making Caroline go to Beechwood. But tell her I absolutely understand. She mustn't see that horrid man. Hugh keeps on saying he isn't a bad chap, but all men are such idiots except Father. Hugh is divine, but he is a frightful idiot. Why on earth does Hugh like James, Father?"

"Because James is a charming fellow, my dear, and it isn't all men that are wise enough to see through a charming fellow, as your old father is. Francis can see through it and so can Wilfred. George can't, nor your mother, Anna. I am not sure about your dear father. He is so good that he doesn't see much evil."

"I think Father sees everything, though he says very little. How I wish you were with him, William."

"If you'll promise not to count your chickens, I'll tell you that I think I will be, and quite soon. But this is deadly secret till you hear it from someone else."

"Cross my heart and wish I die," said Anna piously. "Julia, darling, what a shame it is that we aren't talking about your wedding the whole time. I am quite ready for shopping."

"Bring Anna back to lunch," said Colonel Beaton to his daughter, "and remember Caroline is coming."

The two ladies shopped happily and violently for two and a half hours and then returned to the hotel. Here they found Caroline and they all had a pleasant lunch, talking mostly of Julia's plans and what she would buy in Paris. While they were having coffee, Hugh came in.

"Oh, Hugh, have you heard the awful news?" cried his affianced. "Caroline isn't coming to my wedding."

Hugh looked astonished. Anna and Colonel Beaton tried to turn the conservation to a more general topic.

"But why?" asked Hugh rather loudly. "You can't desert us, Caroline."

"I'm afraid I'll have to," said Caroline with surprising coolness. "We'll discuss it afterwards if you like, not now."

Hugh, almost alarmed at his gentle cousin's self-assertion, moved his chair around next to her.

"Caroline," he said in a lower voice, "what's this fancy? You must come. Julia and I can't be married without you."

A few months ago Hugh's pleading voice would have made Caroline do whatever he liked. Now she said: "It is not comfortable for Mr. and Mrs. Danvers when James and I are under one roof, even for a few hours, so I am going to Beechwood. And Hugh, please don't tell James. When you and Julia are back in London I shall probably be in town again and we'll have heaps of fun."

"But Caroline, we can't do without you."

"I am so sorry, Hugh dear, I really am. But I can't. And I have your word about not telling James?"

"Oh yes, if you like, I promise. I never thought you could be so selfish, Caroline. James is only too ready to make it up and forget the past. You've no idea how he speaks of you."

"I have every idea, Hugh," said Caroline quietly, "because I have heard it often before. It usually ended in some kind of assault."

She got up and went over to Anna, leaving Hugh indignant both on James's behalf and his own. She and Anna then went to a cinema and walked home together. By silent consent they entered the house very quietly, but James's hat and coat had gone, so they went upstairs where tea was still waiting.

"I hope you had a happy lunch," said Anna to Mr. and Mrs. Danvers.

"James isn't well," said Mrs. Danvers. "He had very little appetite and seemed feverish."

"Poor James," said Anna, catching a wholly disbelieving glance in her sister-in-law's eye. Both she and Caroline were conscious of the reproof implied in Mrs. Danvers's remark. If Caroline were not so unreasonable James might be tucked up in bed in the house instead of depending on bachelor hospitality.

"I don't think he enjoys being with Francis," continued Mrs. Danvers pouring out tea. "You see, Rose is rather spoilt, and she has been terribly rude to him."

"Couldn't you have him here?" said Caroline. "I would rather like to go to Beechwood."

"He does not want to come," said Mr. Danvers, who had been sitting apart with his face turned from the light.

"Darling Father," said Anna going over to him and stroking his hair. "I don't expect he does. Young men do like to be free, don't they?"

"And another thing that made James very unhappy was your attitude, Caroline," continued Mrs. Danvers.

Caroline stiffened but made no answer.

"After all, it's all so long ago now. Wouldn't you like to see him just once and tell him it is all forgotten?"

"It isn't," said Caroline softly. "My baby isn't forgotten."

Mr. Danvers got wearily out of his chair and walked slowly to the tea table.

"Caroline must do as she feels, Evelyn," he said. "Whenever you want to go to Beechwood it is open to you, dear Caroline."

Mrs. Danvers made a choking sound and went quickly from

the drawing room, following by Anna who cast a whimsical glance of despair at her father and Caroline as she went.

"Poor Evelyn, she can't understand, and perhaps all the better," said Mr. Danvers. "Sit down my dear. I am an older man than I was a few days ago. I hoped so much from James's return and now—Caroline, what would you feel if you had a child whom you loved and thought for, whom you tried to bring up with justice and love, and then you saw your life's work and love wasted and despised?"

"I never saw my child," said Caroline.

"You may have been lucky. Who could have guessed that James, our first baby, was to become what he is. We have so little power over our children, Caroline, little for right or wrong. When I saw James at lunch today and we were alone together afterwards, I saw a lost creature. God's mercy may save him, but man can do little. I love my eldest son, Caroline, more than my own soul, but I would be glad never to see his face again. He knows he has only to ask me for money, but he pretended he thought I was hard and has been borrowing right and left. I shall shield him as much as I can. Thank God his mother can't see what I see; lies, deceit, degradation. Forgive him, Caroline, and forgive me."

Caroline knelt by him, tears running down her face for his grief.

"Father, Father," was all she could say, bowing her head upon the arm of his chair.

Mr. Danvers laid his hand upon her head like a blessing and so they remained till Caroline, kissing him, got up and went away.

Upstairs she found Anna in their sitting room and asked after Mrs. Danvers. Anna assured her that her mother had nearly recovered from her nerves and was at the moment worrying about the clean sheets if Caroline would go to Beechwood. The two sat quietly together, tired with the day's emotions. Presently

Wilfred and George returned from the office and came up to the girls' sitting room.

"You both look full of news," said Anna. "What is it?"

"What do you think?" said Wilfred, trying quite unsuccessfully to hide his exaltation. "I have got an offer from a French firm through that friend of Hugh's, the one that had the ripping sister you know. It means Paris and a bigger salary."

"How lovely, Wilfred," said Caroline. "And your father?"

"I haven't spoken to him yet. I looked into the drawing room but he seemed a bit tired, so I thought I'd wait. But I know he wants Beaton to come in, so I went to see Beaton before lunch and it seems he was only hanging back because he didn't want to get in my way. He *is* a decent chap. So now he comes in with Old Intellect and I go to Paris. Isn't it perfect?"

"What a dear William is," said Anna. "Dear Wilfred I'm terribly pleased. Of course we'll miss you dreadfully."

"But you and Caroline will come over for weekends and we'll have no end of a good time. I want to introduce you both to Susie."

"Who is Susie?"

"The sister of Hugh's friend that I told you about. She's a remarkable girl and she's longing to meet you both."

"Is she the forty-ninth or the fiftieth?" asked George.

Anna, scenting brotherly disturbance, threw herself into the breach as usual.

"Don't say you are going to Russia, George," she said.

"I wish I were. There'd be some sense in going to a reasonable place like Russia. No, I have to stick on at the old office with Beaton shoved in over my head. It's a shame and very unfair, and James quite agrees with me."

"James?"

"Yes, James. I met him somewhere last night and we had a long talk and I got the rights of the case from him. I suppose I was too young to bother about those things then, but I never knew that the divorce was a put up job before."

His hearers looked at him in horror.

"Mind, Caroline, I don't blame you. I'm broad-minded. But you must admit James had a lot to put up with."

"I think, George," said Wilfred with the new authority that had come to him since he broke his heart at Julia's feet and mended it in Paris, "you had better say right out what you are hinting at. What did James say exactly? Then we shall know how to deal with it."

George, rather disconcerted, began to mumble.

"Speak up," said Wilfred sharply.

"Well, James said Caroline was in love with another chap, so he let her divorce him, and then the other chap turned her down for someone with money."

"What names did he mention?" said Caroline in a conversational voice.

"Oh, I say," said George.

"I asked you for the names."

"He said you loved Hugh," mumbled George, "and that Hugh turned you down for Julia."

"Would you like me to tell you a few of the things James did to Caroline," said Anna, beside herself with anger. "Wilfred, take Caroline away while I talk to George."

"No," said Caroline, "George may as well hear the truth. I did love Hugh, but only after James left me. Hugh never knew that I cared for him. He loved Julia the first moment he saw her, long before he met her here. They both were fond enough of me to tell me about their engagement before anyone else knew, and I was overjoyed. And if Hugh were as free as I am, I wouldn't marry him. There is one man that I would marry, but I am not fit to be his wife. Does that explain it at all?"

"Do you mean James was telling lies?" said the bewildered George.

"She does," said Anna. "He never does anything else. Ask Francis, ask Colonel Beaton, ask your own father."

"I say, I'm awfully sorry," said George, now bitterly repenting his unnecessary intercession on his brother's behalf. "Caroline, I'm awfully sorry."

"I am glad," said Caroline gravely. "Now let us forget it. Only remember that there are two sides to every question. Oh, these men!"

"And you may care to know," said Anna, "that after that delightful evening you had with him James didn't get back to Francis's house till six o'clock in the morning, and then he was so drunk that Rose had to put him to bed. She also gave him Epsom salts," said Anna, determined to spare no pains to disabuse George about his hero.

"Now, George," said Wilfred, "come and change for dinner and leave the girls alone. You've been enough trouble for one night, not to speak of the way you frightened the parents yesterday by blurting out things you had promised not to talk about. And let me tell you," he added as they went towards their rooms, "that if you weren't my brother I'd push your face down your throat. If you want to make up to Caroline for believing those damned lies of James's, promise to repeat them when I ask you to."

"To whom?"

"Never mind. Is it a promise?"

"Oh, all right," said George sulkily.

"By the way, who paid for the drinks last night?" Wilfred shouted from his room to George's.

"I did."

"And likely to remain so," said Wilfred cryptically as he dashed into the bathroom and slammed the door in George's face.

CHAPTER 12

GEORGE MAKES AMENDS

Next day Wilfred rang Francis up and asked him to lunch. Francis said Colonel Beaton was lunching with him at his club and he invited Wilfred to come too.

"I have been mean enough," said Colonel Beaton to Wilfred when he arrived, "to tell Francis your news."

Francis congratulated Wilfred warmly and spoke of the advantage it would be to him to get experience abroad and the advantage it would be to Mr. Danvers to have an active partner.

"Of course if you want to come back into the firm, later, my partnership will make no difference," said Colonel Beaton. "I have no sons and you have first claim to the family business. You would have to start as a junior partner in any case. What did your father say?"

"He was too tired to talk business last night, sir," said Wilfred. "I saw him for a few moments this morning and he seemed frightfully pleased at you coming in, but Caroline was just going and we hadn't time to talk."

"Going where?" said Francis.

"Beechwood. She gave me a letter for you," said Wilfred, feeling in various pockets. "After yesterday she felt she had better go. I don't see what else she could do, poor girl!"

Colonel Beaton and Francis fell upon Wilfred with demands for an explanation. Wilfred said he had gathered from Anna that their mother had been rather resentful of Caroline's attitude towards James.

"But that wasn't the only trouble," he said. "George had been with James the night before, at some club or somewhere, and James had filled him up with the most outrageous stories about Caroline. George then felt it his duty to come and tell Caroline more or less to go down on her knees and beg James's pardon. I expect you know the sort of things, Francis."

"I do. James sits on my stairs in tears and tells Rose what a bad wife he had, and Rose tells me. She doesn't believe him. She hasn't much opinion of men."

Francis then hastily opened Caroline's letter, his heart pounding with fear of her displeasure so that he could hardly read:

"Dear Francis, I am going to Beechwood to be alone. I have heard what you are doing for James and I choose to think that you are doing it for me. Bless you. Loving Caroline."

"I am concerned about George," Colonel Beaton was saying when Francis emerged to consciousness again. "He is a good boy, but too easily influenced. James has charmed him without any effort. When James goes away—if he does—it will be easier. At any rate I can keep an eye on him at the office and perhaps more closely than your father could. I shall be there every day for the first months and it is always easier for an outsider to pull people up than for a relation."

"I expect old George will get on better without me, and I shall certainly get on better without him," said Wilfred with brotherly candor. "We are awfully fond of one another but we do get on each other's nerves a bit. And this James business had fairly put the lid on it as far as I am concerned."

"I'm afraid we are all in for a difficult time with James," said Colonel Beaton.

"The trouble is," said Wilfred, "that he is such a damn plausible chap. Already he has managed to set Mother and Hugh and George against Caroline. That's why she thinks she had better clear out."

"I am sorry if Hugh believes what James says," said Colonel Beaton gravely.

"He can't help it, sir. People nearly always believe him. But you and Julia don't. Julia is as straight as they make them and you can't pull any wool over her eyes."

"I get you," said Colonel Beaton with such seriousness that Wilfred felt more than ever that he was a man of understanding. "Well, I'm glad Caroline is out of it. Beechwood suits her, and she will have Herbert to look after her."

"Is there anything wrong with her?" asked Francis, panic in his heart.

"I don't think so—nothing serious. But Herbert and his wife are coming up for the wedding, so you can ask him. Till then we three must look after James. I hope he won't want to follow Caroline."

"If that young blighter George can hold his tongue," Wilfred began angrily, but Francis interrupted him.

"George has made lots of trouble already," he said, "but I don't think he will make much more. Besides, if James wants to find where Caroline is, he only has to ask his parents. But I don't think he wants to give himself the trouble of going after Caroline. It is much more restful for him to stay in town and poison people's minds against her."

"I think you are right, Francis," said Colonel Beaton. "We mustn't be over-anxious about Caroline. Even if she did see him she could hold her own, though it would do her no good. I can't tell you how much I admire her. Next to your sister, Wilfred, she is the most steadfast, lovable woman I know."

Francis liked Colonel Beaton more than ever. Not everyone could discern Caroline's merits, and if Beaton placed Anna above her, why that was just as Francis would have wished. Let others think that Caroline was less than perfect: for him the joy of knowing her imperfections to be perfection itself. As for Wilfred, that evening he gave his sister a résumé of the conversation at lunch. When he came to Colonel Beaton's words, which he repeated verbatim, he felt obliged to apologise for them, apparently on the grounds that the speaker was on the verge of senile decay. Anna, realizing fully how improper any praise of a sister seems to a brother, listened without comment, except to say that it was very nice of William. And though her father looked tired, her mother was inclined to cry, and George was suffering from ostentatious gloom which his family combined to ignore, Anna thought she had seldom passed a more pleasant evening.

If, as Julia very truly remarked, James had just taken the trouble not to be born, a great deal of trouble would have been saved. Colonel Beaton, Francis and Wilfred were in perpetual anxiety lest some mad folly of James's should bring notoriety upon his family and irremediable disgrace upon himself. George avoided James, but made it up to himself by being very disagreeable at home. Hugh saw a certain amount of James and continued to think he had been misjudged. James slipped like quicksilver through Francis's fingers and even baffled Rose. She on her side treated him with scant consideration when he was in the house, refusing to give him anything stronger than a whisky and soda that she had mixed herself and, it was reported by Maud the housemaid, had on two occasions undressed him and put him to bed. Francis did his best to entertain his guest, but he had work to do that could not be neglected and a few engagements that could not be broken. He never put his latch-key into his door without wondering wretchedly what had happened in his absence. Once he went to see the Danverses, but did not stay long. James had visited his parents the night before and had arrived in a condition that even Mrs. Danvers could not mistake.

"He was not violent," said Mr. Danvers to Francis, "only

stupid and half insensible. Wilfred took him back to your house in a taxi and your parlormaid kindly took charge of him. My poor Evelyn had never seen anything of that kind before. The one thing we have to be thankful for is that Caroline is away."

"Do you think there is any chance of James taking a job in South America? Beaton is almost sure he can get him one there, right away from the towns, where he might have a chance to pull up."

"I am grateful to Beaton, more grateful than I can say, but I don't know that it is any good. If the poor boy couldn't get himself in hand for Caroline, why should he do it in South America? But I hope he will take it. Frankly, I would be thankful for him to be out of the country, away from London where the temptations are so many. We can never thank you enough, Francis, for looking after our poor boy."

"That's all right, sir. I would do anything to help Caroline and all of you."

Of all the people in this story Julia was the least affected by James. Having labelled him as horrid, she abstracted her mind from him altogether, and her father refused to invite him to the hotel again. A few days before the wedding Hugh had taken James out to lunch. Late in the afternoon he dropped in to see his Julia, who was sitting with her father and Wilfred.

"All well?" asked Colonel Beaton, whose anxiety increased as the wedding drew nearer. After that ceremony he had great faith in his Julia's powers of choosing her husband's friends.

"Quite all right, sir. But don't worry. You all seem to have an idea that James is going to make a nuisance of himself somehow. I do assure you you are wrong. All he wants is to see Caroline and then go away for good."

"I suppose you know he has absolutely refused the offer of a South American job that I found for him," said Colonel Beaton.

"Well, sir, he felt he simply couldn't leave England unless Caroline forgave him. After all he has a lot to put up with. You must admit that. Caroline hardly gave him a fair deal. By the way, Julia, he is rather upset because it appears that he hasn't been invited to the wedding? Was it a mistake?"

"Oh, Hugh," said Julia, "we can't invite him. He would be troublesome. You don't want to spoil the only wedding I may ever have. And after all there's no law about inviting your distant cousin's divorced husband."

"But, darling, he is one of the Danverses, after all."

"He is not being invited," said Colonel Beaton decisively.

Hugh was going to make a further protest when Wilfred interrupted him.

"Colonel Beaton is quite right, Hugh," he said. "James is my brother, but he can't come to the wedding, it is out of the question."

"It is hardly your business who comes to the wedding," said Hugh. "No one stands up for James and I really must protest," he added to his future father-in-law.

"I'm sorry," said Wilfred, "if I'm butting in, but you don't quite understand, Hugh. If you knew that James had been telling lies about Julia, just as he has about Caroline, would you still want him at your wedding?"

"In that case the affair would concern me," said Colonel Beaton. "Wilfred, you are making a very serious accusation. Are you prepared to substantiate it?"

"Yes, sir, if I may ring up George."

Permission was given and Wilfred rang up his brother and told him to come round to the Beatons' hotel as soon as possible. There was an uncomfortable interval, consisting of uneasy small talk punctuated by even more uneasy silences. During one of these silences Julia, whose mind was never idle, suddenly screamed.

"What is it, darling?" said Hugh.

"Father, Father," cried Julia, "do you realize what Hugh's name is?"

"Considering that his name will be yours the day after to-morrow, I may say that I do."

"Yes, but Father, don't you see? I shall be Julia Mannering! I had never thought of it before. At least I had thought that I would be Julia Mannering, but I didn't quite think that I would be Julia Mannering!"

"Thank heaven you are not as uneducated as I thought," remarked her father.

Wilfred and Hugh were all attention though not comprehension.

"But what is wrong with Julia Mannering?" asked Hugh rather indignantly.

"Nothing, darling," shrieked his bride. "It's perfect. And Father is rather like Colonel Mannering, don't you think, only his name is William, not Guy. But you aren't in the least like Vanbeest Brown, Hugh darling."

Before Hugh could go quite mad, George came in. He said how do you do to everyone and looked nervously at Wilfred.

"Sorry to bother you, George," said his brother, "But you promised me something. George," he said to the company in general, "spent an evening with James not long ago. James told him a lot of things which he naturally believed. One does believe one's brother. He came back and told them to Caroline, and after that she went to Beechwood. Now, George, that brother of ours wants to be asked to Julia's wedding and Hugh thinks he ought to be invited. So I want you to tell us again exactly what James said. I'm sorry, old boy, but it will clear the air a bit, and you promised to make up for Caroline."

George looked very uncomfortable, eyed the door as if he contemplated flight, but seeing no means of escape, resigned himself.

"James said," George wretchedly began, "that Caroline divorcing him was a put-up job. He said she cared for another man."

"James is *horrid*," said Julia. "Don't let's hear any more."

"Be quiet, Julia," said her father.

"I'm sorry, Julia," said Wilfred, "but you and Hugh and your father had better hear it. If you had rather not listen you can go away till George has finished."

"Oh, no, no," shrieked Julia, composing herself to attention again.

"Just say the names, George," continued his implacable brother.

"James said," mumbled the unhappy George, "that Caroline was in love with Hugh, so he, I mean James, let her divorce him. And then he said Hugh turned her down for Julia because she had some money, I mean Julia had!"

There was complete silence while George went bright red and shuffled about.

"Thanks, George," said Colonel Beaton at last. "We all apologise to you for asking you to repeat this, and I personally am grateful!"

"And if Caroline had been in love with Hugh, it would have been very good taste," said Julia indignantly, and obviously thinking the money consideration entirely below her notice. "In fact I asked her why you hadn't wanted to marry her, Hugh, and she explained. It was rather complicated, but first she was married to that horrid James, who I dare say was not so horrid then though he must always have been excessively horrid, and then you fell in love with me."

"Of course I did, and as for Caroline caring for me," said Hugh, much embarrassed by the thought, "good lord she never thought of it in her life. Why, we have known each other ever since we were children. If James can't think of anything better to say, he had better go and tell lies somewhere else. I'm through with him."

"And you don't want him asked to the wedding?" said Wilfred.

"Certainly not. George, it's a damned shame to ask you to repeat all that, but I'm glad you did. Now I know what to think of James. I don't suppose any of us will speak to him again."

"George and I shall," said Wilfred. "He happens to be our

brother. But we would prefer him to be a private disgrace, not a public one. I think, George, we'd better go along now."

The Beatons said good-bye to George in a manner which considerably raised his spirits and presently he left with his brother.

"How much money has James taken off you?" said Wilfred as they walked along.

"About fifteen pounds."

"Can you afford it?"

"Don't be a fool, you know I can't."

"Well, I'll help if you're in difficulties. I get a bigger salary next month when I go to France. And don't go doing it again."

"I jolly well won't, and it's awfully decent of you. I say, do you think poor old James really believed all he said?"

"I can't tell."

"I suppose he's got a kind of swelled head like Hitler," said George, brightening up.

"Or Lenin," said Wilfred.

"You don't even know if Lenin is dead or alive," said George scornfully.

"I bet I could smell him a mile off, dead or alive."

So, brotherly discord amicably re-established and the question of James happily laid aside for the time being, the two brothers had a mock fight on the doorstep and both fell into the hall together.

CHAPTER 13

LOSS AND GAIN

Colonel Beaton's words about Dr. Herbert looking after Caroline had seriously alarmed Francis. He had so often seen her looking exhausted, only sustained by politeness, but he had put the dispiriting vision away at the back of his mind. The mention of Dr. Herbert roused these slumbering fears and he brooded miserably till he could bear it no longer. He knew that the Herberts were to come up for the wedding, he knew that they were not well off, so he wrote to Mrs. Herbert, asking her and her husband to stay with him for a night or a couple of nights as suited them. He also explained that James was more or less a resident in his house and throwing himself on Mrs. Herbert's mercy begged her to help him with his erratic guest. He also asked in a careless way after Caroline.

Mrs. Herbert answered him by return of post, accepting with joy and fully prepared to help with James. She said she had not seen much of Caroline since she came down. This gave little satisfaction to Francis who was able to give himself a good deal of misery by imagining Caroline ill at Beechwood, too careless of herself to send for Dr. Herbert. He thought of telephoning, but a certain diffidence in intruding on Caroline's voluntary seclusion held him back. His only comfort was an almost daily exchange of letters with his cousin. Her letters seemed to him more like her old self than she herself had ever been since her marriage. They were usually about nothing in particular, written from a wish to share some thought, some small experience with him, or for the sake of writing. Sardonic, fantastic, moving, affectionate, rambling, allusive, they showed Francis facets of Caroline's mind that he had hardly suspected before, that had been lost and dulled in the few past years. Sometimes Caroline appeared to be conscious that her unbridled pen was running too mad a course.

"I can't help writing wildly,' she wrote to Francis, "because ink is fatal to me. I can get drunk on a pennyworth of ink with blotting paper and hairs in it where a bottle of champagne would leave me unmoved. I don't know which is the real Caroline, the cold champagne drinker or the lunatic ink-fiend. I have just the wits to know that I am drunk, but I do get a drunkard's pleasure in letting myself be a little débraillée in letters to you. I live in a kind of mummy case and if I don't break out occasionally I shall become as dead as my case. I take a mean advantage of you and let loose to you because I believe you care for me as myself, as your cousin Caroline, and wouldn't change your opinion of me however madly I wrote. I try to protect you; I tear up five sheets of paper for every one that I send. I walk for hours on the downs, mostly alone, but fast as I walk I can never outstrip my thoughts. It is my ambition to walk to the edge of the world and the end of time and fall into an absolute nothingness for ever and ever—no feelings, no dreams. But one always has to be back for tea alas! at least at this time of year."

Francis was disturbed by her outpourings. He did not like to think of her trying to drown her thoughts in physical fatigue. He longed to be with her and be some kind of help. At least he could restrain her from these feverish walks, make her rest, find music and books to interest her and keep her mind from its ceaseless whirling, let her release herself in talk with him instead of imagining, wondering, fearing. But affectionate though her letters were, there was never a word asking him to come, and he was not willing to force himself upon her, or even to make a suggestion that she might care to see him.

Meanwhile he read and re-read her letters and cursed himself because he could not adequately answer them. Ink to him was no loosener of the tongue.

On the day before Julia's wedding Dr. and Mrs. Herbert came up to town. Francis was still at work when they arrived and Rose, much to her gloomy pleasure, was able to give them a graphic account of their fellow guest.

"He's not been so bad today," said Rose with some pride. "He's having a bit of a lay-down before dinner. Mr. Francis is taking you to the theatre, madam, and Dr. Herbert and Mr. Danvers. I gave Mr. Danvers a nice cup of tea and told him to get to sleep. I'll get you some tea now, madam. I don't know if I ought to mention it, but Mr. Danvers is a bit upset about Mr. Hugh's wedding. It seems it's quite private like, just for the family, and Mr. Danvers hasn't been asked and rightly too, as the poor gentleman couldn't be relied upon, if you take my meaning."

As tea was brought, Francis came in. It was impossible to avoid the subject of James, and Mrs. Herbert was all anxiety to discuss it. She had, it appeared, from her stage experience an infallible eye for the first signs of young men taking to the bottle and these signs she had detected in James soon after she and her husband came to Beechwood.

"My husband didn't agree with me," she said. "He said a happy marriage would make James settle down. Oh, you men! Marriage isn't a cure for alcoholism. If James was to marry he needed a wife like myself, someone who has knocked about the world and knows how to stand up for herself. If I had married James," said Mrs. Herbert who was about fifty-five and of massive and imposing build, "I would have knocked the non-sense out of him."

"I'm sure you would," said Francis respectfully. "And how is Caroline?"

"Caroline," continued Mrs. Herbert, ignoring or not hearing Francis's last question, "was the last person he ought to have married. If his parents had had more sense they might have stopped it. But Mrs. Danvers adored James and could never deny him anything and as for Mr. Danvers he is an angel and quite unfit for a world where you have to keep your wits about you. He may be a good business man, but he hasn't an idea how to bring up a difficult boy. He just didn't believe that his family could go wrong. I must say they both of them made it up to Caroline as well as they could."

"How is Caroline," Francis asked again, but again Mrs. Herbert overwhelmed him.

"I must say," she continued, "that if there were any justice in this world, James would have died in a fit of D.T.'s. My husband says he had the best constitution of any man he knew. He must have it still by what your parlormaid tells us. Drugs too, I imagine. I suppose you are taking him to the theatre to keep his mind off things. I'd let him drink himself to death if I were you. Caroline will never have a day's peace till he is dead. She doesn't say anything to us, poor child, but we have known her long enough to see what is in her mind."

"How is she?" said Francis patiently.

"But don't you bother about James while we are here," said Mrs. Herbert rising majestically. "I didn't have fifteen years on the provincial stage for nothing and if anyone can manage drunks, I can. I have given it up of course since I retired," she added explanatorily, as a prima donna might say she had given up opera since marrying a duke, "but don't let James try it on with me. Besides he may be useful. My new villain, Sir Morton Maltravers, is a drug addict, and I may get some copy. Now I must go and unpack if we are to dine early."

When she had gone, Francis, seeing time slipping through

his hands, turned to Dr. Herbert and asked him about Caroline's health.

"I'm anxious about her," he said, adding rather unnecessarily, "you know she is my cousin and Hugh's, and we are very fond of her."

"The trouble with her is that she doesn't know what she wants," said Dr. Herbert, getting out his pipe. "Do you mind this in your drawing room? She isn't ill. I could give her a tonic or a pill but that wouldn't do anything."

"Is there anything I could do to help?"

Dr. Herbert looked at him as if about to speak, but when he spoke Francis had the impression that he had changed his mind and altered what he was going to say.

"If I were you, I'd go down and see Caroline," he said. "She is lonely and frightened and she won't admit it. Your cousin is a fool, Lester. First she puts up with that unspeakable young Danvers—mind you I've seen him in one or two of his bad times and I know what I'm talking about—till she is half-killed. If you hadn't brought her to Beechwood when you did, it would probably have been the end of her. Then instead of marrying again like a sensible woman and having a husband and children to worry about, she goes about looking like a tired ghost, frightening herself about nothing."

"But perhaps she didn't want to marry again."

"I told you, Lester, she doesn't know what she wants. What she needs, and I speak as a doctor and a friend, is a husband. She probably thinks all men are brutes because of James. They aren't. If she had a husband who could adore her and be firm with her, there wouldn't be much wrong with her. Of course," said Dr. Herbert, walking over to the fireplace and finding some matches on the mantelpiece, "it would have to be a man who would be prepared to go very gently at first and not be impatient if she was sometimes nervous and difficult. There is no more difficult person to live with than one who, like her, has been living alone with herself. But she would get over all that."

The glimpse which Dr. Herbert had of Francis's face in the looking-glass over the mantelpiece apparently satisfied him, for he added, "What time do we dine?"

"A quarter past seven, if you don't mind, because of the play."

"Right. Then I'll go up now and have a look at our friend James on my way up. It would save a lot of trouble if I gave him a good strong hypodermic tonight, but I suppose that would be unprofessional."

The wedding was to be at ten o'clock, so that the bride and bridegroom could get away at once for their brief honeymoon. At half-past eight Francis turned up at Hugh's flat looking so worn that his cousin made him sit down and have a large drink.

"By rights," said Hugh indignantly, "it is I who ought to be a gibbering wreck and you ought to be giving brandy to me. What's up?"

"I'd like to tell you, if there is time," said Francis. "Don't give me any more brandy. I've had no breakfast."

"Great fool," said Hugh affectionately, and telephoned for breakfast to be sent up immediately. "I needn't start till after half-past nine, so fire away. Is it our dear James again?"

"It is."

"Well, I am in charity with all men on my wedding morn," said Hugh, "but I wish James were cremated. I say, Francis, I feel I've let you down a bit over this, but I really couldn't have him here with the chance of Julia coming in. I hope he hasn't been too awful a nuisance."

"It's all right," said Francis.

Breakfast then came in. Francis, eating very little and talking a good deal, managed to tell Hugh the events of the preceding night.

"You know I've got the Herberts staying with me for your wedding," he began. "Well, I thought I'd take them and James to a play. She always snorts like a war-horse at the sight of the stage, and theatres don't encourage heavy drinking, so I thought with the three of us he'd be all right. I would have asked you, but I knew you wouldn't want to come when James was there."

"Frankly I wouldn't. But you might have known I'd have come for you," said Hugh, hitting his cousin on the back. "I've been a hell of a fool about James. First I believed him and when I found he was being a nasty piece of work I rather dropped him. I ought to have thought of you."

"That's all right, and certainly you couldn't have him about with Julia there. Well, Rose had kept James off the drink all day, except when he went round to the local pub, but they are decent people there and look after him, so he must have had some other dope, I don't know what. The Herberts were splendid. She seems to have been a female chucker-out at one stage of her theatrical career and I could see the light of battle in her eye as I told her about him. She was longing to try her hand at him. So we all had dinner and went to the theatre quite respectably and I was just beginning to feel relieved that the whole thing was over so well, and we could get James back and give him some cocoa and put him to bed, when just as we were leaving the theatre he said something about drinking to the happy pair and dashed off. Neither Herbert nor I could leave Mrs. Herbert alone, and before we could collect our wits or knew what to do, James was entirely lost."

"Have another kidney," said Hugh sympathetically.

"No, thanks. There was nothing to do, so we three went home. Herbert, like a sensible man went to bed, but Mrs. Herbert—who I must say was rather enjoying the dramatic situation—and Rose and I sat up all night waiting for the wanderer, blast him."

"No wonder you look a bit washed out. But don't worry like that, Francis. He'll come back all right. Even if he did turn up at the wedding, there are vergers and people to keep him out. Now don't worry, my dear old fellow."

"It's all very well to say don't worry, but wait till I tell you the rest. You see I hadn't the faintest idea where he had gone and what was at the back of my mind the whole time was that he might go to Beechwood. Well, he didn't. He came back about seven o'clock this morning in a taxi, in about as unattractive a state as I ever seen him in."

"I know," said Hugh. "You and I saw enough of that when poor Caroline was still with him. My poor boy, what a time."

"I must say," said Francis laughing faintly, "Mrs. Herbert and Rose had the times of their lives. They reclaimed the prodigal to that extent that he must have repented for the first time in his life, especially as I don't think he remembered who Mrs. Herbert was. They put him to bed and Mrs. Herbert volunteered to stay with him for the morning. She said you would forgive her for not coming to your wedding, and she thought her absence would be better than her and James's presence. She is a brick. So then I had a bath and a shave and came round here."

"It was jolly decent of you," said Hugh. "Are you feeling better now? We needn't go just yet."

"I'm all right now. Hugh, suppose he did go to Beechwood and frighten Caroline. I can't get it out of my head. He is all right for the moment, but I can't look after him night and day, and he won't leave England."

"Now, listen to a little sense," said Hugh, taking a seat on the arm of Francis's chair. "Do you still love Caroline."

"Don't be a fool," said Francis wearily.

"That isn't on the face of it a very helpful answer," said Hugh, "but I think I get you. Why don't you go down to Beechwood yourself today, after the wedding, and see Caroline? Your office won't fall down if you miss a day there. Why don't you marry her and stand no nonsense? Then perhaps James will retire to the Colonies or a lunatic asylum, and anyway it won't matter if he doesn't."

"I did ask her to marry me," said Francis.

"And do you mean to say you never asked her again?" said Hugh. "Then you deserve all the trouble you get. I would have asked Julia twenty times, but she is a sensible girl and saved me the trouble."

Francis got up, looking a little less haggard and weary.

"Look here, old fellow," said Hugh, putting his hands on Francis's shoulders and shaking him kindly. "You go down to Beechwood today, in your car, the minute the register is signed. Is that understood?"

"I suppose so. As a matter of fact I did get a special licence a week or two ago when things looked a little brighter. Oh, Hugh, if you only knew—"

"I do. I know absolutely everything about being in love, only I've got more sense than you have. I must say you show a gleam of intelligence about that special licence though. Come on."

The bridegroom and his best man arrived at the church in due time and greatly disappointed the handful of onlookers, who felt defrauded by the sight of two men in ordinary clothes. Nor were they given any more satisfaction by the bride and Anna who had not even a spray of orange blossom between them. Colonel Beaton, Dr. Herbert, Wilfred and George who were wearing top hats slightly raised the standard, but on the whole it was felt that the money should be returned. Julia and Hugh went through their part of the ceremony with perfect self-possession, the register was signed, and the married pair drove off to Waterloo.

"It feels a bit flat," said Colonel Beaton. "I'm going back to the hotel. I go down to Whitelands tomorrow, unless anything turns up to keep me here. Shall I see any of you again?"

Wilfred and George had to go back to the office. Dr. Herbert and Anna said they would go back to the hotel with Colonel Beaton. Francis took him aside for a moment.

"I'm going straight down to Beechwood," he said, "to see Caroline. I'm worried about her. I wish to God we could get James away. He is all to pieces and Mrs. Herbert is looking after him like an angel. They are staying on till tomorrow to keep an eye on him."

"I will try him about South America again," said Colonel Beaton, "though I'm not hopeful. I'm glad you are going to see Caroline. She needs you—much more than you know."

Francis wrung Colonel Beaton's hand gratefully and drove off.

Colonel Beaton with Dr. Herbert and Anna then walked back to his hotel, where he got into more comfortable clothes and they all celebrated the wedding in a mournful way with sherry.

"One ought to be allowed to go straight to bed after a wedding,' said Anna yawning. "All that emotion so early and then nothing to do. It's too early for a cinema even. I wish something exciting would happen."

The telephone bell rang. Colonel Beaton took off the receiver.

"Your wife wants to speak to you, Herbert," he said. "I hope she's all right with James."

Dr. Herbert went to the telephone. What his wife had to say was evidently extremely disturbing. He said hardly anything, but his ejaculations showed that something unusual had happened.

"I'll be round at once," he said and rang off.

"One of your patients come up to London and had a stroke?" said Anna.

"No," said Dr. Herbert, getting his coat on. "I haven't time to try to break this to you, Anna. It is your brother James. An accident of some sort."

"I'll come with you," said Colonel Beaton taking Anna's arm.

They got in a taxi and drove in silence to Francis's house where a red-eyed Rose opened the door to them.

"Oh, Miss Anna, oh, sir," was all that she could say between sobs and sniffs.

Dr. Herbert put her not unkindly aside, shut the front door and ran upstairs. Colonel Beaton and Anna followed him, not knowing where to go, nor whether they were wanted.

"We had better go into the drawing room," said Anna. "I feel frightened. What do you think it is?"

Before Colonel Beaton could answer, Mrs.Herbert came into the room, looking agitated.

"Has Rose told you?" she asked.

"No one has told us anything," said Colonel Beaton impatiently. "What is it?"

"My dear, it wasn't my fault," said Mrs. Herbert tragically to Anna. "I was very fond of James in old days and I wanted to help him. So I stayed with him this morning to let poor Francis, who looked like death after the dreadful night we had, go to Julia's wedding, and I was more disappointed than I can tell you to miss it myself, but I felt I could do more with James than anybody and now it has come to this. You will need some wine or something. I'll ring for Rose; but she does nothing but cry and makes the other servants cry too."

Colonel Beaton checked her as she was about to ring.

"Mrs. Herbert," he said, "what has happened to James?"

"Yes, please what is it?" said Anna, holding tightly to Colonel Beaton's sleeve with both hands to keep herself steady.

"It was the bath," said Mrs. Herbert. "Rose and I had got him to bed and my husband gave him something to make him sleep before he went to the church. But it didn't work and James said he must have a bath and shave himself. If I had any sense I would have locked the door, but Rose and I were arguing with him and he suddenly burst out of bed and almost knocked us over and he went into the bathroom and bolted the door. And then we heard him fall."

"Is he dead?" said Colonel Beaton, holding Anna's hands firmly in one of his own.

"We couldn't tell. We couldn't get in. So I thought you would be back from the wedding and I rang up the hotel. My husband broke the door open."

"Sit down, darling," said Colonel Beaton to Anna, though neither of them noticed the word, so anxious and exasperated they were by Mrs. Herbert's method of breaking the news. To everyone's relief Dr. Herbert came in.

"James is dead," he said in a matter-of-fact voice which braced everyone. "It was the bath. One of those old-fashioned ones with a marble step up to it. I don't suppose the house has been touched since Lester's people died. He must have slipped and hit his head and been killed instantaneously. I can't say how sorry I am, Anna, for your parents. It will be a frightful shock to them. Otherwise I think you will all agree that it was the best thing. Come up with me, my dear," he said to his wife. "I want you to see about a nurse and a few other things. Then we shall have to tell his parents," he said to Colonel Beaton.

"I'll do that," said Colonel Beaton. "And what about Francis? It is his house after all. I'd better send him a wire to Beechwood and ask him to tell Caroline, but that will do later. Hugh and Julia we needn't trouble till tomorrow. After all James was no relation of theirs and it seems cruel to break their first day together with this sordid affair. And I will tell Wilfred and George. Let me know exactly what to say when you come down, Herbert."

Left alone, Colonel Beaton sat down by Anna.

"I wish I felt sorrier," said Anna. "It is all very horrible, but I can't help a feeling of relief. It is my father and mother I am so sorry about. Wilfred going to Paris, James dead, it is almost like losing two sons. And Caroline can't ever feel quite the same about living with us now. James's death will make a kind of shadow. It will be lonely without her."

"Life is mostly loneliness."

"Yes, you will be lonely too. But you will be very busy in Father's affairs now, so we shall see more of you, I hope."

"Anna," said Colonel Beaton, looking at his watch, "while we have these few minutes to ourselves, I want to tell you how much I need you. I know this isn't the moment with James dead upstairs, but I can't choose my time. I need you so much. I've needed you for a long time."

Anna said, "Is it because you are lonely that you need me, William?"

"No, my dear, I am lonely because I need you."

"Then never be lonely again."

"That is all we may be able to say for the time being," said Colonel Beaton, quite satisfied and making no demonstration of love. "But now I feel a double right to help you, as your father's partner and your husband. The time of marrying shall be for you to say. Whitelands is waiting for you, where you can be near your parents. From now onwards, for some time, we shall have to think of our duty to others, as you have always done, all the time I have known you. When those duties are done, it will be my privilege to think of you and to think for you as long as I live."

Then Dr. Herbert came into the room and all the confusion that cold silent death brings with it had to begin. Anna and Colonel Beaton went straight to Cadogan Square, leaving the Herberts in charge. Mrs. Danvers, at first stunned by the news, found relief in tears and lamentations, and reminiscences of James's childish days till she consented to let Anna take her to her room.

Colonel Beaton glanced at the clock. It was barely half-past one. So much had happened since Julia's wedding, which now seemed a thing of the past. Mr. Danvers asked him to stay to lunch and he accepted, feeling that he might be a help. Anna came down, reporting that her mother was having a little lunch in bed and was calmer. No one could eat much. Mr. Danvers had said little and Anna was afraid for his strength.

Presently a nurse came to look after Mrs. Danvers and then Mr. Danvers said he would like to see James once more, so Colonel Beaton telephoned to Dr. Herbert. He also telephoned to the office to tell Wilfred and George.

Then he and Mr. Danvers and Anna went to Francis's house. Wilfred and George were already there with Mrs. Herbert, who asked them all to come upstairs. There on the bed lay the son, the brother, who had caused so much misery and anxiety. Mr. Danvers approached the bed and looked at the face of his eldest son. Then he knelt down by the bed in prayer. Wilfred and George, full of conflicting emotions, the old affection for their elder brother, the resentment and dislike which youth feels for death, remembrances of James as he used to be and as they had lately seen him, stood close together in silent accord. Anna closed her eyes and pressed her face against her William's sleeve. A nurse who had appeared, asked in a low voice if the lady felt faint, but Colonel Beaton waved her away and putting his arm around Anna gave her the support she needed.

When Mr. Danvers rose they all went downstairs.

"My wife and I cannot thank you and your wife enough," said Mr. Danvers to Dr. Herbert, "for what you did for our poor son. You were old friends of his. We all grieve for what James became and we must forget much that was not his true self. Anna, my dear, we had better go home to your mother."

Wilfred whispered to Anna that he and George were going back to the office, but would come at any moment if wanted, and gladly escaped.

"Come round after dinner, Beaton," said Mr. Danvers. "We shall be glad to see you." And he got into a taxi with Anna and went away.

Colonel Beaton then wrote a note to Hugh and Julia, telling them that it was quite unnecessary to interrupt their honeymoon. He had a thought to tell them about Anna, but decided to leave it till they returned. He felt no doubt as to his Julia's pleasure.

By the time Dr. Herbert had arranged for James's body to be removed it was getting late, so he asked the Herberts to come out to dinner with him. It was a pleasant meal. They all knew each other well enough not to pretend any deep grief for what had happened.

"The person I feel sorriest for at the moment, apart from Mr. and Mrs. Danvers," said Mrs. Herbert, "is Francis. It was quite bad enough to have James living in his house without his dying there. I suppose he will have got your wire by now, Colonel Beaton."

"I forgot it. Also, now I come to think of it, I don't know if he is staying the night there or not. Herbert, if he does come back tonight you will explain to him, won't you. And if he isn't back, I will ring him up at Beechwood first thing tomorrow. Then he can bring Caroline up with him."

"How like a man," said Mrs. Herbert. "Why on earth should poor Caroline who has suffered heaven knows what at his hands have to come up to her ex-husband's funeral?"

"Well, I really don't know why she should."

"I really don't know either why Francis should," said Mrs. Herbert provocatively, "except that he has to come up for his business. Otherwise I would say he had much better stay where he is needed."

"With Caroline, do you mean?"

Mrs. Herbert bowed her head majestically.

"A decline is a good old-fashioned word," said Dr. Herbert, eyeing his wine as he lifted it and sipping while he spoke, "but it is what Caroline will go into if she doesn't settle down. I have looked after her since Francis brought her to Beechwood when that skunk James had done with her—bad taste I dare say to say skunk, but he is no longer in Francis's house so it may be excused—and I know her. Dying for love is another old-fashioned exploded expression, but it is what she is capable of."

"'Und mein Stamm sind jene Asra . . .'" said Colonel Beaton, half to himself.

"Quite right, Beaton. I used to think Hugh was the man, but I have felt for some time that it was Francis. With Francis and a handful of children you wouldn't know her."

His wife who had been looking at him with suspicion, stretched out her hand and took away his glass.

"You have exceeded," she said, with great majesty. "When you get to gossiping about your patients it is time to stop."

Dr. Herbert laughed and Colonel Beaton called for the bill. He then drove them back to Francis's house, keeping the taxi waiting to take him on to Cadogan Square. Voices in the dining room attracted his attention. He opened the door and looked in. Rose and a young woman of pleasant appearance who were sitting by the fire jumped up.

"Friend of yours, Rose?" said Colonel Beaton. "Dr. and Mrs. Herbert have come back, so you'd better see if they want anything."

"I'm sorry I'm sure, sir," said Rose, "but Miss Morton who works at the Rose and Crown just round the corner, a very respectable house, sir, came over to keep me company, it being her half day off. If I had known you would have been back so early, sir, I'm sure I wouldn't have presumed, but I don't fancy being alone much after what has happened, and that Maud and cook do get on my nerves downstairs."

"I would like some hot milk, Rose, before I go to bed," said Mrs. Herbert, advancing into the room. "Good evening, Miss Morton."

"Good evening, madam," said Miss Morton, who seemed to be a well-spoken young woman, "I hope I'm not intruding, but Miss Faggott asked me to step round."

The rest of the company gazed enthralled at Rose whose surname had previously been unknown to man.

"You see, madam," continued Miss Morton, pleased to have an audience, "the poor gentleman used to step across quite often to the private bar, but I never let him go too far, not more than a gentleman should. But what's the good? He only went elsewhere."

"You are a reader, I see," said Mrs. Herbert pleasantly as Miss Morton picked up her bag and a paper-covered book.

"*Cissie's Companion*, madam. A reel good paper," said Miss Morton, her gentility leaving her as her enthusiasm mounted. "There's a lovely serial running in it by Pearl Trotter. I'm a bit partickler about what I read, but she always writes splendid.

Reel life, if you know what I mean. I've just got to the bit where the villain is offering Maisie a trip to Southend. Poor girl, she needs someone like me as knows the world a bit to tell her to mind her step. I do hope the worst won't occur. I should mind ever so."

Mrs. Herbert's heart beat in her bosom with high exaltation. Here at last was the reader of her dreams.

"I can promise you that it will be all right," she said, "because I wrote that story. I used to be on the stage under the name of Pearl Trotter so I use that name for writing."

As she spoke Mrs. Herbert became aware that she had fallen to the lowest point of Rose's estimation, but in her joy at discovering Miss Morton Rose's opinion was of complete indifference to her. Miss Morton's gasp, her devouring eyes, her respectful mien, were honey to the authoress.

"I'm very glad you like the story," she continued graciously. "I'm going to have an even better one about a wicked baronet called Sir Morton Maltravers."

"Morton!" exclaimed the present bearer of that name in an awestruck voice.

"Yes," said Mrs. Herbert, following up her advantage. "And mind you tell your friends to read it, any girl friends you have in your possession. I'm sure they'll enjoy it."

"I will, Miss Trotter, madam I should say. I'll tell Edna Pope that works with me. She's a one for books. She says she can read anything on a Sunday."

Mrs. Herbert, intoxicated by fame, drew a fountain pen from her bag.

"I will autograph your copy," she said, writing a large 'Pearl Trotter' on the cover. "And now, good night, Miss Morton."

"Pleased I'm sure," said Miss Morton.

Rose followed Mrs. Herbert out into the hall to which the two men, unable to keep from laughing, had retired.

"If you please, madam, I should wish to give notice at once," she said.

"But you can't," said Mrs. Herbert, "I'm not your mistress."

"Then I would wish you to witness, madam, that I hand in my notice now and Mr. Francis will get it as soon as he comes back. Mr. Danvers was one thing, but having such a fuss made about Miss Morton is quite another. I am sure I read every bit as good as Miss Morton, besides which I remember Mr. Hugh and Mr. Francis when they was little boys and it isn't likely I'll stay after this."

"All right, Rose, you can go," said Colonel Beaton.

Rose looked at him, thought better of it, and slowly disappeared towards the kitchen.

"There is one of Francis's troubles solved," said Colonel Beaton. "If Rose leaves, he can sell the house. Otherwise he would go on living here forever sooner than hurt her feelings. Good-bye, Mrs. Herbert. Good-bye, Herbert. I'll see you again at Whitelands in a day or two, and many, many thanks."

At Cadogan Place he found Mr. Danvers and Anna in the library. Wilfred and George had been at dinner and done their best to be cheerful, but their well-meant efforts were so embarrassing that Anna had whispered to them not to bother to come to the library unless they wanted to. So they had melted upstairs.

"It is good of you to come, Beaton," said Mr. Danvers. "My wife sends you messages, but she doesn't feel equal to coming down. Her doctor has been to see her and I think she is to have a sleeping draught. When the funeral is over she will feel better and perhaps I will take her and Anna abroad. I couldn't have done that without you to take my place."

Colonel Beaton told them the story of Mrs. Herbert and Miss Morton which amused them. He also broke the news of Rose's departure, though without mentioning her reasons.

"That is good luck," said Anna. "Now Francis can sell the house and have a nice little house or a flat. Rose has been getting crosser and crosser for the last ten years, and he and Hugh didn't dare to get rid of her. I must say she was always very nice to Caroline and me. But then we weren't her mistresses."

"I hope to be back at business in a day or two, Beaton," said Mr. Danvers. "Now those partnership deeds are signed we can settle things at the office and I shall be free to look after poor Evelyn for a time. I look forward to your help more than I can say, and to seeing more of you. Do you know, Beaton, I thought at one time that you were beginning to care for Caroline. One gets these fancies. Poor child, I hardly see what is to happen to her for the present. I shall see that she wants for nothing of course, but this will hardly be the home for her that it was till my wife is better."

"Caroline has very true friends," said Colonel Beaton, "and I hope and believe she will be well looked after. I admire her greatly, sir, but we never have been, and never should have been more than excellent friends. You see I not only admire but love your daughter, and always have, so Caroline could only take second place."

Mr. Danvers looked puzzled. Anna, though trusting her William to do what was wisest, wondered whether the news would be too much for her father.

"William, how can you perplex Father?" she said. "Dear Father, William wants to marry me and I can't think of anyone else I would rather marry, so I hope you won't mind. And we shan't get married till you feel you can come to our wedding."

She stroked his hand in the old way as she sat on a cushion at his feet.

"I couldn't have wished better for you, my dear," said her father, and he held out his hand to Colonel Beaton. "I am a bad match-maker. Do you know, my dear, I actually thought it was Francis that was in your mind. But this is all I could hope for. Bless you, my child."

Then he fell silent and they did not like to disturb him. Presently he asked them to go, saying he was tired. Anna kissed her father and she and her William went softly upstairs, past the Spider's Den, with pity for Anna's mother, to the old nursery which the boys used as a kind of sitting and working-room.

Wilfred and George made them welcome, though evidently puzzled by their unexpected visit.

"Father all right?" said George to Anna.

"Yes. He wanted to rest, so we came up to tell you the news."

"Not any more news today, Anna?"

"This isn't bad news, at least I hope you won't think so. William and I are going to get married."

Both young men looked at the betrothed, bereft of all power of speech.

"Good lord, you'll be Julia's step-mother," said George, rising to the occasion.

"If Julia hadn't turned me down, you would have been my step-mother-in-law," said Wilfred, awestruck. "Well, I don't grudge it. Julia and Hugh are jolly lucky to have hit it off, and so are you and Colonel Beaton."

"Could you manage William?" said Colonel Beaton.

"Certainly, sir. It's a bit of a shock, but I'm glad. In fact I'm awfully glad," said Wilfred as the facts began to soak into his mind. "Many happy returns of the day and congratulations and everything. You are both in luck."

Anna hugged Wilfred while Colonel Beaton expressed warm thanks for his good wishes.

"George is pleased too, but he's a bit slow in getting it out," said Wilfred.

"Gee, William, that's great," said George, veiling his sincere pleasure and indeed emotion under the words of the newest language. "He's a swell man, the new boss. Proud to woik under you, sir. And Anna's a swell girl too. Heil Beaton," he added looking at Wilfred.

But Wilfred wouldn't rise, and the next half-hour was spent in a happy babel of talk and plans in which James and Caroline were quite forgotten.

Mr. Danvers sat on in the library by his reading lamp, looking into the fire. He felt old, and there were too many thoughts in his mind. Anna and Beaton. She would be happy with him and

Beaton would keep a firm hand on the business when he himself was gone, and look after Wilfred and George. Caroline came to his mind. Caroline as she was when James first brought her to see them, pale and shaken with her love for him, her anxiety to please his parents; as she was when James had finished with her. Then his thoughts stayed with James. His heart was flooded with the self-reproach that every parent feels for a child who has not fulfilled its promise. Had I done this: Had I not done that: Was it my fault? The questions circled through his mind unanswered. Faster and faster the thoughts, the questions whirled about him. He tried to wave them away, to shut his ears to them, but they pressed on him, louder and more insistent. He was looking at James as he had seen him that morning, laid upon the bed. A wordless prayer for mercy for James and himself came from his heart. Then he knew that his spirit had left him and was following the likeness of James as he used to be. Thoughts and questions were left far behind. A silence fell about him, a still clear light filled his eyes. The vision of his lost son passed from him, but peace filled his heart.

When at last Colonel Beaton said he must go, he and Anna went to the library to say good night. The fire had burned low and Mr. Danvers was half asleep. Though he looked old and tired they thought he looked happier than he had been since James's return. Anna took her father up to his room and Colonel Beaton went back to his hotel, thankful for his new-found happiness. He rang up Rose, who said Mr. Francis had phoned up to say he wouldn't be back till tomorrow, so he determined to telephone to him at Beechwood early on the following day.

CHAPTER 14

FRANCIS MAKES HIS LAST MOVE

F rancis, who was obliged to go to his office before starting his journey, had to waste a good deal of precious time over urgent matters of business before he could get away. So he did not get to Beechwood till after three o'clock, anxious and unfed. Here he was told that Mrs. Danvers had been out all day on the downs. Food was offered to him, but he refused, and set off to look for her. By questioning a laborer in a field by the hill and a shepherd who was loitering near a lambing hut, he learned that she had been seen on the ridge of the downs where she and William Beaton had walked one day while Francis had followed with Anna. He sped up the steep hollow lane and came out upon the frosty turf, but there was no way of telling which path she had taken. At a venture Francis walked hurriedly on towards the low sun, breathless with the bitter windless air and the uncertain beats of his heart, till far off he saw a figure which he guessed with a pang of almost unbearable sharpness to be hers.

She, not expecting him, had been on one of her long walks hoping to fatigue herself to forgetfulness. Not till she had lived alone at Beechwood did she realise how constant was her need of Francis. Every day she determined to telephone him but was ashamed to do it. Even to lift the receiver with his number in her mind so shattered her that she had to hang it up again. To write was solace, but she wrote so much that seemed to her diffident spirit too self-revealing that she tore up sheet after sheet, sometimes in despair sending those that she would less willingly have let him see. Francis's lack of response did not perturb her, for she knew of old his inability to express himself on paper, but she read and re-read each of his letters, trying to get from it, to put into it, more than met the eye. Whenever the telephone bell rang, which was but seldom, she rushed to it, hoping to hear Francis's voice. She was sleeping badly again, dreaming of Francis while she lay awake, dreading the dreams of James that haunted her restless sleep. Music, books, Anna's village doings which she had promised to keep up for her, nothing could stop her dreams or her fears. Her terror of meeting James face to face kept her away from London and she wondered what her next step would be. A bed-sitting-room alone would be better than to eat the bread of James's parents as things were now, but she was very vague as to whether her small income would even run to a bed-sitting-room. Her one solace was to be up on the downs and walk for silent miles on the springing grass, coming back as evening fell, tired but refreshed in mind. Then as she neared the house the fear of a letter, a telegram, some sign of James, the waiting for a telephone call from Francis which she yet dreaded to receive, all these undid the good that the lonely hills had done.

Today she had gone out in the morning with sandwiches and had walked six or seven miles along the ridge westwards, dipping to the river and walking on again on the further side. When she had covered most of the homeward path she saw a figure approaching. She recognised Frances with the red light of sunset on him before he could be sure of her. She walked swiftly up to him and stopped a few feet away.

"I hoped you would come at last," she said.

"I could have come before if I thought you wanted me. You never asked me in your letters."

"I hadn't the courage. I hardly knew if you would care to come."

"Caroline, why did you hope I would come then?"

"Because I wanted you so much."

"Then why didn't you ask me?"

"Because I'm not good enough for you."

"Not good enough?" said Francis almost roughly, taking a step towards her.

"No, no, Francis. Don't. It's not that I don't want you so much that it is killing me, but what have I to give?"

"All that I want."

"But what exactly do you want?"

"Caroline," said Francis answering one question with another, "you said to me last time we spoke of this that you couldn't care for any man in the way I meant. What did you mean? I have been thinking of your words, miserably."

"What I meant was what I am trying to say now," said Caroline, cautiously coming near him again and looking at him with her deep gaze. "It is so difficult that I hardly know how to say it. Francis, I have been married before. You know a little of what that marriage was. Can you think, "she said, lowering her glance, "how broken I am, and how afraid of so much that marriage means? Dear Francis you are quite young still. You want a wife who can give you passion for passion, ardor for ardor. I can't. I am dead. Leave me, Francis."

Her hands raised to appeal were trembling. Francis caught them and kissed them.

"Do you think I haven't thought of that?" he said. "Couldn't you trust me, Caroline, for patience, for kindness? Such ordinary things."

"How can I tell? I haven't found them so very ordinary. I wouldn't mention it, Francis, only I love you so much that I can't bear to be unfair to you."

"I think you may let me judge of the unfairness."

Caroline gave him a look half afraid, half grateful, and releasing her hands hurried on. Francis, uncertain whether he had pleased or offended, followed her, but fast as he walked there was hardly a foot between them when they reached the road that plunged downwards into the twilit gloom. Francis drew nearer to Caroline in the heavy dusk and caught her arm as she stumbled on a root.

"Don't take it unkindly, Caroline, if I slip your arm through mine," he said, with his voice very much out of control. "I don't want you to fall in the dark." Caroline submitted without a word, but as they went down the hill her steps became slower and slower, and Francis felt her weight dragging at his arm.

"Caroline," he said, looking anxiously at the glimmer of white that was his cousin's face, "are you all right?"

He could hear a faint sound of "No."

"What is it, then? Did you hurt your foot when you tripped? Are you too tired, my poor darling?"

"It's not that," said Caroline stopping altogether and speaking with the ghost of a voice. "But I love you so much that I can't walk, I can't even stand."

"That settles it," said Francis and gathered Caroline into his arms.

For a moment she stiffened, then let herself melt into his embrace, while he hardly dared to move for fear of frightening away this strange sweetness.

"If you don't marry me after this, it will be the unfairest thing you have ever done," he said at last to the top of her head, for her face was buried in his coat collar.

"How soon could we be married?" asked a rather choked voice.

"Practically almost at once. Would you like that?"

Caroline looked up.

"Yes, please," she said, "if it isn't too expensive. I think Francis, if you are still of the same mind tomorrow you had better marry me as quickly as possible in case I get frightened again, or you change your mind."

"We can quite well be married tomorrow if you like. I thought it was worth gambling on it after that lunch when you became so relenting. Would half-past eight tomorrow morning suit you?"

"Yes," said Caroline, lifting her face to her lover.

"I shall have two boys and two girls," said Caroline cheerfully as they walked home in the dark after a visit to the Vicarage which had excited the Vicar very much, as he lived in a small way and had never seen a special licence before.

"Very well, darling," said Francis, marvelling at the way in which Caroline appeared to have adapted herself to her new situation.

"And what about a wedding ring," said Caroline, "or can we be married with a curtain ring?"

"I was rash enough to buy one. I have always known the size of your finger."

After a blissful but constrained dinner Caroline suddenly had an access of conscience.

"Will it be respectable for you to spend the night here before we are married?" she asked. "Of course I know you are a sort of cousin, but then I have never been going to be married to you before. Only I don't know where you could go. Whitelands is shut up at present, and I know the Vicar hasn't got a spare room, and the Herberts won't be back till tomorrow, and the village pub is impossible."

"Don't wrinkle your forehead, my love," said Francis, "it will be perfectly respectable. I shall tell the servants that we are to be married at half-past eight tomorrow and they will be up all night with excitement, furnishing water-tight alibis. Will that do?"

"I don't know, but I thought I had better just mention it, because, you see, I am very respectable, whatever my misfortunes."

"It would do you a lot of good to be less respectable," said her adoring betrothed.

"I know. But you see my first husband was so disrespectable

that someone had to keep up the standard. Francis, did you notice how well I said that?"

"Said what?"

" 'My first husband.' "

"It's bad taste to say that before you have a second."

But I have—practically."

Francis was as good as his word in telling the servants, by which means he was to his eternal fury woken at four o'clock by an over-zealous housemaid who slept in the room above him and had set her alarm clock to that dispiriting four for fear of missing the wedding. He then spent three hours in having nightmares that he would not be called in time, and did not go comfortably to sleep till seven o'clock when the housemaid, in a state of twittering excitement, brought him his tea.

At a quarter-past eight he and Caroline walked to the church where the Vicar, hoping that a special licence was all that is said it was, married them. They thanked him and walked back to Beechwood, discovering on the way that they both felt extremely shy.

Breakfast was ready, and the whole staff found an opportunity to be doing something in the hall or the dining room when they appeared. Before they had finished the telephone rang.

"I always hoped it was you ringing up when the telephone rang," said Caroline, "and it never was."

Before Francis could thank her adequately, or explain how he had wanted to ring her up and been too frightened, a maid came to say that Colonel Beaton wished to speak to Mr. Lester. Francis was some time at the telephone and came back looking rather serious.

"Oh, Francis," said Caroline, "was the special licence not a good one?"

"You are as silly as Julia," said Francis, laughing in spite of himself. "It was perfectly good and thank heaven it was, or you mightn't have felt like marrying me today."

"Why?"

"It is rather beastly, darling, especially as it happened in my house. James was pretty drunk on the morning of Hugh's wedding—yesterday in fact—and Mrs. Herbert and Rose stayed with him while Herbert went to the wedding. Then he went mad, you know how, and said he must have a bath. They couldn't stop him and he slipped on that marble step—many's the time I've slipped on it myself and cursed the thing—and he hit his head and was killed at once. Herbert came straight back and he and Beaton arranged everything. James has been moved elsewhere till the funeral."

His wife looked straight before her and said rather defiantly, "I am glad."

Francis could not disagree with her, but felt that it was hardly his place to applaud such sentiments.

"You see," she said, "women are more truthful than men about some things. I wouldn't have lifted a finger to hurt James, but I am extremely glad that he is dead."

"So am I," said Francis.

After a pause he went on: "I told Beaton we were married and he was delightful about it. He said he had seen it coming, but people always say that. And he countered with another bit of news; he and Anna are engaged."

Caroline's scream of pleasure could hardly have been bettered by Julia. "Oh, how glorious," she said. "I can't imagine a nicer thing than to marry William, except you, darling. And William being a partner with Mr. Danvers seems all so suitable. Oh, but Francis—Mr. and Mrs. Danvers."

"I know. It will all hit them pretty hard. We must see what we can do. Look here, my love, do you realise that your second husband has an office and can't afford to neglect it unless you want to starve. We must go up today and—oh, what with getting married and one thing and another, I'd forgotten almost the most important news of all. Beaton says Rose has given notice and won't hear of staying on. I gather that Mrs. Herbert managed to offend her, though how I can't think. So we can sell the house and live where we like. I wish I could live on a mountain top for you, my proud walker, but it doesn't go with a solicitor's office."

Mr. and Mrs. Francis Lester drove accordingly to London and went straight to their house. Here they had to break the news of their marriage to Rose, who first had semi-hysterics, then frightened them out of their wits by nearly taking her notice back, and finally announced her irrovocable decision of leaving the house on the following day. She further obliged with a flood of reminiscence of Francis's boyhood which filled him with shame and was impossible to stem, till Caroline said mildly, "Thank you, Rose. And now where am I to sleep, I wonder?"

"I'm sure I couldn't say, Miss Caroline," said Rose with an offended expression, and becoming as stone left the room.

"Are you sure you don't mind living here till we can find a nicer place," said Francis. "I mean, you won't mind about James."

"If I minded living where James lived," said Caroline, "I couldn't have stayed with his people so long. It doesn't much matter where he lived—or died. Where I am going to live with you is the important thing, and if this is your house it is my home. You have a spare room, haven't you, Francis?"

"Yes," said Francis, perplexed. "The Herberts were in it last."

"Well, if there is room for the Herberts in your spare room—" said Caroline, and then looked out of the window.

"Certainly," said Francis and rang the bell. After an interval Maud appeared.

"Where is Rose?" asked Francis.

"Please sir, she said I was to answer the bell."

"All right," said Francis, feeling that the less he asked about Rose's reasons the better, "I want you to get the spare room ready and put Mrs. Lester's suitcases in it."

"Both beds," said Caroline still looking out of the window.

"Yes, madam," said Maud in an awestruck whisper, and withdrew.

"Now," said Caroline, ignoring this interlude, "we really must go to Cadogan Square. Have you time, Francis?"

The days were beginning to lengthen, but when they got to Cadogan Square the curtains were drawn and fires glowed. Anna in the drawing room greeted them with open arms. Francis and Caroline threw themselves whole-heartedly into the business of praising her William till she shone with pleasure.

"What is so delightful," she said, "is that Father approves, just like a real father in a book. He wants to see you, Caroline; William is with him now. He wants to know what you think of doing. William said he thought you had a plan. What is it? Not to leave us altogether, Caroline? When Father and Mother come back from abroad I am sure they will want you here again. And I shall want you too. If only I could stay here with you, but they want me to go with them, and William agrees that I ought to."

By this time Caroline and Francis had fallen a prey to ridiculous embarrassment and were exchanging helpless glances. Luckily Colonel Beaton came in, and after greeting them with a warm handshake he said, "I haven't told Anna your new plans, Caroline. I'll leave Francis to explain them. Mr. Danvers is very anxious to see you and I'll take you to the library if I may."

"William," she said as soon as they were outside the door, "what am I to say to Father? You know I didn't know about James till this morning, or I wouldn't have married so quickly— oh, I don't know, perhaps I would; yes, I know I would—but what will he think? Why didn't you tell us last night, William?"

"Because, my dear, I thought I wouldn't. I have seen so much in the last two years. I have seen Wilfred having a very touching calf-love for my abominable Julia and getting through it like a man. I have seen my Julia fall into Hugh's arms, and I think they will be happy. I have watched Anna in her devotion to you and her parents and learned to value her so deeply—I can't talk about her, Caroline, but you know what her selfless generosity is. And my dear I have watched you doing your best against odds. Do you remember how I preached to you one day on the downs?"

"It was a good preaching, William. I needed beating."

"It was impertinent on my part, but let that pass. May I speak to you frankly? I knew that things were more than usually difficult for you just then. You showed all the best in you; you gave your wholehearted blessing to my Julia in her new-found happiness. I thought I knew where your true happiness lay. I thought that yesterday would be the deciding day for you. So I didn't ring Francis up till this morning."

"My blessed William, it was very wrong of you, but thank God you didn't. Oh, William, I can't do much for Francis, but I can make a doormat of myself and ruin his character."

"You won't do either, my dear. You will bully Francis and improve him. But come, we can't stand on the landing pouring out our hearts for anyone on the stairs. Come see Mr. Danvers. I will help you if you need it, but I don't think it will be needed."

It was with a sinking heart that Caroline went into the library. Mr. Danvers was sitting alone at his desk. At the sight of Caroline his tired, patient face lighted and he came forward to meet her.

"My dear, it was good of you to come," he said. "We won't talk about what has happened. It is the end of a hopeless story. I didn't know what you would feel about it. Sit down, Beaton."

"Father," said Caroline, "if ever I didn't do my duty by James, forgive me."

"Child, there is no forgiveness between you and me, or James. The account is closed."

"I am afraid," said Caroline, taking Mr. Danver's hand, "I have to ask you to be patient with me again. I have done something that you may disapprove. I can only say that I did it in ignorance of James's death."

"I can never disapprove anything you do."

"Father, Francis came to Beechwood yesterday. We met on

the hills. It was nearly sunset. I thought my love had died with James, years ago, but Francis—Francis—"

Her voice sank to a low touching sound on her husband's name. Mr. Danvers said nothing. William Beaton looked encouragement at her and she spoke again.

"He asked me to marry him, Father. I was thankful. He had a special licence. We were married at half-past eight this morning. Then William rang up and told us what had happened. Father, my first thought was selfishness; gladness that I had not known before. Then I thought of you. Will you forgive me and take my thanks for sheltering me, bearing with me for so long? And will you still think of me as a daughter?"

"God bless you, my dear," said Mr. Danvers. "You and Anna are happy. I have no more to say. Go to your husband now. Beaton, stay with me. "There are affairs to discuss before I go abroad."

Caroline went softly out. Too much moved to return to the drawing room she slipped up stairs to Anna's sitting room and there gave way to silent tears, the last she was to shed in that house. Mr. Danver's handsome face lined with grief, his acceptance, his unbelievable understanding, his final blessing, all these mingled to something that touched the sorrow and hope of life itself. Not till she had released herself in tears did she go down to find Francis.

He and Anna had not been for long at cross purposes. It had pleased him to mystify and tease her for a short time, but his eagerness to tell his triumph soon got the upper hand. Nothing could have given him more pleasure than Anna's joyful face; nothing could have given Anna more joy than to know that Caroline was at last in a happy haven. Together they talked over the past two years and laughed at past troubles. But Anna said no word to Francis of the love's cross currents that had tried and proved herself and Caroline, nor would she ever speak of them in the future, even to her William.

Wilfred and George coming back from the office together

were discussing the state of affairs at home, with special reference to themselves, for their young minds had been considerably exercised during the last twenty-four hours.

"I don't want to be a beast," said Wilfred, as he and George emerged from Sloane Square station, "but James really might have thought of other people a bit. I mean he might have known that the parents would be upset. Not that I mean to say he fell down and killed himself on purpose, but to go on the burst in another man's house and then get killed simply isn't done."

"Thank heaven the parents are going abroad," said George. "I'm dashed sorry for Old Intellect, and I'm sorry for Mother too, if only she didn't want one to come and sit with her and hear all about James's childish days. It's so awkward to get away. If you stay too long that wretched Nurse Somebody comes in and says you are tiring her, and if you try to go away she begins to cry, and one feels no end of a beast. It will be a bit brighter when William is in charge and you are in Paris."

"It will be a bit brighter for me to be in Paris, I can tell you. I say, George, how about a wedding present for Anna and William? I thought we might club together and give them a lot of really decent records."

"Jolly good idea. Boris and Prince Igor perhaps."

"Don't be an ass. They won't want that ghastly stuff. Wagner's the chap."

"Better give them a record of Hitler cutting his moustache while you're about it."

The controversy proceeded on well-worn lines till they got home and was continued in the hall, up the staircase and into the drawing room.

"Hullo, Caroline," said George. "Hullo, Francis, Look here, Anna, would you like some records for a wedding present?"

"Oh, George, I'd love them."

"We thought of some Wagner," said Wilfred lightly.

"We thought of some Rimsky," said George carelessly.

"I'd simply love a Gilbert and Sullivan opera," said Anna at the same moment.

The scorn which the two brothers felt for each other was now completely obliterated by the pity they felt for their sister, but they did their best not to let her feel what a brick she had dropped.

It was George who first remembered the anomalous position in which Caroline now stood.

"I say, Caroline," he remarked, drawing his chair nearer to her, "I hope this business about James isn't upsetting you. I know you didn't have much of a time, but I don't suppose you wanted the poor old fellow to go off like that."

"Thank you, George dear. I really don't mind, so don't be sorry for me. And I have something to tell you. Francis came down to Beechwood yesterday and we decided to get married."

In George's ingenuous countenance she could read the surprise of one who finds that his elders are capable of any kind of human emotion, struggling with a kind heart.

"Well, I'm awfully glad and all that," he said nervously, "but I suppose James will make a difference. I mean, don't you want to—I mean, don't you sort of—"

"One doesn't have to go into mourning for one's divorced husband, if that is what you mean," said Caroline a little tartly. But sorry for George, who was reddening uncomfortably, she added, "and anyway it is too late because Francis and I were married this morning."

George looked at her with a face so devoid of any intelligence that she began to fear that the shock of the news had deranged his intellect. His demented appearance began to attract the attention of the rest of the company.

"Hi! George! What's up?" said Wilfred.

George with an effort pulled himself together and said Francis and Caroline were married and he supposed it was all right.

"I wouldn't have believed it," he said, "only Caroline told me."

"Is it true?" asked Wilfred.

Francis said it was perfectly true.

Nothing would then satisfy the young men but that Francis should tell them the whole story from beginning to end. Their admiration of anyone got married with a special licence was unbounded, and having got over their initial horror at Caroline's unmaidenly step, they were voluble in congratulations. George's only criticism of the affair was that in Soviet Russia no licence would have been necessary as marriage had no legal status, while Wilfred applauded a marriage in which both parties were so delightful and would obviously—He then broke off in some confusion.

"I intend to have at least four children, if that is what you mean, Wilfred," said Caroline, reflecting that it was the second time she had had to rescue her young brothers-in-law from impasses of their own making. At this Wilfred looked so ashamed, though more on Caroline's behalf than on his own, that everyone laughed.

They were still laughing when William Beaton came into the room with the depressing announcement that Mrs. Danvers in the first place couldn't understand why the children were making so much noise at such a time, and secondly wanted George to go up and sit with her and tell her what they were all talking about.

"Don't you wish you were going to Paris like me?" said the ungrammatical Wilfred, displaying neither fraternal nor filial piety.

George said he wished he lived in a sensible place like Russia where people's mothers didn't expect them to behave as if they were still in the nursery, and saying good-bye to Caroline and Francis went disconsolately upstairs.

"William," said Caroline, "does Mother know about Francis and me?"

"Yes. Mr. Danvers told her."

"Did she mind? Is she angry?"

"I am afraid she feels it."

"Never mind, Caroline," said Wilfred, "Mother gets such a lot of pleasure out of feeling hurt that you are really a blessing in disguise. When she comes back you'll be in favor again and probably Anna will be in disgrace for wanting to marry William."

"I hope I shall be in favor," said Caroline sadly. "But I don't think people forget about their children that die, and I am afraid I shall always be in her mind when she thinks of James, and she will blame me. We had better go now, Francis."

Wilfred came down to the front door to see them off.

"Good-bye, Caroline," he said. "I shall be off to Paris soon. I shan't forget how good you were to me at Christmas. William told me the other day that it was you that got him to send me to Paris that first time. I do hope you and Francis will be very happy."

"Thank you, dear Wilfred, and you too," said Caroline giving him her hand. Wilfred held it for a moment and with a diffidence which sat well upon him he kissed it. Then he seriously gave it to Francis and returning into the house shut the door behind him.

Francis and Caroline, nervous of the possibility of facing an outraged Rose, dined at a restaurant, the same at which they had dined on the night of the Russian ballet. They lingered over coffee till it was late, talking little, for they had much to say and speech was difficult. When Francis had paid his bill he was going to get up, but Caroline, stretching her hand across the little table, held his for a moment.

"Francis," she said, looking at him with her piercing, unfathomed glance, "I have thought of something."

"What, love?" asked Francis, adding idly, "do you know what lovely hands you have?"

"Yes, because you told me so. Do you want to know what I thought of?"

Francis, his spirit reeling in Caroline's deep gaze managed to say that he would like very much to know.

"I'm terribly glad you married me," said his adored one, "because now I shan't have any more trouble with those horrid apostrophes."

Though Francis's head was among the wheeling stars, he had to look down to earth to inquire into this preposterous remark.

"Apostrophes, darling? I knew I was mad, but it appears that you are too."

"I mean all that trouble about esses," said his idol, not making matters much clearer.

"I am still entirely at a loss as to your meaning, but you look so heavenly."

"Well," said Caroline patiently, "you see with Danvers one never knew what to do. If I wanted to say Mrs. Danvers's car—not that we ever had one except for a few months after we were married because James didn't appear to be able to afford anything but whisky—it was such a hissing noise. And when it came to writing it, I never knew whether I ought to put an apostrophe or lots of esses."

She paused with a rapt expression as of one who has discovered a new natural law, while Francis, feeling unequal to the mental effort required to follow her, sat adoring her with all his might.

"But now," continued Caroline getting up, "it will all be so easy. It is so easy to say Lester's. Francis Lester's wife. Is that a good thing to say, Francis?"

COLOPHON

This book is being reissued as part of Moyer
Bell's Angela Thirkell Series. Readers may join
the Thirkell Circle for free to receive notices
of new titles in the series and to receive a news-
letter, bookmarks, posters and more. Simply
send in the enclosed card or write to the address
below.

The text of this book was set in Caslon, a typeface
designed by William Caslon I (1692-1766). This
face designed in 1725 has gone through many
incarnations. It was the mainstay of British
printers for over one hundred years and
remains very popular today. The version used
here is Adobe Caslon. The display faces are
Adobe Caslon Outline, Calligraphic 421,
and Adobe Caslon.

Composed by Alabama Book Composition,
Deatsville, Alabama.

The book was printed by Thomson-Shore, Inc.,
Dexter, Michigan on acid free paper.

Moyer Bell
Kymbolde Way
Wakefield, RI 02879